For mom and dad,
and all my golfing friends over the years
at the Victoria Beach Golf Course in Manitoba, Canada.
My own little piece of heaven and escape, since I was eight years old.

1

WHO'S COUNTING?

As I pull into the parking lot on this beautiful early summer morning in late August of 1995, the pleased smile on my face that has been stamped there from the moment I woke up, shows no signs of diminishing. It's still early enough in the day that only one car has arrived before me -- a 1990s Cadillac -- and I choose to park directly beside it. Exiting my car, I carefully place my still piping hot coffee on the roof for safekeeping, as I kick my regular sneakers off and exchange them for my new golf shoes waiting in the back seat. I know I won't have much time to hit balls this morning, but I want to take at least half an hour to treat myself before an extremely busy day swings into full gear. As I lock the car and grab back my coffee from the roof, there's just enough coolness in the air that the warm liquid serves double duty. It gives me the early day caffeine kick I so desperately require, and it warms up my slightly cold hands as well.

As I leave my car and walk towards the golf course grounds, everything around me is just how I like it. Silent and still. The only significant sound is the gentle rhythmic click-clack of the spikes on my shoes striking the asphalt.

Click-clack, click-clack, click-clack, click-clack, click-clack, click-clack...

Oh, how I love that sound reverberating all around me! A sound that any early morning golfer would know and appreciate in an instant. As I leisurely walk and take in the dawning day, the rhythmic sound is both hypnotic and soothing to me.

The sound and repetition continue, slightly changing in pitch, as I move from the asphalt pavement in the parking lot onto the concrete path that leads me into the beautiful green world I'm so very familiar with. As I stroll along, suddenly, in all but an instant, my idyllic moment evaporates as the click-clacks are intruded upon by the sound of a loud "crack"! Like a doe in the forest, I instinctively stop and react.

While most people would turn their gaze towards the source of the sudden shot of sound, I do the opposite. Instead, I turn my head to the much closer, dull thud following it. In doing so I see, just in time, a white golf ball with a red line running through it, land on the ground, spraying up a stream of dew behind it. Located closely by is a dented and pockmarked black-and-white yardage sign marker that reads: Two-Hundred Yards. The ball gently rolls barely a few yards past it, before coming to a complete rest after it kisses into another previously struck ball.

Off in the distance, I hear a voice call out.

"Two hundred and ninety-four!"

Barely a second passes and I hear another crack, identical to the first one. As if I'm Bill Murray in the movie Groundhog Day, a ball comes to a gentle thud on practically the same spot, only this time the ball hops directly at the sign, gently hits it square on, and bounces inches beside it.

It too is followed by the same high-pitched, haunting voice.

"Two hundred and ninety-five!"

With military timed precision, there is a repeat of the exact sound, and another ball gently lands, tenderly mimicking the kiss I just witnessed on another ball already resting there, until it too comes to a final rest. Off in the distance, the tally grows by one more, proudly announced by the same singsong, bird-like voice.

"Hoo! Two hundred and ninety-six! Hoo! Two hundred and ninety-six! Two hundred and ninety-six swings and two hundred and ninety-six shots, right at the target. Right at the target, every time."

Before waiting for another replay, I turn my head in the opposite direction of the huge cluster of golf balls to discern exactly where this voice is coming from. What I see standing off in the distance is what would be an odd-looking sight for most. But for me, it's exactly what I expect.

There stands Moe.

Murray (Moe) Irwin Norman, perched on a driving range tee-off box, golf club in hand, where he's been robotically hitting all of the previous golf balls with such repetitive precision. He's short and stocky in stature with a strong torso and a neck like a tree stump. He would make a good, albeit short, football linebacker. On the top of his head is a thick and scattered longish crop of grey-white hair trimmed tightly at the sides, standing straight up, around a pair of exceptionally large ears. When you combined the hair and ears with his twinkling eyes it always made him look like he was in a state of great surprise. He's in his sixties now, but still, a very fit man, deceptively younger-looking than his age should dictate. He's wearing a pair of colourful orange, yellow, and brown well-worn plaid slacks -- that are much too short for him – and a colourful and sweat-stained bright red turtle-neck sweater that looks to be made of the same material as a cheap motel carpet. Both of his sleeves are rolled up, revealing three wristwatches on one arm and two on the other. He also wears a pair of golf shoes that are well worn and there is a hole in the front of one that his socked foot sticks through.

Moe spots me and with gleeful recognition waves heartily to get my attention.

"Hey, Nick! Over here! Over here! Nick, over here!"

One of the many unique and interesting things about Moe is his voice. He didn't need to wave at me to get my attention as the shrill carry of his voice does it all by itself. He was born with an odd, high-pitched, sing-song kind of voice. The timber would rise even further and higher than his regular high pitch whenever he got excited or nervous. It reminded me of a fictional character from my past that my grandma would read to me at bedtime. That "chubby little cubby all stuffed with fluff" Winnie-the-Pooh. But on steroids.

Moe also has a habit of repeating words and phrases when he speaks. Interestingly, when you first meet him it's the first thing you pay attention to and it's what you think might be what you will remember the most. But the more you're around him, the more it disappears into the catalogue of everything else unique about him until it becomes both normal and fitting for him to sound the way he does.

I wave back with a smile and start walking toward him.

Moe is still, staring fixedly down at me like a statue. Only the anxious tap-tap-tap of a golf ball, skillfully bouncing on a golf club, gives away any sense of bodily motion, as he impatiently waits for me to make my way over.

I barely even take ten strides before Moe yells out to me again, "C'mon! Pick up the pace! Pick up the pace! I don't have all day you know! Don't have all day!"

Knowing completely well that unless I break out into a full-out sprint -- and that no other speed would be adequate for him -- I determinedly keep my chosen leisurely morning pace.

Moe points towards all the balls he has hit and hollers to me, without any intentional boasting, "Look, Nick! Two hundred and ninety-six. Look! Every ball right at the target. Two hundred yards every time. Just like a walk in the park for me. A walk in the park! That's what happens when you're the greatest ball-striker the game's ever seen. Not that I'm the one saying that. Oooh no! It's the best players in the game who say that about *me*. Sure! It's not me saying that. Oooh no! I'm just repeating what they say! Repeating what they say."

As I continue my trek towards him, Moe becomes increasingly

4

agitated with the speed of my unacceptable gait. Unable to wait any longer, he tees up another ball and strikes it confidently in my direction. Upon hearing the large familiar crack again, I don't flinch or remotely worry about getting hit. In fact, I don't even bother to watch this time, knowing full well the ball will land within a few inches or feet of the distance he has chosen to hit at, and it will reside placidly with the other two hundred and ninety-six balls off in the distance.

Moe watches his shot until it comes to rest.

"Two hundred and ninety-seven. Two hundred and ninety-seven. Right at the target. You missed it! You didn't look! Two hundred and ninety-seven right at it every time!"

"I'm quite sure it was a carbon copy of the rest of them," I state matter-of-factly. "I must have seen you swing a million times already. I'm sure it's okay to miss a shot now and then."

Now that I'm close enough, I notice there is a see-through wire trash can nearby. A healthy portion of its contents is empty Coca-Cola cans. As well, I spot six empty range ball buckets stacked with precision on top of each other, piled neatly off to the side. I also note that only three golf balls are left, laying directly in front of him.

"I thought for sure I was going to beat you to the golf course today, Moe. How long have you been here?"

"Not too long. Not too long."

"Six empty range ball buckets say differently," I point out suspiciously.

Moe looks down at the three remaining golf balls and kicks them a little with his foot.

"Not quite six empty. Not quite six. I still have three more balls left. Three more swings until a half day's work is done."

"I get that, but you promised me today was going to be one of those days you take it easy. I'm quite sure putting in half a day's work before the sun gets well over the trees is not exactly what anyone would call 'taking it easy.'"

Shaking his head firmly in disagreement he says, "Oh, I can't be doing less. Can't be doing less. Can't be taking things off my plate.

Oh, no. If you want to achieve, if you want to get better, it takes work. Oooh yes! A good long day's work. Day after day, year after year. I hit six hundred balls a day to keep getting better. Oh, sure! Six hundred balls a day. At least that many. It's my labour of love. Oooh yes! My labour of love!"

Smiling, Moe picks up a Coca-Cola, finishes it, throws it in the trash can, and immediately opens another.

I point to the trash can. "Are those all from just this morning?"

"Oh, you know me! I drink twenty or more of these a day. Twenty at least! Breakfast, lunch, and dinner of champions!"

With a big, wide-open, and unabashed grin he states the obvious. "My teeth aren't too thankful for it though! Hoo! Oh no! Not too happy! Hoo! Not too happy at all!"

He follows it up with a good shrill hearty laugh and blesses me with a big toothy smile revealing all his teeth. A less than gentle visual reminder of what years and years of Coca-Cola's sugar carnage can do to this kind of "breakfast of champions."

There's no gentle way to share with you how big of a disaster this poor guy's teeth are. They're all cruelly twisted and crooked and have been ever since he was a young boy. Once you added on the decades of sugary deterioration to the twisted mess, you had before yourself a dentist and an orthodontist's walking nightmare. I wouldn't be at all surprised if Wes Craven has based a character or two on that smile. I must have told him a hundred times he needed to get them fixed -- or at least get them looked at -- but getting Moe to a doctor of any kind was a battle you would lose. He always took considerable pride in saying that he never went to see a doctor in all his life. Not ever. Boasting that since he never had a toothache, a headache, or an earache, why bother? He was adamant that he never even got colds, so what was the point? And when you witnessed his never-ending diet of foods like liver and onions, hotdogs and hamburgers, potato chips and chocolate – on top of gallons of Coca-Cola -- you had to wonder how that possibly could be true. But he wore it like a badge of honour. I had no idea if there was some underlying reason for why he was so obstinate to avoid doctors at all costs, but I did know how stubborn he could be about certain things. And I mean bullheaded, no-chance-in-hell-you're-going-to-change-my-mind, so-just-drop-it, kind of stubborn. So, I did just that. I learned long ago to know when to drop it and find better battles to fight.

"Want a sip?" asks Moe as he holds out the can, playfully taunting his sugar addiction in my face further.

"No. I'm good, thanks," I reply as I hold up my cup in a cheers gesture. "I've got my coffee... *black* coffee," I strategically point out.

"Yuk. Your loss. Your loss," he rebukes, quickly following with one final air-sucking swig, inhaling every last drop for his satisfaction -- and my torment -- and lobs the can into the trash. He immediately opens another one with a slightly teasing Cheshire Cat smile tossed my way for good measure.

Fully aware that Moe is having fun trying to get my goat, I refuse to take the bait and change my tactics.

"You must have been here quite a while already...well before daylight. By hitting three hundred balls already, I'm extremely disappointed, to be honest."

"No, you're wrong!" Moe defensively bleats back.

Moe does not like to disappoint his friends.

"Really? Then why are all of these lights still on?" I counter, with a knowing look to back it up.

He gives me no response in return.

I walk over to the driving range light control panel, rummage around in my pockets, pull out my key ring and find my master key to open it. Moe also has a set of keys that I loaned him earlier in the week and therefore he also has access to the panel. I insert the key, and with a good tug, the door creaks open. There are a series of ca-chung, ca-chung, ca-chung sounds as I pull each breaker switch and each section of lights shuts off.

"No way these lights are on unless you got here so early that you couldn't see well enough to see your shots in the darkness and needed them on."

"You're still wrong," Moe insists.

"Really?" I doggedly question him back. "So? What? Are you going to blame it on the poor guy closing up last night? That it was Karl's fault? That he left them on? That he forgot to turn them off? Because that sure doesn't sound like him to me. And he's the only one with keys outside of you and me."

"No, I'm saying you're wrong about the number! It's two hundred and ninety-seven. Two hundred and ninety-seven! *Not* three hundred. I've only hit two hundred and ninety-seven golf balls. *Not* three hundred like you said. Not even half a day's work is done yet. Long way to go yet! Long way to go."

"The number is not what we're talking about, and you know it," I shoot back.

Moe isn't overly thrilled with the easy dismissal of my rounding-up counting error -- and even more so of my lack of contrition for it.

"People don't realize that owning the perfect swing and being the best ball-striker in the game didn't just happen by accident. Oooh no! I have to practice. And practice hard! Day after day! To earn it. To own it. Oh sure! Every practice swing out here counts. Every single one. There's a big difference between three hundred and two hundred and ninety-seven. Those three remaining swings could mean everything! Change everything!"

Having heard how important it is for him to hit many golf balls every day, ad nauseam, I know it's going to be almost impossible to get him to back off, if even for one day. But I have to at least try.

"I know you need to hit these balls, Moe. I get it. I was just hoping that today you would hit a few less. For me. Something more for me and something less for you. Just for today."

"You bet I do it for me. And all by myself too! Oh sure! Nobody else can help me or do it for me. Learning the perfect swing is a journey you take alone. Sure! All by yourself. Golf isn't like a team sport. Oh no! It's not like hockey for instance. You're on your own in golf. All on your own. In hockey, if your team's defenceman back-checks, he can make you look good after you're the one to goof it up and make the dummy pass. Sure! But in golf, it's just you, mister. Just you and you alone. You and the golf ball."

Moe takes a sip of his Coca-Cola and continues, "Best of all, in golf, nobody else is allowed to touch your ball. Just how I like it. Just how I like it. Just me and my ball. Nothing else and nobody else."

After another guzzle of the Coca-Cola he grins, "Most people would cry if they could hit it this good," as he puts the beverage down, bends over, places one of the three remaining balls onto a tee, and without any hesitation or a practice swing he strikes it.

We both watch intently and the golf ball -- as expected -- gently lands, bounces, and rolls up to the target.

"Two hundred and ninety-eight. Right at the marker every time. Two hundred and ninety-eight!"

Now, before we talk about his next shot, there's something I really must take a moment to clarify to you. He *is* making these terrific shots. Time after time. He does have the best golf shot in the history of the game. And it's not just my opinion either. The biggest names in all of the game of golf have said it too. Here are just a few of the many quotes I can share:

Lee Trevino with eighty-nine professional wins and six Majors: *"Moe Norman is the best ball-striker I ever saw come down the pipe. I don't know how anyone could hit the ball better than Moe Norman. He is a genius when it comes to playing golf."*

Ben Crenshaw with twenty-nine professional wins and two Majors: *"Remarkable. You have to see it to believe it. The ball going to the target every time. Every time."*

Nick Price with fifty professional wins and three Majors: *"I've seen Moe hit balls. It's golf in the purest form as far as I am concerned."*

Tom Watson with seventy-one professional wins and eight majors: *"I'll tell you about a guy who can hit it better than anybody. His name is Moe Norman."*

Vijay Singh with fifty-nine professional wins and three majors: *"Best golfer I ever saw. He was incredible. Anything he said he could* do, he could do. God gives people little gifts and Moe had a gift for golf."

Paul Azinger with twelve professional wins and one major: *"He'd start ripping these drivers right off the ground at the two-fifty-yard marker and never hit one more than ten yards to either side of it, and he hit at least fifty. It was an incredible sight. And when he hit irons, he was calling how many times you would see it bounce. After he hit it – sometimes before he hit it –and he'd do it. It was unbelievable."*

And yes, even Tiger Woods with eighty-two PGA wins and fourteen majors had something stellar to say: *"Only two people ever owned their swing. Ben Hogan and Moe Norman. I hope one day to be the third. Moe woke every day knowing he was going to hit it well. He just knew he was going to hit it well. Every day. It is frightening how well Moe hit the ball. He's like Iron Byron the golf hitting machine."*

I wanted to take the time to share these quotes with you to make sure you didn't think I was exaggerating or blowing Moe's ability out of proportion. That I was embellishing, or even worse, that I was pulling your leg before going forward with this story.

Moe Norman is the real deal.

And now that I have taken a moment to point that out, there is one other nugget I have to share with you before proceeding any further. While it's one of those you-have-to see-it-to-believe-it kind of things, I will do my best. It's about Moe's golf swing.

By now I'm sure you have envisioned a graceful, beautiful, powerful, balanced, flawless, silky-smooth, God-like swing. I mean how else could anyone strike the ball with such perfection, right? Yet nothing could be further from the truth. His swing was like no other professional golfer. It was unconventional and unique, just like him.

As Bob Goalby with eleven professional wins and one Major said: *"He had an odd-looking swing. Sort of short. Sort of quick. But it didn't make a damn difference. He could hit the ball as straight as any human being who ever lived."*

So, there you go. A short and stocky, tooth-handicapped, fashion-challenged, Winnie-the-Pooh kind of guy, possessing one of the oddest swings in the game, produces the most accurate golf shot in the history of the sport. Bar none. And now, should you choose to stick around to read more, you'll see that all of what I've shared so far, is just the tip of the iceberg. Only a sliver of what made up, and what challenged, this unsung and often misunderstood, one-of-a-kind, Canadian sports hero.

2

POETRY IN MOETION

Just as Moe finishes hitting his ball, getting himself up to his self-imposed three-hundred-balls-half-a-days-work quota, a random golfer strides onto the driving range. He's a well-built younger lad, barely a day into his twenties, looking like a model directly out of the latest issue of Golf Digest's golf fashion trends. As he puts down his clubs and a bucket of range balls, he looks over at us. I receive nothing more than a fleeting glance, while he reserves a long-studied look for Moe.

Mere seconds pass and already I'm beginning to feel uncomfortable with the first impression I'm getting from him. Or to be clearer, at the look on his pretty face as he judges Moe as if he was a down-and-out squeegee person about to bother him for some spare change. It's both a smirk and a sneer that is not exactly a ringing endorsement of Moe's fashion sense. I'm able to quickly determine that what you are wearing would most likely be the first key step as to whether this silver-spoon-in-the-mouth kid may like you or not.

I interrupt his runway evaluation of Moe with, "Good morning. Perfect conditions to hit some balls don't you think?"

"Yeah, perfect indeed!" he agrees. "But then again when isn't it, right?"

"You've got me there! Still, it's easier to work on shaping a shot when there's no wind like this morning."

Moe's reaction to the young man's presence is the exact opposite of mine. He doesn't say anything. He just keeps enjoying his Coca-Cola. It's as if the other golfer isn't even there. Moe makes no effort to engage him or acknowledge him whatsoever. Not even as much as a cordial nod of the head.

Now, so you know, this isn't Moe being rude. Not at all. It's just that if Moe doesn't know you and the topic wasn't strictly about golf, he wouldn't have much time for you. You wouldn't exist in his world. Once you factored in his shyness and compounded it with his myopic desire to only want to engage in hitting a golf ball perfectly, most strangers didn't stand much of a chance of getting any interaction out of him. Unless it was one hundred percent his decision, of course.

Sensing this guy must be pretty good since he seems to have all the right equipment and "the look", Moe and I decide to sit for a bit – Moe drinking his Coca-Cola and me sipping my coffee -- and watch the fellow hit.

Sadly, for all of us, he's not a particularly good golfer after all. He surely has the look down pat but little else to accompany it. He has no form and no sense of balance -- before or after a shot. It also appears that thus far in life he has somehow avoided being told the number one rule in golf: To keep your head down. (Although, in his defence, if you are a golfer, you know that this is quite literally the hardest thing to learn. That, and don't try to kill it.)

Moe quietly chuckles to himself each time the guy swings as the shots spray everywhere but where the poor guy intends. To exacerbate his problems, he's trying so hard to kill it that he almost falls over after every shot. (As I just mentioned...the number two hardest rule to learn in golf.)

It doesn't take long however before Moe's noncommittal gaze turns into a steely glare. After every swing, there's a whopping piece of earth dug out of the ground by any one of the clubs he's using, and a grass pelt goes hurtling forth following his ball. Sometimes it goes even further than the shot itself! And the repetitive slamming of his club into the ground that starts to emerge, after each bad hit, which was often, isn't helping the situation much either.

Finally, Moe is unable to take it any longer. Without directly looking at the golfer he chides loudly, "What the heck do you think you're doing? You got it all wrong. All wrong!"

And with that commentary launched, I knew exactly what the poor guy was in for. Let the games begin!

I've seen this scenario many times over the years and sure, I could have tried to intervene as I have before in this kind of situation, but sheepishly I have to admit that today I'm childishly in the mood to let this one play out in the way I expect it will. So, I remain silent and watch.

"What do you mean, what am I doing?" replies the golfer.

"For starters, how the heck are you supposed to hit the ball forward when you're falling back all the time? Right after you hit it! Every time, you're falling backward! Makes no sense. You gotta swing through the ball, ya dummy. Swing forward. Through it. Not at it. And swing the same way each time. Why are you changing your swing every time you try and hit the ball, ya dummy? Makes no sense at all. No sense at all."

Moe gets up and purposely retrieves one of the many massive divots the golfer has made.

"And how about a bit of respect for the course while you're at it. Don't take such a big divot! You're not digging your way to China! Hoo! You want to caress the grass. Oh sure! Caress the grass. Greenskeepers love me. I try to never leave a mark when I play. And if you do decide to leave a divot, you want your divots to be bacon strips, dummy. Not pork chops. Bacon strips, of course! Bacon strips, ya dummy."

I internally grimace each time he uses the word dummy. I know Moe doesn't intend it maliciously and that it's just the way he speaks, but this guy doesn't know that. It's a term Moe uses in particular when he's frustrated. He often uses it regarding himself. And for the record, this isn't me making an excuse so he *could* use it. Not at all. I'm just trying to let you know he isn't trying to be antagonistic. Not intentionally anyway. It's just that his demeanour in situations like this, compounded by his complete lack of self-awareness in realizing how he might be coming off to others, often led to bad outward reflections of him rather than good.

You can immediately tell that hi-hoe-silver-spoon-in-his-mouth, who has most likely spent his entire life being told by his parents and friends that he *was* perfect, isn't taking a shine to being called a dummy. Not at all. Although, I mean, who would? Whether you were a prima donna or not.

"What did you just call me?" the young golfer challenges.

Moe dismisses the question since for him it's irrelevant. While still avoiding making eye contact, Moe questions him some more.

"I bet you use a golf cart when you play golf too, don't ya?"

"Of course, who doesn't use a cart?" he responds, with a slight growing annoyance in his voice, implying a history of not liking being challenged.

"I don't, that's who! See, I'm not like you. I'm not always going back and forth, shooting side to side, all over the course. I swing *through* a golf course. Swing *through* it while everyone else swings *around* it. I see my target and I swing to it. No hooks or slices. Everybody else is hitting the army swing. Left-right-left-right-left-right. But not me. Mine is always straight down the middle, every time. Why would I need a cart?"

It's becoming quite obvious at this point that Moe's enjoyment of this impromptu golf lesson is beginning to increase exponentially, and his shyness is quickly dissipating in correlation.

"You know, if I were in a tournament at night, I'd be the only one shooting par. Sure! Everyone else would be saying 'I think I went right' or 'I think I went left'. But not me! Hoo! Oooh no! Not me! I'd know where my ball went. Right down the middle. Right down the middle every time! I'm poetry in motion! Poetry in motion!"

With a twinkle in his eyes he clarifies further, "And do you know how to spell that? Spell 'poetry in motion'? You spell it P-O-E-T-R-Y, I-N, M-O-E-T-I-O-N. That's right! M-O-E-T-I-O-N. Get it? Hoo, hoo! Get it?" as he lets out a gleeful belly laugh.

The golfer looks at me with a wide-eyed annoyed skepticism, and blurts, "Is this guy for real?"

At this juncture, I'm beginning to think that maybe, just maybe, I should step in and smooth things out. But Moe was on a roll now and there was no stopping him. And let's face it, this guy has been rubbing me the wrong way, right from the start. So, I just shrug my shoulders and sit back and watch. I can be the ringmaster another time. Now it was time to be the audience.

Sensing that words are not going to be enough, Moe begins to physically demonstrate what he is explaining to the golfer.

"Here are some tips for you to hit the ball straight and precise. First thing, feet wide apart, outside the knees. You may lose distance but you're going to be dead straight. And I want both feet on the ground. On. The. Ground. Most guys are always up on their right foot. Way up! But I want my swing to balance me. I don't balance my swing. My swing balances me. And you roll your ankles! Don't lift them. Roll them! When I swing you won't ever see a spike under my shoe at contact. Not on my backswing either. Oooh, no sir! Not one spike."

Just as the golfer is about to interject, Moe puts up his hand like a stop sign and continues.

"Second, extend your arms. Make a 'V' and don't do anything to change that 'V'! Don't bend your elbows at all. Pretend there's no club head. And hit with the handle. Hold it extra tight. Strangle it. And third, when you swing, you swing through to the target. Pull with your left hand to the target. It's a swing, not a push. The right hand just follows along. Follows forward. You should have a pulling sensation. And don't try and kill it! Everyone else is so busy using brute force. Oooh yeah! Brute force. Always trying to kill it. When smooth force is the key. Smooth force."

Moe gestures with his hand and requests, "Hold your club up for me. Show me how you hold it."

"What?" the golfer questions with a growing perplexed look on his face.

"Your club. Show me how you hold your golf club."

The guy looks at me again, with the same befuddled look, and the kindest thing I can do is tell him, "You want my advice? You're way better off if you just do it and show him how you hold your club."

Hoping this is the quickest way to the end, the golfer acquiesces and begrudgingly holds the club out for Moe, with a growing scowl on his face.

"WRONG!" chastises Moe. "Hoo! Wrong, wrong, wrong! Oooh no! Not in the fingers! Fingers are fast, fingers are fast. Palms are calm, palms are calm. Hold it in your palms!"

"That feels completely wrong," as he tries the new suggested grip.

"How does a baseball player or a tennis player hold their bat or racquet?" confronts Moe back. Without letting the poor guy respond he answers his own question. "In the palm of their hand, of course. The palm of the hand! Not the fingers! Where the meat is! Now, show me your hands."

"I'm not showing you my hands."

"C'mon. I just want to see your hands. I'm not going to bite you."

The guy looks over at me again and I sheepishly respond, "Sorry, all I have is the same advice. Just show him."

With an audibly annoyed sigh, he holds out both his hands.

"Palms up," corrects Moe. "Palms up."

He flips them palms up and Moe grabs them and caresses them.

The fellow instantly pulls them back and Moe bellows with high-pitched laughter, "Oooh! Oooh my! Oooh my! Those are so soft. Soooo soft. What do you do? Use ladies' hand lotion every day? Hoo!

You must be like that Jergen's lady in those dishwashing commercials! 'I'm just soaking in it...'"

Before the kid can even take offence, Moe thrusts his hands close into the guy's face. They are worn, leathery, and full of calluses. They look like rawhide and if you touched them they would feel like sandpaper.

"*These* are a golfer's hands," he proudly declares. "If you don't have the scars, the scars like these, of hard work, you haven't pushed hard enough. That's how you get calluses like mine. Hard work. Hard life calluses! Hard work calluses!"

The bemused look on the golfer's face at this point is impossible to miss. Moe takes a quick look at him in the eyes, for the first time, and sees the confusion behind them.

"Ah, here, let me show ya better then. Let me show ya better."

Moe turns to me. "Hand me my driver, Nick. Hand me my driver please."

Without any input from me, I see I've officially been designated as Moe's accomplice for this portion of the lesson. Without arguing I dutifully go over to his golf bag, pull out the driver, and bring it over to him.

"No, no, no. I want the other one, the other one," as he points to the other bag.

I grab the correct driver this time and Moe quickly snatches it from my extended grip.

"Watch!" he orders.

To be honest, at this point, I have to admit I think the guy is being remarkably cool about all this, despite my initial dislike of him. Once you factor everything in so far, I'm quite sure if it were me in his position, I would have had a few choice words already. At the very least, I would found a way to have walked away and extricated myself from this bizarre situation by now.

"And three, make sure the clubhead is well behind the ball. About twelve inches."

The golfer incredulously interrupts Moe. *"Twelve* inches?! Twelve inches behind the ball?! That's ridiculous!"

I guess I spoke too soon and I'm wrong after all. The kid has met his limit.

"Now I know you're full of it!" he declares.

"Yes, twelve inches! Twelve inches!" commands Moe, standing his ground. "Not with the club right behind the ball like most duffers, but back further. Twelve inches!"

Moe shows him the difference and places his club on the ground, going back and forth to each position.

"Here is me and here is everyone else. Me. Them. Me. Them. I put it twelve inches back behind the tee and the ball. That way you're already drawing the club back properly when you start. Oooh, sure! Why not make it easier for yourself? Don't overcomplicate everything. Keep it simple, stupid! Keep it simple!"

Having seen and heard this last tip -- which contradicts pretty much everything he has ever been told -- the golfer is beginning to conclude that Moe is indeed a bit of a whacko. He laughs at the last bit of advice and mumbles as he turns away, "You're an idiot."

"LOOK!" demands Moe, stopping the kid in his tracks, as he places the driver twelve inches behind a tee, rather than right up to it, demonstrating his entire stance, placement, and swing but without hitting the ball. He mimics the action three or four times.

Interpreting the lesson he's getting as being increasingly ridiculous by the second, the golfer chuckles to himself, shakes his head, and looks at me with pity in his eyes. A look that assumes I'm being punished for unknown sins, having been assigned to be Moe's babysitter or his caregiver as my sentence.

Having heard the young guy's chuckle, it triggers something deep within Moe, and his demeanour changes.

"Oooh, I know what you're thinking. Thinking that I look different than most golfers when I'm swinging. Oh sure! Thinking that's an odd-looking swing. No way he can hit it good. Oh, I know. Oh sure! Oooh sure! But once I hit it? Oh, man! No more comments.

Oh, man, no sir, nothing but stunned silence! And that my friend is a feeling of greatness. MY feeling of greatness. I'm the only golfer who has it. A greatness that happens every single time I hit the ball."

Moe bursts into a laugh, "I'm probably the only golfer on the planet you can't help. You wanna know why? Because I don't need it. I don't need help! I can't hit the ball crooked. My swing won't let me! In all my years of tournament golf, I hit the ball out of bounds once! Just once."

Moe bends down puts a ball on the tee but doesn't hit it yet.

"One of the secrets is that before you even hit the ball, you need to see what you want it to do. Oooh sure! You don't just hit it! You see it! Like life. You should see what you want. Visualize it. If you can't see clearly what you want, before you even start, then you're never going to get it! Cloudy vision equals cloudy results. And don't see bad things when you hit the ball! Bad things don't exist on Moe's golf course. No sir! Only good things. I see only good things."

Having finally had enough, the golfer tries to wrap up the unsolicited lesson. "Thanks, old-timer, but I think I'll be fine doing it my way. You have a good one."

With a devilish grin in his eye, Moe challenges him right back. "What? You don't think I'm telling you the truth? Not telling you the truth on how to hit a ball right?"

"Look pal, hit it whatever whacky way you want. Whatever floats your boat. I need to go practice."

"Whatever floats my boat? Whatever floats my boat? I'll show ya what floats my boat. What marker do you want me to go for out there?" pointing to all the markers scattered out on the driving range.

"What do you mean?" the young golfer says.

"Which marker do you want me to go for? Which marker?"

The golfer looks incredulously at me. "Is he serious?"

"Go ahead and tell him which one and see for yourself," I say, desperately trying to hold back an all-knowing grin. Things are about to get *really* fun now.

"You want me to tell you which marker to hit a ball to?"

Moe shoots me his best devilish impish grin and winks at me, "Maybe not such a dummy after all."

"Do you want to put some money on it smart guy?" the golfer contests, sensing an easy bet.

"No. The look on your face will be good enough son. Which marker? What distance?"

Purposely picking the furthest marker, "The two-fifty."

Moe takes a ball from the golfer's range basket, tees it up, and with no practice swing, he strikes it. It flies perfectly towards the marker on the left. As you may have guessed, it lands right by it and stops on a dime.

"Lucky shot," snaps the golfer.

"Or maybe...you meant the other one? The marker to the right?"

Moe takes another ball from the golfer's basket, tees it up, strikes it, and it also flies perfectly towards its target on the right side. This time it kisses it and comes to a rest just inches away.

"So, what do you think? What do you think? Just lucky again?" Moe teases.

The young golfer purses his lips, saying nothing this time.

"How about the two hundred then?" quips Moe as he grabs another one of the kids' balls, tees it up, strikes it, and has it land within a few feet of the two-hundred marker.

The young golfers' eyes grow wide with wonder. He's starting to have trouble processing the accurate shot-making he's seeing.

"Or maybe the one hundred? Yes, the one hundred. One of my favourites. One of my favourites."

Moe nonchalantly turns to me. "Can you pass me my wedge please, Nick?"

I respond obediently, getting up and grabbing the requested club from his bag. I'm glad I'm asked to get it as it gives me a moment to turn my back on them both and compose myself. Watching this cat and mouse fun is a real treat. We've arrived at the point in the proceedings, where I'm finding it exceedingly difficult to not burst out laughing at the poor kid's predicament.

I hand the club to Moe.

"The one hundred it is! Here she comes. Here she comes."

Moe drops a ball on the ground, strikes it and hits it about fifteen feet past the sign, and cautions, "Wait for it, wait for it," as it sucks backwards to within mere inches of the marker.

Without taking as much as a second to appreciate the shot or to luxuriate in the kid's bewilderment, Moe demonstrates he's not finished yet. "Now, of course, it would be rude to leave the one-fifty out of this game, wouldn't it? Wouldn't it?"

Looking like one of the three pigs about to be caught by the big bad wolf, the wide-eyed young guy is silent. His face is full of shock, awe, and wonder.

Enjoying this fully now, Moe repeats pointedly, "Wouldn't it?!"

With an ever so slight tremble in his voice, the young golfer manages to utter, "Look mister, it's okay. You don't have to --"

"Of course, I do. Of course, I do!" bellows Moe back. "Seven iron please, Nick. Seven iron."

I grab it from the bag, take the wedge back and he quickly strikes another ball and hits it right to the target once again.

"What do you think now? Huh? What do you think?" queries Moe as he cockily tosses the club upon his shoulder and rests it there like a rifle, satisfyingly studying the young man from head to toe.

The kid looks at me, then to Moe, then at me again.

Sensing it's my help he desires, I shrug my shoulders and say, "He told you..."

Moe gets a big toothy grin as an idea strikes him. At the same moment, I can't help but notice a slight flinch in the kid as he finally gets to see the no-one-is-ready-for-that-prime-time Moe smile. I knew he wasn't getting away clean from getting a peek at that.

"Let's try one more thing. One more thing. Whad'ya think?" proclaims Moe. "Nick, can you grab a Coca-Cola bottle out of that middle bag for me, please?"

I can't contain my glee. I know exactly what is coming next. I know precisely why he has a Coca-Cola bottle hiding in his bag.

I dutifully run over, eagerly pull it out of the zipped-up compartment, and hand it to him.

He sets it on the ground, takes one of the guy's golf balls, and places it on the top of the glass bottle.

"Driver again please," requests Moe as he extends his hand out like a surgeon. I hand it to him as any dutiful assistant would in any operating room. He gives me the wedge back and I hold it. He stands in front of the ball and places his driver in front of the Coke bottle.

"Ready?" he relays with relish, as he bears down on the kid with an evil smile.

"Dude, you're not serious," blurts the young golfer.

"Ooh! One-hundred percent serious. Hoo! One-hundred percent. How about we go for that two hundred and fifty again shall we?"

The golfer is mute.

"Which one? Which one? Right or left?"

"Huh?" the guy mumbles back.

"Right or left? Right or left?"

"I...uh...I dunno...left?"

"Left it is!" and without an ounce of fear or a moment of hesitation, Moe immediately swings at the golf ball.

Instinctively, the kid flinches and covers his face, fearing a furious blast of glass shards flying through the air which will impale his still perfectly unwrinkled face. As he cowers, he yells out, "You're nuts!"

In direct contrast to the duck-and-cover lad, I placidly sit there, calmly watching, barely moving a muscle. This is all turning out way better than I ever would have thought!

In one fluid motion, Moe strikes the golf ball, and there is not even the slightest wobble to the Coca-Cola bottle. The ball is picked off of it clean and flies perfectly straight towards its target. The young guy uncovers his face just in time to see the ball as it lands directly in front of the sign, about ten feet short.

Moe matter-of-factly deadpans, "A little further away than I would have liked. But not bad."

"Not bad...not bad," I giggle to myself.

The young man stutters, "That's...that's...that's crazy man. That's some crazy shit. Sorry I didn't believe what you were saying."

"No offence taken. No offence taken," Moe replies nonchalantly, with the lesson now completed and the lesson learned. Mission accomplished, the Moe Norman way.

The young guy extends out his hand in an attempt to shake a truce with Moe. "That was some crazy good ball-striking mister. Nice shots."

With an ever so slight hesitation at the outstretched hand, Moe reaches out in return and says "I'm the best ball-striker in the game they say. That's not me saying it though. Oooh no. It's everyone else saying it about me. Everyone else saying that about me."

They shake hands and the poor guy immediately grimaces in pain.

Oh yeah, sorry, that's another thing I haven't mentioned yet about Moe. The guy has a killer handshake. He easily has the strongest pair of hands I've ever seen from gripping his golf clubs so tightly all these years. When he shakes your hand you may as well be a golf club to him. So be warned and be prepared.

After releasing the handshake and shaking out his hand to relieve the tingles and even massaging it a bit, the young man looks at me one more time and nods his head in a "we're good now?" kind of way. I nod back in kind. All good.

Without saying another word, he straightaway goes back to his bucket of balls, picks them up, along with his clubs, and moves over to the farthest edge of the range, to get as far away from us as possible. As much as he is impressed by Moe's dazzling display of shots, he didn't want to have to risk spending any more time in the crazy town golf academy.

I quietly point out to Moe, "You've been keeping that Coke bottle in there for a while now, for just the right moment, haven't you?"

"Maybe," Moe shrugs. "Maybe."

We give the golfer a few minutes to himself, letting him lick his wounds and recover from Moe's school of hard shots. Eventually, he gets around to teeing one up for himself. He shoots a quick sly glance our way to make sure that we aren't paying attention – but oh yes, we sneakily are -- and he puts his club about twelve inches behind the ball as Moe suggested. Sadly, for him, it's not just another routine bad shot, but he whiffs it, missing altogether, almost falling completely over. Slamming his golf club into the ground in anger, we hear him mumble to himself, "That doesn't work at all! That's bullshit! Twelve inches behind the ball. My ass!"

Both of us try to quickly turn away, to avoid being caught watching, as he shoots a brief frustrated look our way to see if we just saw what he did.

I'm not sure if we were caught, but after that, he refuses to look our way again, doggedly continuing away on his determined self-flagellation.

He may have been done with us, but we continue to be quietly entertained by his arrogant ineptitude and slowly enjoy our beverages, secretly watching from afar. It's like watching a car accident happen. You know you should turn away, but you just can't.

After a few more disastrous shots, Moe points to the golfer, offering to me quietly, "Nowadays everybody wants something right away. Right away. No desire to put in the effort. It's always just 'I want it, I want it now, I want it, give it to me.' No hard work ethic at all. And then, people are always seeing the bad too. Thinking the bad. Jeez, yes. Never seeing the positive. Just beating themselves up. It's such a shame. Such a shame."

Moe takes another drink of his Coca-Cola and continues.

"You know, playing golf is better than being in jail, isn't it? Oooh sure! Think about it! The guys in jail would love to be free. Be out here, playing on the bright green fairway. But they can't. Then what do *we* do when *we're* on the fairway? We go put ourselves in jail! Sure! In jail! We throw our clubs, call ourselves names, get angry for missing a two-foot putt or hitting it in the sand trap or the water! Idiot! Loser! Choker! Sure! Never patting ourselves on the back but instead, just kicking ourselves in the behind. Always downgrading ourselves. But not me, I only see the good. See the good *before* it even happens. I've never slammed down or thrown a golf club in my life nor swatted a ball in anger. Oh no! Never! What's the point? Why get upset? All you can do is try. All you can do is try. Why beat yourself up for trying? I say good for you for trying! Good for you! Bad thinking is worse than a bad swing! Good thinking, good golf. Bad thinking, bad golf. Hope and fear. That's how most people play golf. How they play life. Hope and fear. But not me. I believe. Fear is what defeats you. Sure! Fear! Not me. I just believe in my swing. I believe in me. Every time. I only see good things. Pars, birdies, and eagles. There's no bogeys in my bag."

Moe calculatedly waits for a beat before adding, "And maybe just a few Coca-Cola bottles. Maybe just a few Coca-Cola bottles."

He winks at me, gets up and grabs the Coke bottle he was using for the shot moments ago and returns it to his golf bag. I hear the clink of more than one inside as he places it back in. He zips it up and gently pats the spot where they are hidden when he's done. It dawns on me that he sneakily has a conveniently secured, well-prepared stash in there. Each bottle patiently waiting for its turn in being a part of a whoop-ass golf lesson for an unsuspecting random student to be.

3

YOU GOTTA BELIEVE

As we sit enjoying our quiet timeout with our cola and coffee, now trying to ignore the increasingly angry and frustrated young golfer hacking away at his shots, I begin wondering more about Moe's last comment. About how he believes in himself and his swing every time.

"I guess what you're saying is that ultimately, confidence and belief go a long way to hitting the ball well. Even more than the mechanics of it all?

"Oh sure. Oh sure," Moe pipes up. "Mechanics are a must. Mechanics are a must. But belief is one of the biggest pieces of the puzzle. Know *how* you're going to hit first, then see *where* you're going to hit, see it happen in your mind, and then put all other thoughts out of your mind and *believe*. Like them Nike folks say. 'Just do it.'

"Let me give you a good example," Moe continues. "In 1960, I was playing an exhibition golf match with Sam Snead and another pro named Porky Oliver. Porky's real name was Ed, but we all called him Porky. Now, Sam, you called him Sam. Or, Mr. Snead, even. There was no messing with that name unless you knew him well. If you were close to him you could call him 'Slammin Sammy'. But otherwise, no way. Oh, no sir. No way. No way you messed with that name. Sam was a legend.

"The three of us were out there having a good time playing. A good time. We're all competitors and so we always want to win but since it was an exhibition match there was a little bit of wiggle room to have some fun too. A little fun with each other. A little wiggle room fun. We purposely kept the match close and quietly agreed amongst each other that we were gonna decide the winner by the best play on the last four holes. We all had just parred the fifteenth and now we were at the sixteenth hole. It was a long par four and there was a creek that ran straight across it at about the two-hundred-and-forty-yard mark.

"Now you have to remember that back then, unlike today with all the fancy-dancy golf clubs and long-distance golf balls, two hundred and fifty yards was a long way to carry. It would take at least two hundred and fifty yards to carry the creek. Before pulling out any golf clubs from our bags, the three of us stood there and looked out at the hole, thinking about what to hit...

"You're up Porky,' said Sam. 'What're you going to be hitting?'

"If it was earlier in the round I might have gone for it, but I think I'm going to go with a three wood and put it in a good spot for my second. I'll put it somewhere right in front, but short of the creek,' Porky answered back.

"Smart play,' Sam agreed.

"I didn't say anything.

"Porky went to the tee-off, teed up his ball, and took a step back behind his ball to line it up properly. When he was ready he got up to the ball, took a couple of practice swings, and addressed it. He struck a fine shot that went right up the middle of the fairway and landed perfectly, rolling to about twenty yards short of the creek. The crowd politely applauded him.

"Good one. Smart shot,' said Sam.

"Nice one,' I agreed.

"Thanks, boys,' said Porky. 'You're up Sam. What're you going to hit?'

"Well, I'd like to think that I'm one of the smart ones too, so I'll go with the three wood as well.'

"From out of the crowd a voice shouted out, 'You're the smartest of them all, Sam!'

"Hoo, Sam liked that! Hoo! He liked that a lot.

"Then Sam tipped his trademark pork pie straw hat to whoever it was in the crowd and yelled, 'Why thank you! Can't argue with the paying public now can we?!'

"The crowd laughed and roared its approval for him even more after that comment.

"Sam went to his bag and took out took his three-wood. He stood behind the ball, took a good look at the fairway, and took two methodical swings before solidly striking his ball. Just like Porky's, it was a fine shot, right down the middle. Right down the middle of the fairway and finished up just to the left of Porky's ball. Of course, the crowd roared their approval again. Even louder for Sam though. He was their favourite, after all.

"Porky applauded, 'Nice shot!'

"Then I added, 'Yeah Sam, nice shot. Nice, safe, shot.' Sam turned to me, saw what was already in my hand, and said, 'What're you hitting, Moe?'

"Driver, Sam. Hitting my driver.

"Driver? Are you kidding me? It's two hundred and fifty yards easy to carry the creek. You're going to get wet.'

"Some people in the crowd laughed out loud at what Sam predicted would happen.

"You think?' I said.

"Sam knowingly smiled back, 'I *know*.'

"Then Porky chimed in, 'I have to agree with Sam on this one. No way you're going to make it over the creek.'

"I just smiled and said, 'We know what happened the last time I took your advice don't we, Sam? I think I'll stick with the driver, stick with the driver.'

"Sam shook his head at me and repeated, 'No way you'll carry the creek with a driver, Moe. But do whatever you want. It'll just take you out of the chance of winning the hole. So, no complaints from us!'

"Not to worry Sam, not to worry,' I warned him.

"I got up on the tee-off and without wasting time checking out the fairway, lining up my ball, or taking a bunch of silly practice swings, I hit my ball. Just hit it. Plain and simple. Swung and hit it. Like I do every time. Every time. Right at the spot I was thinking of.

"The ball landed just short of the creek.

"It seemed clear to everyone that Sam and Porky were going to be right. That it would go into the creek and cost me a stroke. The crowd oohed and aahed as they all eagerly anticipated what was going to happen. I bet some of them were even being poor sports, praying for my ball to go into the water to prove that their favourite Sam Snead, was right. Some of them even laughed as it got closer to the creek.

"I told you, there's no way you were clearing the creek,' chuckled Sam as my ball landed.

"Yessir, you're going to be wet,' said Porky.

"I just kept watching my shot.

"THEN, the ball bounced right before the creek, hit the bridge going over it, took a huge bounce forward, and rolled over to the other side of the creek by about thirty yards.

"I turned back to Sam and was feeling pretty good when I said, 'I was never thinking about the creek, Sam. The bridge was my target all the time. The bridge was the target all the time.'

"Then the crowd went crazy with applause again. But this time it was for me. This time it was for me!

"Keeping my attention on Sam I asked, 'Any more advice?'

"Sam took a good moment before saying anything. Then he shook his head and wiggle finger pointed at me and said, 'If it wasn't you hitting that ball Moe, I'd say you just got lucky.'

"But it was me,' I said.

"Yes, it was,' Sam managed with a nod of his head.

"Sam smiled, tipped his hat to me and walked away, still shaking his head as he mumbled, 'You're one of a kind, Moe. One of a kind.'

"Sam never gave me a suggestion on how to play a shot again. Never again. And I never forgot what he called me that day. 'One of a kind! One of a kind!' Hoo! Sam Snead calling *me*, 'One of a kind!' That was a great day. A great day. One of the best players there ever was calling me, Moe Norman, Moe the Shmoe, one of a kind!

"Yup, you gotta believe in you, if you're gonna make others believe, Nick. You have to do it to yourself first. You gotta believe in you first or there's no chance for you to ever convince anyone else."

4

DUMMYING IT DOWN

JUST AS MOE FINISHES TELLING ME HIS AWESOME SAM SNEAD story, mister fashionista cranky-pants simultaneously finishes hitting his bucket of range balls. Appearing less than enamoured with his session, he angrily thrusts his clubs back into his bag and briskly strides past us in the direction of the clubhouse. Interestingly, I notice he doesn't take his clubs back with him. I assume he's keenly aware that he needs to hit a few more balls and will be back shortly.

As he marches off, Moe waits until he is out of earshot before he repeats his opinion of the frustrated golden boy.

"What a dummy!"

While I didn't want to chastise Moe in front of the other guy earlier, this is now a once-too-many usage of the word dummy for me today. I could not let it go. Nor would I.

"I don't think it's very fair or nice to use that word just because someone can't hit a ball as well as you. That doesn't make them dumb, it just makes them not as good a golfer as you. Does that make everyone else in the world dumb then? Me included? Am I a dummy too?"

Moe sheepishly turns away from me and mumbles, "I've never called you a dummy. And I never would. I never would."

"When you act like that, it tells me you don't have to say it, but you certainly must think it."

Looking down at his feet and not at me he defiantly repeats, "I don't think it. I'd never call you that."

"Moe, my point is that I don't think *anyone* wants to be called that. Not ever. Not for any reason. Whether they're the smartest person or not. Whether they're a good golfer or not. It's just not a very nice thing to do or say. It sure doesn't make anyone feel good does it?"

He knows I'm right, but Moe isn't ready to give in easily.

"He's still a dummy...trying to hit it a ball forward and falling backward...," Moe smacks himself in the side of the head, "What a dummy. Oh what a dummy."

"As I said, not everyone can hit a ball like you," retaining my patient tone of voice.

Moe digs his heels in further, "You bet they can't. I'm the best ball-striker there ever was. That's what they all say. You saw my shots today already. Right at the target. Three hundred. Every time!" Moe chuckles, "For me, hitting a ball is just like falling off a log! Like falling off a log. For that dummy? He just falls. What a dummy."

"He is practicing and trying to get better, is he not?" I try and reason. "You said yourself that trying was important. You said it was to be applauded."

Moe contemplates for a second as he drains his Coca-Cola, swishing some around in his mouth before swallowing. "You can't just practice now and then. You have to practice all the time. All the time."

"Most everyone can't practice all the time."

"Then they won't get better. Simple as that. They won't get better. They certainly won't become great," he defiantly insists.

Despite the endless stubborn go-around Moe is clinging to, I know I'm making headway. Moe is not a mean person and purposely bringing someone down for the sake of it is nowhere in his genetic makeup.

"I just thought I'd put that out there. Something for you to think about," I state matter of factly.

Moe keeps silently sipping his drink, not a fan of being in the wrong. I can't tell for sure if the silence is a sign of his giving some consideration to my argument or whether he is just biding his time to let this discussion blow over.

We sit for a short while longer as the sun moves higher into the sky and a few isolated puffy clouds start to arrive, casting shadows on the ground here and there.

"You know what? I think I will have a Coke after all," I decide.

Moe eagerly rushes over to his stash.

"Sure thing. Sure thing. Here you go. My last one. All yours," as he enthusiastically hands me the pop.

"Oh, no. I don't want to take your last one. I don't need it that badly," not wanting to have him make that big a sacrifice for me.

"Should have asked earlier then," Moe replies. "Should have asked earlier when there were plenty more. You can have it though. I don't care. Take it. Really. Take it, please," as he stretches out his arm further, aggressively shoving it at me.

I highly suspect the Coke is also being offered as a peace offering. He knows full well that we shouldn't have had to have had our "dummy discussion" in the first place. This is not our first go-around on the subject.

"No, it's okay, seriously. You finish it. Besides, I tell you what. I'm going to go and grab some more cold Cokes and bring them back for you. I have tons of things I need to start to do for the big event later today. I can grab them at the same time and bring them back when I have the chance."

While Moe would love to have some fresh ice-cold Coca-Cola to devour and placate his proud addiction, he is not so fond of the idea of losing his audience and one of his biggest fans.

"No, Nick. No! Stick around. Do that later. Let me hit a few more for you. Watch me hit!"

Moe eagerly jumps to his feet, grabs the empty buckets, and picks them up. "Let me run over to the clubhouse and get some more balls to hit! You can watch!"

"I'd love to Moe, but I really don't have the time. Why don't you just sit and drink your pop and I'll be back with more before you know it?"

"I know, I know. But every second of every day counts. You sure you can't stay? Let me hit some for you! Let me hit some more for you! Please! Please!?" he continues to beg.

Knowing I'll be stuck here for the better part of the day if I don't stand firm and make my immediate getaway, I sugar-coat my escape. "I would love to keep watching the most perfect swing in golf all day long Moe, but I have lots to do to prepare for tonight. Maybe later okay? I won't be gone too long I promise. You know I like to watch you hit your shots."

As I turn and leave, once again hearing the click-clack of my new shoes on the path and realizing I won't have time to hit some balls in them after all, I can feel Moe's eyes boring into my back, desperately pleading for me to stay. However, I don't bend to the gnawing power and continue on my way.

"Wait up! Wait up for me then!" yells Moe suddenly, hastily following after me. "I need to get more balls to hit. I'll walk with ya."

"Sure, c'mon then," I agree, happy that walking with me will at least keep him from hitting more balls for a while. If I'm extra lucky, I may even find something less physical for him to do, to distract him with, when we get to the clubhouse.

Within twenty seconds into our walk, Moe is no longer walking with me, but rather, he is well in front of me, already creating a gap between us that precludes normal talking voices. I shout out to him, "I thought you said you wanted to walk with me?!"

"I do, but you're too slow!" he complains back.

"Okay then, see you later, I guess."

Moe begrudgingly stops and waits for me to catch up, just as I suspect he will.

As we slowly walk at a pace that I am determined to set and maintain -- because if I let Moe be in charge, we would already be starting a slight sprint again -- I bring up his part on this special day.

"I've been wondering...have you given any thought to what you're going to do tonight? Have you written anything down? Do you have anything to show me or to run by me yet?"

It seems that Moe has suddenly turned blind, deaf, and dumb on me all at once.

I repeat, "Have you?"

Doing his best Helen Keller impersonation he offers me nothing in return.

I repeat louder, "Moe?!"

"What's that?" he innocently replies.

Knowing full well he heard me the first time, "Do you know what you're going to say tonight? Have you written anything down? Do you have anything to show me or to run by me? I'm happy to hear it if you want."

"I'm still thinking about it. Still thinking about it" he deftly dodges.

"I need you to stop just thinking about it and I need you to start writing something down," I express to him with a more firm tone in my voice. "It'll be much easier if you write something down now. I don't want to have to be doing it for you, in a panic, at the last minute."

Showing an absolute, stubborn infused, dismissive disinterest, he gives me a vague and all telling "Mhmm," to placate me.

Just as I'm about to dig into this further, refusing to drop the subject whether he likes it or not, my attention is distracted by some loud hooting and hollering in the distance. It grabs my focus as this kind of behaviour isn't the sort of thing you see and hear on a golf course. As I look toward the source of the revelry my stomach drops a bit and I come to a halt.

I don't like what I see ahead of us.

Off in the distance, I spot the young golfer from the driving range earlier. But he's no longer walking, and he's no longer alone. He's driving a golf cart by himself, and another two buddies are in another one close beside him.

When I first see them, they're not coming our way and they seem to be racing off in another direction. But then, they stop. I see the main guy rise in his seat and point in our direction to his two friends. To my dismay, they immediately swing their carts around and change their direction. They are now coming full tilt at us.

This can't be good.

5

HIT AND MISS

The faster the boisterous posse of three hurtles towards us, and the closer they get, the quicker I must assess what is rapidly evolving before my eyes. Fortunately, I can see that my first impression was right. There are only three of them instead of the usual four expected for a pair of golf carts. One less to worry about. Not surprisingly, his buddies are almost carbon copies of the ringleader, nearly identical triplets in their carefully chosen golf ensembles. I'm quietly praying that I may have miscalculated after all and that he was pointing them in the direction of the driving range behind us and not towards Moe and myself.

As the distance between us continues to shrink, as a safety, I move Moe and myself off to one side of the path. As I do, the leader mischievously decides to take the same side. Like good soldiers, his friends follow into enemy formation. There is no question now that the sensation in the pit of my stomach, upon first seeing them, was spot on. Their target destination isn't the practice range. It is the two of us.

As my panic begins to swell, Moe is completely oblivious to all that is happening, and I start to feel like I'm a mother bear who needs to protect her young cub. When the three get within a few paces of us the lone ranger quickly swerves and narrowly misses us, as does the other duo. While in reality we were never in any critical danger of being hit and he was never that close to us to cause bodily injury, it was damn close! Enough so, that both Moe and I instinctively jump further to the side at the last minute to avoid being struck and both of us tumble hard onto the ground.

The main young guy -- who I'm now quickly concluding is a dummy, if not a complete asshole – screeches his cart to a halt and shouts, "Why don't you guys watch where you're going?!"

His buddies roar with laughter.

Without wasting any time to make sure Moe nor I have been hurt, I jump up and angrily confront the leader.

"You almost hit us! What were you doing? You knew darn well we were there! You saw us all along! That wasn't funny if that's what you're thinking. Someone could have got seriously hurt!"

"Calm down," one of them pipes up. "He wasn't anywhere near you."

Completely ignoring my comments, the ringer leader points at us. "That's the two guys I was telling you about earlier."

"You aren't too hard to miss are you!" chimes in one of his pals, looking directly at Moe.

Not wanting to be left out from being a dickhead, the other buddy in the pack offers his own two cents. "You got that right. That's some look you got going there, grandpa! Are you doing a show for the kids later? Working the event they're setting up for in the banquet hall at the clubhouse tonight? Going to add a big hat, some white face make-up, and a red nose later? Be the clown entertainment for all the kids?"

Another one adds for good measure, "You sure have the goofy shoes to complete the look!"

All three of them howl with laughter. One of the guys gives his buddy an appreciative high-five for his supposedly clever clown joke.

Moe doesn't say or do a thing. He just sits there and takes it, looking despairingly down at the ground.

"Stay here," I instruct Moe, walking menacingly closer to their carts.

There's not a chance in hell they are getting away with this.

Now, I'm not a physical confrontation kind of guy – heck, I've never even been in a real fight before, outside of some scuffles in the playground during my grade school days – but if push needs to come to shove in this case, I'm all for it. Bring it on!

Predictably -- being the cowards they truly are – all three quickly begin to drive off as I get close to them, laughing while they do. Before getting too far away I yell at them with my fist pumping in the air, "You've got another think coming if you think this is over!"

That makes them laugh even more, and one yells out, "Fucking clown!" as they speed off. "Both of you!"

I'm so angry right now, I could spit.

To be honest, I don't care about myself being called a clown. But I don't have any patience for them calling Moe one or treating him like that. Deep down I know it's just a bunch of young rich kids who think they own the world and can do and say whatever they want. That, in their arrogant little minds, everyone else is beneath them, and there is nothing I can do to change that. Even more so, I know they aren't worth the time of day and most certainly not worth the anger I'm giving them at this second. I'll get over it, I know. But in this exact moment, I can't help but notice how tightly clenched my fists are. If a golf club was in my hands right now, Moe would be very pleased with my grip. I have to firmly, inwardly, instruct myself to calm down and relax my fists.

As the goons drive off into the distance I turn and look over to Moe. What I see tugs at my heartstrings. He's completely deflated. The three stooges have taken a huge bite out of him. He sits sadly on the worn grass beside the cart path, saying nothing.

But his face?

It says everything.

6

THE CLOWN PRINCE OF GOLF

As skilled as I normally am at smoothing things over, I'm not quite sure what to do at this particular moment. Do I say something to Moe? Do I try and cheer him up? Do I go after the three little monsters and eviscerate each one of them, one at a time, limb by limb? Do I tell Moe that he was right after all? That the kid is a dummy? A dummy-asshole, to be precise.

After brief contemplation, I decide the best plan of attack is to go with "none of the above" and choose plan "E" instead.

I elect to sit beside him, say nothing, and wait.

And wait.

And wait.

Finally, Moe quietly speaks up.

"I have the swing. The best swing in the game. The best swing in golf. No question about that. Everybody says it. It's not me saying it. It's everyone saying it about me. And I figured it out all by myself. All by myself. My mind is the generator, my body is the motor, the club is a trigger, and the ball is a bullet. Before you shoot you take aim."

"You do!" I immediately encourage back. "You have the best swing in the game. You have a lot to be proud of. You're way better than those three losers will ever be. And I don't just mean about golf but about everything. Everything that matters anyway."

Unfortunately, my honest praise does nothing to change his sad face. He continues staring down at his wiggling toe sticking out of his worn shoe.

"And yet, for some reason, everyone wants to laugh, don't they? Everyone wants to laugh at me. Everyone."

He goes quiet again and I echo the silence.

When ready he repeats in a sad, deflated, little voice, "Oh, yes. How they laugh. How they like to laugh. How they like to laugh at me. Like I'm nothing but a big joke."

"C'mon, you know that's not true."

As if I just pressed a magic button, Moe comes roaring back to life.

"Oh, sure they do! Oh sure! They do! They all say the same thing. There's Moe the Shmoe! Moe the Shmoe! There goes the clown prince of golf! Oh yes! That's what they call me! All of them. Moe the Shmoe, the clown prince of golf! It doesn't matter if I shoot a sixty-three, a seventy-three, or an eighty-three. Doesn't matter. Whatever I shoot they're gonna laugh. Seems everyone thinks that I'm not a golfer but a comedian. A CLOWN! I'm the laughingstock of the country. Me in golf and Eddie Shack in hockey. Laugh at me....laugh at *me*? What a bunch of lunch pailers! Who was paying money to see me golf in a tournament? Who? They were! Guys just like those three. That's right. *They* were paying to see *me*. So, who's the freak?! Who should be laughing at who? I hit at least six hundred balls a day. Six hundred a day! Day after day. Over four million golf balls in my lifetime to be the best. And yet, they all laugh. Only seeing how I look or how I talk or how my swing isn't the same as everybody else's. Not seeing the shots! Not seeing the perfect shots! Nope. Just seeing the differences between us. Even the RCGA wouldn't give me any credit. No credit at all. The Canadian Golf Hall of Fame has been around for twenty-three years, and in all that time and I didn't even get a sniff of getting in. Not a sniff."

Moe stops for a moment to gather himself together before continuing. He's not always well equipped when emotions hit him hard.

"And it hurts. It hurts. They may as well put a sign at the front door of The Hall of Fame that says, 'Sorry, no clowns allowed! No clowns allowed. Don't even think about it.'"

I try to interrupt, "But Moe, that's about to --"

That's all he allows me to blurt out, determinately powering right on through with his much-needed rant.

"Lots of people in the Hall of Fame don't have nearly half of what I've done! Not nearly half! Ha! Most don't even have a quarter as many wins as me! Why, just two years ago, this Dorothy Howe woman got inducted. She was born in Scotland, won the U.S. and British Amateurs and then immigrated to Canada in 1910. She lives here for three years...winning the Canadian Amateur three times...and then? She moves to Pittsburgh! Yeah! Moves to Pittsburgh! Doesn't even stay here in Canada. And *she* is in The Hall! A long-since-dead, unknown Scottish woman, who lives in Canada for three years is in the Canadian Golf Hall of Fame. But not me. Oooh no! Not me! Not the clown prince of golf. Not Moe the Shmoe. Not me. Argh!"

Moe stands up, throws his arms into the air in frustration and begins to pace back and forth in agitation.

"The RCGA hasn't been fair to you in the past, Moe. I admit that. You're fully entitled to those feelings. It's okay to have them. But you're going to be --"

Cutting me off again, "I know I shouldn't say anything about it. I know. I know I shouldn't care so much. Golf is about yourself. No one else. So why should I care? Why should I care what them others think? A lot more people would be better golfers – and better people -- if they worked harder on being themselves. Finding their own swing. Finding their own selves instead of trying to copy each other. Oooh, of course! Just be yourself, be yourself. Don't try to be me. I don't try to be you! Besides! You can't be me Oh boy, so much time wasted on trying to be like someone else. What's the point in that? Who wants everything to be the same?"

I attempt to object to several things he has just said, but it's abundantly clear the subject is now closed and any opinion I may have in response is irrelevant as Moe turns his back on me and marches quickly off towards the clubhouse leaving me in his dust. It's as if a switch was flipped and the last few minutes with those three morons that triggered this meltdown has evaporated. However, I know it's not the case and the emotions I just witnessed are still intently bubbling below the surface and out of sight. It's not the first time Moe has tried to make me think everything is all fine and done, by turning the channel and swallowing the remote.

"C'mon, enough of this blather! Let's get going!" he hollers as he scurries off. "I need to get more balls. I need to get back to the driving range. Time is ticking. Only half a day's work is done so far. Half a day's work done."

As he hurries off, I take a brief moment to fully brush myself off and make sure I look presentable for the clubhouse. I quickly realize doing so is an error, and that my earlier anticipated leisurely pace is no longer an option, as he is quickly building a huge gap between us. I break out into a fast walk that quickly evolves into a jog to catch up to him.

"Moe, wait! Slow down!" I beg as I chase after him.

He doesn't of course and he's at the front doors of the clubhouse in no time, vanishing inside before I can get anywhere near him.

7

ORANGE IS THE NEW WHITE

As I push open the large front doors to the main clubhouse I'm instantly engulfed by the cool conditioned air, assaulting me as if I'm being hit with a bucket of cold water. It serves me to notice that it wasn't just those young men that were getting me heated up but that it's already starting to get deceptively hot and humid outside. The morning chill in the air is now long gone. Somehow the heat always seems to tiptoe upon you until you come inside, doesn't it? It takes the cold knowledge to wake you up with a firm smack in the face. It also gives more weight to my realization that I desperately need to get those cold Cokes back to Moe and keep him well hydrated. I need to find a way to keep a closer eye on him for the rest of the day, otherwise, he would be sure to overexert himself. The last thing I needed is for him to get sunstroke and derail everything we have planned. And now, to complicate matters, I've gone and lost him altogether!

I look around to both my right and left and Moe is nowhere to be seen. Suspecting he may need to use the washroom after all those plentiful consumed morning Coca-Colas, I head directly down the main stairs towards the locker room.

I take a passing look around and don't see Moe anywhere. Not giving in easily, I proceed to the washroom area where it's more isolated and obscured from where I stand. Alas, no luck. No Moe. It occurs to me that he may have instead gone to replenish his Coca-Cola stash by himself or go grab a bite to eat. I immediately head off to the kitchen to see if I'm right.

Moe always prefers to sit in the back of a kitchen if he can, at a table just beyond where the kitchen staff busily worked, to eat his meals. A bit like a mafia don who has a space in the back of a restaurant to eat and attend to his "business" at the same time. With Moe though, it's the opposite. He doesn't opt for it so he can conduct discussions in private but so he can avoid them altogether. This way he doesn't have to talk to anyone. He can just swiftly eat his meal – usually something quick and simple like a hot dog or a hamburger with some barbecue potato chips -- without interruption. Once satiated he could deftly sneak back to the range or course unimpeded by any boring chit-chat with others that could in any way delay getting him back to feeding his never-ending hunger for golf.

Unbeknownst to me, as I head back up the stairs to check the kitchen, Moe has bypassed both of my assumed destinations and has gone directly to the Pro Shop to get more balls. By the time I am climbing the stairs, Moe is already at the Pro Shop counter talking to the club pro.

"Hey, Lloyd! I need six tokens, please. Six tokens," trying to hide his impatience -- and failing.

Without blinking twice at what would normally have been an extreme request, Lloyd toys with Moe, replying with a question he already knows the answer to. "Six small ones, Moe?"

"Ohhh Lloyd, large! Large! You know I need large! I have three hundred more shots to go today. Only half a day's work done so far. Only half a day's work done so far!"

"I know that's the usual Moe, but I saw Nick yesterday and he pointedly told me that you were supposed to take it easy today. So, I thought today, maybe you just wanted some small ones."

"Ohhh, who's overdoing it? Who's overdoing it? I need to hit six hundred balls a day to do a good day's work. Six hundred balls. It's the only way I can be the best ball-striker there is. And that's not me saying it about me. No, sir. That's everyone else saying it about me. Until I hit one ball over that number, there isn't any chance I'm overdoing anything. Not a chance. Six hundred balls isn't overdoing anything. Hoo! Six hundred is the minimum!"

Knowing full well it's pointless to argue and that he has now fulfilled his promise to me, to watch out for him, he hands over the six tokens to Moe. He also makes a mental reminder to avoid me the next time he sees me.

"Thanks, Lloyd! Thanks!" Moe politely tosses over his shoulder, immediately exiting through the door and out to the machine that doles out the range balls outside.

As he's leaving, Lloyd yells out, "I'm looking forward to later this evening!" but Moe never hears it as he is already off, laser-focused to complete his range ball gathering mission.

Once outside, Moe stands in front of the large green monster of a range ball machine that sits jam-packed with his precious cargo. A Brinks truck full of gold bars could not be any more valuable to him. He reaches to the side of it and grabs six large empty buckets from the stacks that reside there. One at a time he places a bucket under an opening and places a token into the slot, hearing it drop into the token counter. There is a momentary whirring and gurgling sound inside the green monster as if it is having indigestion and is about to throw up and then, it essentially does. The loud sound of clunkety-clunk-clunk-clunk rings out as the machine spits fifty balls into a bucket. Moe has a big smile on his face as he sees each ball drop. I imagine he fleetingly thinks in a rapid-fire succession of the shot he will make with each one as they plummet out. The endless clunkety-clunk-clunk-clunk sound of them dropping and filling the bucket is like a soothing song to him. It practically hypnotizes him. I would wager it's probably his second most favourite song in the world.

47

Second only to his absolute favourite song: My Way by Frank Sinatra.

Moe repeats this action six times. On the filling of the sixth and last bucket, a frown that borders on disgust abruptly forms on his face, shattering his smile.

Until the sixth bucket, all of them have been perfectly filled with white golf balls. But as the sixth one is filling up one lone orange ball plops out and is added to the otherwise white harmonious blizzard. He spots it instantly.

Just so you aren't confused, there's no significance for this orange ball. It's not like a gumball machine scenario whereby if you get the featured coloured one you win a prize. In most driving ranges they are apt to use only one colour of a golf ball – usually white -- with some using only yellow ones. If there is a random coloured one mixed in it's usually because a customer pulled it from their own golf bag and hit it and it didn't get weeded out. In the grand scheme of things, this orange ball would have been of no consequence to most anyone.

But Moe is not everyone.

Spotting the lone orange golf ball mid-way through the loading process, he quickly pulls the bucket away to get at it. By the look on his face and the way he so quickly reacts, you would think it's somehow riddled with a contagious virus and it will contaminate all the other balls unless it's immediately quarantined. This manoeuvre, however, is a significant miscalculation on his part.

As he pulls the bucket back, the remaining balls continue tumbling down the chute and they rain out onto the pavement below. Each ball that misses the bucket ends up ping-ponging about, scattering everywhere, as you would expect if someone suddenly pulled the top off of a lottery ball mixing machine. Realizing his mistake, but temporarily paralyzed watching the boing-boing-boing carnage for far too long, he tries to shove the bucket back under the chute. By the time he does, quite a few balls have escaped, and the machine utters one final clunkety-clunk-clunk-clunk, and the few remaining balls drop.

"Oh, ohh, ooohhh!!!" Moe flusters out loud as he realizes the extent of the mess he has made, witnessing a number of the escaped balls rolling down a nearby slope running further and further away from him. It's as if they are running for their lives as escaped convicts would after a prison breakout. Instead of immediately trying to retrieve the runaways he takes the half-full bucket and with a determined aim goes to a soft spot in the grass nearby. He dumps them all out, gets on his hands and knees and picks up the orange golf ball. The blazing orange culprit that caused all of this chaos! He holds it and looks at it with a growing scowl on his face and talks to it.

"What are you doing in here? Oooh boy! What are you doing here!"

Having heard all the commotion, Lloyd appears from inside the pro shop and sees the scattered balls and a frustrated Moe on the grass.

"What's going on? What's wrong?" questions Lloyd.

"What's wrong? What's wrong?!" Moe shrieks. "This! This is what's wrong!" holding up the orange ball. "What's it doing in here with all the white ones?!"

"I guess someone hit some of their own balls on the range and it got picked up by the ball collector. It happens now and then."

"I don't know why anyone would hit an orange golf ball. Who came up with this orange golf ball nonsense anyway? What a silly idea. So silly! Golf balls are supposed to be white! White! It's the easiest to see, easiest to hit, and easiest to find. You'd think the way most people hit a golf ball all over the golf course they'd want to use the best and easiest colour to see. White! Sure! White! The easiest to see and find. I'll never understand why people fool around with things that already work. I figure once something works, it works. Don't fool with it."

"To each their own, I guess. Whatever works best," Lloyd offers, choosing to be Switzerland on the topic and not wanting to stir up any confrontation.

Moe holds up the orange ball and looks disparagingly at it one more time. "Sometimes I think people just like to do things or change things to cause trouble. I really do. I really do."

With a frown of disgust, he shoves the ball into his pocket.

"No sir! Not gonna be using that orange one! No, not that one! I'll leave it back at the driving range and let one of them lunch pailers have it, and they can take it home! That's not a Moe Norman kind of colour of a golf ball."

Having removed this singular blight from his bounty, Moe stands, puts his hands on his hips, and sizes up the carnage before him, letting out a desperate sigh as his focus returns to the scene of the crime. He sees the lost balls are scattered everywhere.

Acknowledging Moe's frustration, "Looks like some of the balls took off pretty far. Do you want me to help you gather them up?" Lloyd graciously offers.

"No! I'm good" Moe warns. "I can do it myself. I don't like anyone else touching my golf balls."

"Alright then. But if you change your mind, I'm inside if you need me" he reiterates as he returns to the pro shop.

Increasingly frustrated, Moe begins to gather the balls up one by one, knowing that every minute wasted here collecting golf balls were minutes that he wouldn't be on the range hitting them. With each ball he retrieves he places it back in that last bucket for which they were originally intended. Much to his chagrin, some of them rolled or ping ponged quite a distance down the pavement in their desperate escape to nowhere and it takes him much longer than anticipated to congregate them. When he finally believes he has them all, he goes back to the spot on the grass, dumps them all out again and gets back on his knees, counting them as he puts them back in, one by one.

"One, two, three, four, five, six, seven..."

8

COME OUT, COME OUT, WHEREVER YOU ARE

Still sitting on the grass counting out loud to himself, Moe places the last balls into the last bucket. "Forty-six, forty-seven, forty-eight...forty-eight? FORTY-EIGHT?!"

Having plopped the last ball into the bucket, Moe whirls around to see if he has accidentally missed any and continues to talk out loud to himself.

"Oh no! No! I knew it! I knew it! Not fifty! NOT fifty! But forty-eight!? I thought there would be forty-nine since I'm not using that stupid orange one. I expected that...but forty-eight? There must be another white one around here somewhere that I missed. Must be one somewhere..."

Looking like a little kid late to the easter egg hunt, after his siblings had already been there before him, gobbling up all the eggs and chocolate, leaving him nothing but empty surprises for them to snicker at, Moe frantically starts reinspecting the entire area for the lone lost ball. Every time he comes to a spot where he thinks for sure he will find the ball, he peers in with the anticipation of success, which is quickly followed by a furrowed frown of failure when the answer is no. After exhausting all possibilities and almost feeling ready to capitulate that all hope is lost and it's gone forever, he crosses his arms and does one last stubborn final scan of the area. Eventually, his eyes lock on the big green machine again. He studies it intently.

"Maybe it didn't give me all fifty balls?" he thinks to himself, quickly dismissing that thought as the machine has always been precisely correct before in its payout.

His eyes drop to the lower part of the machine, and he realizes there is a fair-sized opening under it.

"I wonder," he considers to himself.

Bending down on one knee, he takes a peek into the shadows below it.

Sure enough, there it is! Victory is in his sights!

He gets down on both his hands and knees, trying to reach it. It's even further back than he anticipates, forcing him down even more, onto his belly, stretching and reaching under as far as he can. The tips of his fingers brush up against it and he almost has it in his hand like a toy prize in a vending machine claw. And just like those gimmicky machines, where instead of the contact being helpful, it pushes the prized ball further away from him and frustratingly rolls back even more beyond his desperate grip. Determined he must be close, he squeezes under, even more, sucking in his breath to make himself as thin as possible, lying flat under the machine as much as physics says he can go. Still not enough! No matter how skinny he tries to will himself, he can't reach it. All he's accomplished is to exacerbate the problem. The renegade ball is much too far to the back now and there's no way to move the heavy machine to get at it.

Just as he lets his body go limp and as a frustrated resignation begins to set in, another golfer comes up to fill his range bucket with balls. He looks down at Moe. Or to be more accurate Moe's plaid legs.

"You okay buddy? Is everything all right?"

Without wasting any precious time coming back up from under the machine, Moe takes quick advantage of the situation. "Do you have your golf clubs with you?"

"My clubs? Yeah, why?"

"Pass me your putter will ya? Pass me your putter."

"You want my putter?"

"Yes, your putter. Your putter. Do I have to ask you twice?"

Being a good-natured fellow and recognizing this perfect opportunistic opening for a little levity with the stranger lying below him, the golfer teases, "You already asked twice."

With an impatient and loud shrillness in Moe's voice, "Just give it to me will ya, funny guy? Just give it to me!"

Sensing the urgency that he was previously unaware existed; the good-natured soul goes to his bag and pulls out his putter and hands it to Moe.

"Be careful with it," he pleads as Moe's hand sticks out, takes it, and disappears with the other half of him back under the machine.

Meanwhile, having not found Moe in the kitchen as I'd hoped, I arrive at what I think might be another possible destination: the pro shop. I ask Lloyd if he has seen Moe and he sheepishly tells me he's at the ball machine. As soon as I get outside I spot the unmistakable orange, yellow, and brown plaid plants sticking out from under the green ball machine, with a man staring down at them.

I needn't wonder where Moe is any longer.

"What the heck is going on?" I impatiently inquire. "What are you guys doing?"

I turn my attention specifically to the golfer who is staring down and looking at Moe.

"What's going on?" I ask.

"You've got me. I came to get some range balls and I found him under the machine like that. Then he took my putter," responds the man innocently.

"For heaven's sake, what are you up to? Come out from under there!" I say to Moe, realizing this guy is just an innocent bystander and not an accomplice to whatever is taking place.

Moe does not move nor answer back.

"Moe? Can you hear me? Come on out from under there."

"Yeah, I can hear you."

"Then come out! This nice guy wants his putter back."

"Graham," the golfer clarifies. "My name is Graham."

Correcting myself, "This nice guy Graham would like to have his putter back."

"He can't," says Moe tersely.

"What do you mean he can't? Look, get out from under there and stop fooling around and give the man his putter back. Now!"

"He can't have it. Or at least, I can't give it back to him."

"What do you mean you can't give it back to him?"

Graham begins to worry. "Hey, that's my lucky putter. I need that back. Seriously."

Moe's reply is the same, "I just cant."

"Why can't you?" I ask in exasperation.

"I don't want to tell you."

"Moe, just tell me."

"But you'll be mad."

"Tell me! I won't be mad."

"Promise me?" he begs.

"Tell me!!!"

"You sound mad already."

Calming myself down, I state very clearly, "Please just tell me why Graham can't have his putter back. I will not be mad."

There is a moment of silence before he responds.

"Because I'm stuck!"

Knowing he's stuck tries my patience to its fullest. Here I am worried I wouldn't find him, and now I have, and he's in a much worse situation than just hitting too many golf balls.

"Stuck?!" I yell out with a little less compassion than I would have liked and definitely in breach of my not-getting-mad promise. "What are you doing under there in the first place!"

A weak resigned voice squeaks out from below, "See, I told you. I told you, you'd be mad."

I look to Graham for some kind of explanation, and he just gives me a stumped look. "Sorry, I haven't the faintest idea."

From under the machine, a firmly trapped Moe finally lets them both in on the selective facts he chooses to share.

"One of the balls fell out of the basket and it rolled under here. I tried to get it myself, but it was too far back. So, I asked this Graham fellow to let me use his putter. It worked. I got it. But now I'm stuck."

"I'm sorry for all this," I apologize to Graham. "Do you mind grabbing a leg and seeing if we can pull him out?"

"Sure, no problem."

"Okay, Moe," I start to explain, "Each of us is going to grab a leg and pull. Hopefully, that works. You okay with that?"

There is a beat as Moe contemplates the suggestion. Normally it would be a no-brainer kind of question for most of us, but Moe does not like to be touched. Particularly by a stranger. *Ever.* So, he needs to give it serious thought. You can insert the entire Final Jeopardy theme music here if you like, to get a gist of how long it takes.

"So?" I ask, breaking the silence and trying to maintain my cool. "Are you okay with that?"

"Can't you just pull me out by yourself?" he bargains back.

My patience is now beginning to reach its breaking point. "No, Moe. I can't pull you out all by myself! And Graham is being a swell guy offering to help."

Another few irritating seconds pass before we hear, "Yeah, okay then. Go ahead and pull. Go ahead and pull."

We both grab a leg and Moe doesn't budge. We try again and still, no movement. At this point I am so frustrated that I fantasize about getting another bucket -- but this one full of cooking oil -- and pouring it all over him, using the lubrication to extract him. Because he *is* coming out! Fortunately, on the third try, out he comes with the putter in one hand and the golf ball in the other.

With sweat pouring down his face, he bleats out, "Thanks, guys. It was really hot under there. It was getting hard to breathe. Hard to breathe."

With the extraction complete, I wholeheartedly thank Graham for his help and give him back his putter. As to not waste any more of his time than we have to, I assure him that Moe is fine and that I will look after him from hereon. I also insist that I will reimburse him for his range balls for all the inconvenience.

"Don't worry about it," Graham dismisses, as he grabs a bucket, digs into his pocket, drops his token into the machine, and the familiar clunkety-clunk-clunk-clunk of the golf ball drop begins anew. "Glad I could help."

Meanwhile, in the brief moment I took to return Graham's putter to him and to say thanks, Moe disappears again!

In a panic, I whirl around and see that no, he hasn't gone as far as I thought. He has merely gone back over to the last of the six buckets he filled and drops the rescued ball from under the machine into it. Once he does he crosses his arms, glowers, and stands there, muttering, "Forty-nine. That's only forty-nine."

My first thought is, what could possibly be bothering him now? But what was tugging at me, even more, was that I wanted to know how all this happened in the first place.

"Do you want to tell me what on earth this was all about?" I demand.

"Ohhh sure. Sure! I just had some problems with the ball machine. Some of them got lost when a stupid orange ball dropped out. Stupid orange ball! But the real problem is that now I only have forty-nine balls in this bucket. Only forty-nine! Which means I only have two hundred and ninety-nine golf balls. Two hundred and ninety-nine! Which means I can't do a complete day's work! I need six hundred balls for a full day's work. You know that! Not five hundred and ninety-nine!"

Moe quickly becomes increasingly disturbed over the new crisis he finds himself immersed in and I can sense a potential meltdown is in the offing if it's not resolved pronto. While this isn't a big problem for most of us, this is for Moe, and I know it. In consideration of all of the drama this is causing, I let most of my anger dissipate and try to use my energy to home in on a solution instead.

"No big deal Moe. We'll just get another bucket – a *small* one – and you can take one ball from that and add it to the one with forty-nine. Problem solved and you're back to your three-hundred."

Moe beams and his defeated attitude completely reverses itself.

"Hooo, and then why not just take that extra basket too? Hooo! I'll hit those too! I'll hit those too! You can watch!"

"No!" I state firmly, kiboshing his instantaneously deployed devious plan. "I've already asked you to do less today. Letting you hit six hundred is bad enough. You're not hitting any more than that! Not one more or forty-nine more! Nor do I have the time to watch you hit them all!"

With a slick move that would make me even smarter than Sam Snead, I dig into my pocket and pull out my wallet. I extract a twenty-dollar bill and stop Graham just as he is leaving for the range.

"Do me one more favour, Graham? Give me one of your range balls and I'll give you this twenty."

"Twenty bucks for a ball that isn't even mine?" he questions skeptically.

"That's the favour. Nothing more to it," I assure him.

"Done!"

I hand him the twenty, he hands me a ball, and Graham walks off. I proceed to Moe's sixth bucket, looking like the cat who caught the canary and proudly drop it in.

"There you go. Three hundred balls. There's the last remaining one you need to get you to your six hundred. Happy?"

"Sure thing, Nick. Sure thing! Thanks! Now, can you help me get them back to the driving range?"

I look at my watch and see that too much time has already been wasted this morning and I still haven't had the chance to barely accomplish anything that I must, for tonight. Frustrated at the position I have placed myself in, it occurs to me that if I play this right, this conundrum I find myself mired in right now can provide me with a much-needed solution.

"Yes, I will help you," I commit, "But then you have to do as I say. No questions. Deal?"

"Sure. But will you watch me hit some? You have to watch!"

"I said no questions. Deal? And the longer it takes for you to agree, the longer you won't be hitting balls."

"Okay fine," Moe instantly gives in, "I'm all ears. I'm all ears."

And looking at the pair that God gave him I think to myself endearingly, "Yes you are, my friend. Yes, you are."

9

LET'S MAKE A DEAL

As Moe eagerly picks up two of the buckets he looks at me with a what-are-you-waiting-for expression as if to insist I do the same. I submit to the look and leisurely go to get two of them as well. Once I have them in hand we both stand staring at each other and simultaneously look down at the two that remain unattended on the ground.

I explain, "There are six buckets and each of us has only two hands. There's no way we can get six of these buckets back in one trip. Not unless each of us can suddenly grow another arm. But you see, fortunately for you, I have a plan. A plan to do it all in one trip. It's the deal you just agreed to."

Moe quickly morphs a what-have-I-just-got-myself-into look on his face.

"I want you to sit here and wait for me. I have to go grab something. I'll only be gone for a few minutes and I'll be right back!"

Not liking how this is playing out he interrogates my barely laid out plan.

"How long are a few minutes? How long? Is it gonna be longer than me just making the trips and doing it myself?"

"Hey now, wait a second!" I challenge him back. "I thought we had a deal? We have a deal, don't we? No questions. That was part of the deal."

"Yes, but..."

"Uh-uh. No yes but's. NO questions."

Moe gives me an I-don't-like-this look but gives in. I know darn well that if we made a deal he won't back out. One thing about Moe is that if he liked you, he wouldn't want to disappoint you. Not ever. Sure, his behaviour with those he didn't know can be lacking in grace and predictability at times, but once you knew him and he knew you – which was a very small circle -- a deal was a deal.

"I'll be right back. Promise me that you'll stay here and wait. Okay? Promise me."

Begrudgingly, Moe agrees with a nod of his head.

"Not good enough, I want to hear you say it."

Like a petulant twelve-year-old who has been scolded he whines, "I promise. I promise I will stay here and wait," as he goes over to the sixth bucket, dumping out the balls back onto the lawn again. "I'm going to make sure all fifty are here again while you're gone. Just in case. All fifty." He adds sarcastically for good measure, "It's not like I don't have the time."

"Good. You do that and I'll be right back," purposely not acknowledging his sarcasm.

As I walk off towards the clubhouse I can hear in the background, "One, two, three, four..."

10

TWO OUT OF THREE AIN'T BAD

Moe doesn't know it yet, but this deal we've just struck is going to play perfectly into my plans for the rest of the day. One of the top things on my agenda is that I need Moe to get cleaned up and to be looking good for later. If you think of it along the lines of "before and after" shots in advertisements, I need him to become the "after Moe". Just as importantly, I have to convince him to give some serious thought as to what he is going to say later this evening. This plan should go a long way to accomplishing both.

I quickly head back into the clubhouse, down the stairs to the locker room, and go directly to my locker. I open the door and pull out a freshly pressed brown suit, with a check pattern dress shirt and a green tie. I also grab a box containing a new pair of shoes and some socks from the bottom shelf. It's difficult to manage it all, but I do, and take them upstairs, making a quick detour to the ballroom coat check area. I place the bundle of items down on a wooden empty side table and poke around trying to find what I'm looking for, to no avail.

I spot Allison who runs the ballroom.

"Hey, Allison! Do you have any extra rolling racks kicking around that I can use?"

"Sure, there's a bunch of them at the back of the hall in the storage section. I won't be needing any until later tonight."

"Awesome, thanks."

I find a rack, snag it, and I hang the clothes on the top rail, placing the shoebox on the bottom shelf of it. With this step completed, I head over to the canteen area.

When I get there I ask Doug, who works behind the counter, "Can I get a case of Coke please?"

"A whole case?"

"Yes, please."

"Let me guess, for Moe?" he chuckles.

"That obvious, huh?"

Doug disappears into a back area beyond the canteen counter, quickly returning with a case of Coca-Cola and hands it over to me. I place it securely on the bottom of the rolling rack beside the shoe box.

"Thanks, see you later," I wave, as I trundle back to Moe in my best bellhop imitation stride.

Clothing, check.

Case of Coca-Cola, check.

Two tasks down and one to go.

11

RACK 'EM UP!

I ARRIVE BACK OUTSIDE THE PRO SHOP, CAREFULLY PUSHING MY rolling rack with the items I've collected and find Moe still on the grass, his back towards me, passing the time recounting the balls. *All* of them this time.

"Two hundred and eighty-seven, two hundred and eight-eight, two hundred and eighty-nine --"

"I'm back!" I shout out, interrupting his count.

"Oooh, finally. Finally!" he says with a startle. "Just a second. Just a second," quickly finishing up the last count, "Two hundred and ninety, ninety-one, ninety-two, ninety-three, four, five, six, seven, eight, nine, three hundred! Three hundred. All here! All here!"

With that important undertaking concluded, his attention draws back to me. His expression of relief in finding that all three hundred balls were accounted for, quickly shifts into a healthy dose of cynicism, when he sees what I'm pushing.

"What's that for?" his eyes narrowing.

"It's a brand-new suit, shirt, and tie. For you!" I pat the shoebox on the bottom. "And a new pair of shoes and socks."

Completely disregarding all that I have proudly presented, every bit as effectively as any of the models on The Price Is Right, he only sees what he wants to.

"Oooh, good! Good! You got my Cokes. You got my Cokes. Thanks!" getting up to grab one from the case.

"Not just yet," I stop him in his tracks. "Our deal hasn't been fully revealed yet. You can use this rack and place the six ball buckets on the bottom of it, beside the shoes and the Cokes. Then we can take it all to the driving range area at the same time, all in one trip. After that, you can even go hit some more balls. BUT, you have to promise me, that you'll clean up and put all these great new spiffy clothes on in the next little while."

Moe grabs two of the buckets and brings them over to the rack, appearing to ignore me.

"Okay?

"Mhm," he barely audibles, as he sets them down on the rolling rack shelf and goes back for two more.

Unconvinced I try again, "Okay, Moe?"

"Oh, sure! Sure!" he replies, not in an assuredly kind of way but rather more as a toss-off dismissal.

"I want you to look good tonight. I want you to shine."

I get another grumble as he brings the two buckets over, "Mhm. Mhm."

"Promise me you'll change into these," I repeat, replacing the tone with more demand than questioning.

Moe places the two buckets on the rack and goes back for the last two.

I remain patient with my tone. "Moe?" And then a bit more irritated, "Moe! Stop and promise me!"

"I'll never understand what the big deal is with all you guys and clothes. What's the big deal? We only really put them on to keep warm or keep the bugs off."

"There's more to them than that and you know it."

He goes to pick up the last two buckets, stops, and turns to me with a big grin.

"Or to cover up your...well...you know...your you-know-what's," as he plucks two balls from a bucket and puts them between his legs, dangling them and laughing out loud.

Refusing to let something this important be reduced to something this juvenile I hold my ground and refuse to give him back the smile he's cutely trying to elicit from me.

"Please just remember to put them on, that's all I'm asking. That's part of the deal."

"Why always all the fuss about what we look like? Huh? What *I* look like? Who cares what colour goes with what colour? With what goes with what? Why don't my yellow pants -- the ones Irv and Ken called my banana pants – not look okay with an orange shirt? They're both fruits. Fruits are fruits, right? Fruits should go together! Right?"

He shakes his head and picks up the two last buckets. "It's not like we're comparing some fruit against a vegetable! It makes complete sense they would go together. Fruits with fruits. Why can't the fruit colours go together? It all makes no sense to me. No sense at all."

"The way you put it may sound like it makes sense, but sometimes the rules are the rules."

This particular comment strikes a sensitive chord with Moe, and he mutters back to me in a mocking childish sort of way, "The rules are the rules... The rules are the rules..."

Then with a strong and sudden surge of pent-up anger, he looks me directly in the eyes and adds, "Sometimes the rules need changing!!!"

As quickly as the glare is given it is retracted, as he slams the last two buckets onto the rolling rack and off he goes, marching back to the driving range, pushing the rack as fast as it can go. His behaviour right now is eerily reminiscent of what we last encountered with the three guys earlier in the morning. It's like he pulls some kind of internal emotional switch, thrusts everything back into neutral and when it's pulled, you're left in the dust. Keep up or be left behind.

As he bolts off, the wheels on the rack spin straight most of the time but they also intermittently go madly around in circles at times too, making it veer off course. It almost falls over more than once, and I cringe in horror each time it does so. It's eerily reminiscent of every grocery cart I tend to get stuck with when I go shopping. And when I do, I exacerbate the torture by determinately pushing it around the store, too lazy and stubborn to exchange it, thinking it will miraculously somehow fix itself on my grocery rounds. As a result, my grocery shopping experience often includes at least one near-miss experience on an aisle display. I'm terrified that he's going too fast and that the rack is going to go flying end over end, ruining the suit, and cracking open some Coca-Colas to christen it. I envision Coke foam spraying everywhere, destroying whatever part of the suit that doesn't get soiled or torn by impact. Not to mention *all* the balls this time, bouncing off everywhere and anywhere to attain their once again short-lived parole.

"I will not let that suit be ruined!" I scream internally as I run off in hot pursuit of him.

12

THE ART OF THE DEAL

ONCE I CATCH UP, I BEG MOE TO SLOW DOWN SO EVERYTHING doesn't end up scattered and destroyed on the ground. Thankfully, he concedes without argument, and I do not say a word after that. I figure a quiet walk will do us both good and hopefully calm everything down. But the topic at hand is obviously still eating at him as barely a few moments pass before he breaks the short-lived unannounced truce.

"I really tried to make an effort with clothes you know. Oh sure! Tried to make people happy and have them stop saying I looked like a clown. Oh sure! I did! Even had my pal Irv help me. He made me a chart. I took it out every day. Day after day. I checked it, followed it, and made sure I didn't make a mistake. It told me what to wear and with what. It told me that if I was wearing a blue shirt I could wear navy or black pants with it. A navy or a black. But not an orange or a purple or a pink. Oh no! Not those. Just a navy or a black. That chart helped a lot I must admit but, I also have to tell ya, it sure was a lot of work and took a lot of my time. *A lot* of my time. Time that I put in to make everyone else happy. Time that could have been spent hitting golf balls. Making *me* happy. But you know what? It didn't do much to stop the laughing. Didn't do much of anything. People still did. People still laughed at me. Sure. I always had to hear 'Look, here comes Moe the Shmoe! Look, here comes The Clown Prince of golf!' What I was wearing – whether right or wrong -- didn't change a thing."

Moe stops rolling the cart, looks right at me and holds the gaze. Remember, this is something he didn't do very often and here I am, being given it twice in a matter of minutes. I pay attention to these kinds of things.

"I tried. I really did. But after a while, I just threw that chart out. Ripped it up into a million pieces. A million pieces. I decided there are lots more important things to worry about at the start of the day than what you ought to be wearing. Oooh boy! Way more important things! Steve Jobs and Albert Einstein didn't waste time with clothes. Oh no, they wore the same clothes every day! Same things, every day. Day after day. No one laughed at them."

Moe begins pushing the rack again, not so quickly as before, and I don't have much to say about that last comment. I'm not sure if he's telling me the truth about Jobs and Einstein or if he made it up. I'll have to check that out later. But since I don't know for sure I don't want to contest it. I also know that he reads a lot and listens to a ton of self-motivation tapes, so the odds are he isn't making it up and it is a piece of trivia he picked up to use in his defence when needed. He loved to find a quote or piece of information and then extensively use them down the road when the right time arose.

"Besides," Moe deadpans, "doesn't everyone say that golfers dress funny anyway?" as he tosses his arms in the air and resumes a more spirited pace again.

In my head, I think to myself, "Touché my friend, touché."

As he picks up the too fast pace, the rolling cart lurches, and the cans of Coca-Cola almost fall off.

"Better slow it down partner," I warn. "If you go too fast, you're going to lose those Cokes!"

That does the trick. He instantly tones down the semi-run into a brisk -- but relatively safe -- speed walk.

We fast pace walk a good chunk of the rest of the way in silence. As we get closer it suddenly hits me that the pretty boy and his buddies might still be hitting balls. I dread the thought. I finally have things under control, and I don't want things running off the rails again. Fortunately, when we get there, they are nowhere to be seen.

Phew.

As Moe begins to unload two of the buckets, I delicately bring up the last part of our deal.

"Do you know what you're going to say tonight? Are you ready? Have you written anything down?

Moe dumps the first batch of balls by his clubs and goes for the next two.

"Did you hear me?"

No response. As I stare at him, he picks up the next two buckets and he tosses me a soft "maybe" as he passes.

"What do you mean, maybe?"

"I've been thinking about it. I've been thinking about it," he grumbles.

"You better be writing it down too. Not just thinking about it. That's the last part of our deal."

He goes to get the next and final two buckets, "Mhm."

"I'm serious, Moe."

"Mhm. I know. A deal is a deal. A deal is a deal."

Relieved to see we have made some legitimate progress, "Great. I'll check in on you later then."

"Wait! Where are you going?" he protests. "Aren't you going to watch me hit some?"

"I told you I have more things to do. I'll be back later. Maybe if you take your time and don't hit them like you're a machine gun, you'll have some left that I can watch you hit when I get back. But as for now, I really must go."

I walk away with the firm intention of not looking back to prolong this any further, but I reconsider to make sure all my points have been made.

"Don't forget. Don't overdue the practicing, clean up, write something down, and get those on sooner than later," pointing to the clothes. "They are part of the deal too."

Without any further arm wrestling or allowing him any room for protestation, I'm on my way back to the clubhouse. In doing so, I fail to see the look on his face as he turns his attention to the suit and scrutinizes it from a distance. He makes sure I'm out of sight and long gone before he dares to tiptoe up to it for a closer inspection. He grimaces, scrunches up his nose and cautiously sticks out a single finger, touching the suit once, and then reacting as if it may be covered with the plague and now death is imminent.

This isn't going to be easy for him.

13

YOU GOTTA PAY TO PLAY

With the suit, shirt, tie, and shoes stored safely at a distance, purposely abandoned far off to the side – out of sight but not necessarily out of mind – and the Coca-Cola calculatingly close for comfort, Moe has transported once again to his happy place. The perfect utopian world where he is simply surrounded by buckets of golf balls, his clubs, and a case of good old Coca-Cola. If you were to ask Moe what he wanted heaven to be like, this would come darn close.

As we are well into the day now, a few more golfers have arrived and they too are hitting balls.

"Three hundred down and three hundred to go!" he says to himself with excitement and purpose as he eyes the first two buckets he brought to his driving spot.

"Hoo! Lugging these is hard," he grunts to himself. "Harder than hitting them! Harder than hitting them," as he wipes the sweat from his forehead, pausing for a moment, and looking at the three watches he is wearing on his one arm to check his whereabouts in his day.

"That's interesting. Why the three watches?"

Moe whirls around, surprised from hearing the unexpected voice and realizes it's Graham, the key player in all of the golf machine drama just moments ago. At this point, Graham is more than halfway through hitting his bucket of balls.

"Hoo, it's you! Graham, right? Thanks again for helping me out back there. Thanks for helping me out. Nick would have killed me if I didn't get unstuck."

"No problem, glad I could help. So, what's the story with the watches?"

"Hoo! You'd think I needed to know what the time was in every part of the world wearing all these watches don't ya! But nope, just got used to having two or three on each arm. Just got used to it is all. I'd feel naked now without them."

"Why did you have to get used to it? I still don't understand."

"Oooh. Well, you see when I was young and playing in the amateurs as a golfer you never won money. No sir. You won prizes. And they didn't seem to have much of an imagination when it came to first, second and third place prizes. Lots of watches. At one point I owned twenty-seven watches. I kid you not. Twenty-seven! Hoo! What is someone supposed to do with twenty-seven watches? I'll tell you what. Wear more than one at a time, that's what. I could barely afford to eat back then, but I sure could tell you what time dinner was on all the seven continents!"

"You were an amateur golfer back in your day were you?" asks Graham. "A pretty good one too, it sounds like."

"Oooh! Sure! Sure was! Real good! It wasn't just the watches that I was piling up either. Oh no. I also had seven TV's. SEVEN! I had no place to keep them! I asked the RCGA what am I supposed to do with seven TVs? Watch them all at once? Their answer? 'Yes.'"

Moe shakes his head and gets two more of the full buckets while continuing his story, "So, I kept putting them in different rooms in my folks' house. Their house only had eight rooms. I swear, if I won one more TV, we would've been the only house in all of Kitchener that would be able to say we had a TV in every room of the house! Hoo! Every room in the house! Oh, it was endless the useless things I won.

Luggage, silver trays, radios, golf bags, fancy glasses, toasters, lawn-mowers....even rocking chairs. I won a rocking chair from the same tournament four years in a row! Four years in a row! Only the Friendly Giant on CBC would have been jealous! What the heck do you do with four rocking chairs!? All a bunch of junk. Just a bunch of junk. I didn't need all this stuff. Oh no! What I needed was some money. Needed something in my pocket so I could pay for my next meal or an entry fee! Of course!"

He comes back with the two buckets, sets them down, and goes back for the final two.

"It didn't take long though to learn that there was a way around all this. I saw that lots of the other guys were selling their prizes in the parking lot after the tournaments. Trading them for cash. Sure! For the things they really needed. You know, food, entry fees, gas, or hotel rooms. So, I started selling my prizes too. Sold them in the parking lot after, to the highest bidder. Just like the other guys. We all did it. Sometimes, I even had one of the fans come up to me *before* a tournament and tell me what they would pay me for a second or third place prize. Then, I would purposely blow a few shots if I was winning, to come in second or third. Oh sure! That way I could sell the prize! It didn't matter that I didn't win when I knew in my head that I could have if I wanted to. Oh sure! I knew I could have won if I wanted to. But selling the prize for the extra money was way more important. Times were hard. Times were hard."

As Moe returns with the final two buckets he concludes, "It was like my dad once said. I was a golfer; I wasn't running a warehouse!" shaking his head in frustration.

He drops them down with the other four buckets and is about to crack open a Coke when he looks at Graham, "You want one?"

"Sure, don't mind if I do."

Moe hands him the one he's about to open, and as Graham cracks it open, he's instantly sprayed in the face with a torrent of Coca-Cola foam.

"Whoa!" exclaims Graham as it streams right for and into his unsuspecting face.

"Hooo!" counters Moe, pausing from grabbing another for himself, seeing Graham's Coca-Cola shower as a clear warning not to.

They both look at each other for a beat and then Graham, looking like a kid having a light brown bubble bath, laughs. Moe joins in with laughter.

"Sorry about that. Must have got themselves a good shakeup on their way over."

Not to be denied his heavenly elixir, Moe grabs another, extends his arm out as fully as possible and cracks his can open, far enough out and pointed away from him so that the same torrential spray doesn't get him. He takes a sip and continues his story.

"So yeah, even though I wasn't supposed to as an amateur – because it was breaking the rules -- I sold the prizes and took the money. But just like the other guys! Just like everyone else who needed to. You know what they say...sometimes you do what you gotta do. You do what you gotta do. And I *had* to play golf."

Moe holds his three-watch arm up for Graham.

"So, you wanna buy one? Wanna buy a watch?"

Graham is taken aback and unsure what to say as Moe lets out one of his high shrill belly laughs.

"Oooh, I got ya! Oooh, I got ya! You shoulda seen your face. Don't worry I'm not selling anything anymore. Not selling anything. I'm just pulling your leg. Pulling your leg! These aren't for sale."

Looking relieved, Graham gives him an awkward chuckle and goes back to practicing.

As Graham strikes a ball, Moe gets one of his buckets and gently kicks it over with his foot. A bunch of the balls roll out of it to allow easier access when he starts hitting.

Now that everything was perfectly organized, Moe was finally ready to commence his second half of a good day's work. He begins to loudly whistle the old theme music that played for years on CBC Hockey Night in Canada. He's a surprisingly good whistler when you consider all those crooked teeth, and if you knew the theme song, you knew immediately what he was whistling. He saunters over to his bags of clubs, pulls a driver out of one of them, and stops to watch Graham hit another ball. It's a rather good shot and Moe is impressed.

"He shoots! He scores!" laughs Moe. "Good shot! Good shot! Still, some stuff you could work on, but good shot!"

Graham cheerfully receives the backhanded compliment. "Thanks."

"You like hockey?" Moe asks.

"What red-blooded Canadian doesn't?"

"Then let me tell you a story..."

14

HOCKEY NIGHT IN CANADA

"Remember when I said it was hard to make ends meet back in my amateur days?" began Moe.

"You mean when you could keep track of the time on all the continents at once, as you sat in whatever rocking chair you wanted?" Graham laughs.

"Exactly," Moe laughs back. "Hoo! Exactly. Well...had it not been for Connie, I may have had to sell even more of those prizes than I did. Even all of them. Connie got me out of more than one money pickle over the years. Oh yes, more than one. He was one of the first people to stand behind me and give me a real chance. A real chance. Connie was a saviour. He was one of my first angels."

Moe's impish grin grows exponentially. "Oh, I'm sorry...you probably know Connie differently. You probably know him under a different name."

"To be honest, I have no idea who you're talking about. I don't know any women by the name of Connie," confesses Graham.

"Hoo! Hoo!" giggles Moe with glee. "Connie isn't a girl! Hoo! Connie isn't a girl! It's a boy!

I'm talking about Mr. Smythe. Mr. Conn Smythe!"

While Moe radiates with relish, Graham starts putting two and two together, but he's still not completely buying it.

"*The* Conn Smythe?" questions Graham.

"Yes...*that* Conn Smythe."

"The owner of the Toronto Maple Leafs?"

"And the same one who built The Gardens in Toronto. But he liked his friends to call him Connie. Yes sir! Liked his friends to call him Connie."

Moe gets a ball and sets it on a tee but doesn't strike it.

"I met him in '54 when I won the Labatt Open in Scarborough. I had just finished the tournament and he came up to me afterwards. Came up to me just as if he knew me and said, 'Congratulations on your big win today, Murray. Well done.'"

"C'mon. You're pulling *my* leg now!" interjects Graham.

"Hoo! It's true! One hundred percent true. And when I said, 'Gee thanks, Mr. Smythe,' he corrected me right away. Oh sure! Corrected me right away. Said, 'You can call me Connie. All my friends do.'"

"That's an awesome story!"

"Oooh, but that's not the half of it! Not the half of it!" warns Moe, as he takes a sip of his Coca-Cola, milking the moment of expectation he has so expertly set up.

"The next thing I know he says to me, 'You're quite the character, son. You've got a lot of colours. I like that in a person. Tell me, are you going to go play the amateur circuit down south this year? Give them Americans a sound thrashing!? Show them who's boss?'"

"Did you?" queries Graham, completely hooked now.

"I'll tell you the same thing I told him. 'No, sir.'"

A puzzled Graham shoots back, "Why not?"

Moe bursts out loud with delight, "Jeez, it's like I'm talking to Connie again for the first time. He asked the same thing. The same thing! I told him 'No, sir. It would cost way too much. Way too much. I'll go back to The Strand over the winter and work at the glove factory to save up money for next summer's golf season.'"

"Those were your winter jobs I'm guessing?" ponders Graham.

"Sure were, I had two of them. Spent every winter setting pins at The Strand Bowling alley and making gloves at the leather factory when I wasn't setting pins. I hear they still talk about me back at the bowling alley. Said they never saw anyone before or after who could set pins up as fast as I could. People would come in and specifically make sure they got me working in their lane. Plenty of times they would give me a tip afterwards too. Tipped me for my speed. But anyway, back to the story, back to the story," continues Moe. "Connie says, 'You're too good a golfer kid, to be setting pins all winter or wasting your time in a glove factory. How much would something like that cost? You know, to play down south on the amateur circuit for the winter?'"

"I told him 'Oooh...at least two or three thousand dollars, Mr. Smythe.' Oh, sure! I told him, 'Two or three thousand! A lot of money.'"

"'You're right, that is a lot of money, Connie replied.' And just as he was leaving he said to me: 'I wish you luck, kid. I think you have what it takes to go far in this game. You keep working hard. Those who work hard reap their rewards. Congratulations again on your win today! That was quite the show.'"

"Then as he left he shook my hand. And when he did, he said I should ease up on it a bit. The handshake, I mean. Said it was a little too eager. Too eager. Said that I could have broken one of his fingers."

"Wow," what an amazing memory for you to have," Graham shares back.

"Oooh, I'm not done! Not done by a long shot," as Moe waves his hand dismissively at Graham.

"I can't imagine it gets much better than that!" replies Graham, eager to hear more.

"Well, sure, all that was something. Sure, it was. I know it. I know it. It was pretty neat. I mean meeting someone like Connie? Now, that doesn't happen every day, does it? Oh boy, no! Sure, doesn't happen every day. I'll never forget it. I knew I wasn't gonna wash that hand for a few days!"

Graham laughs out loud at the thought.

"Then, about ten minutes later," Moe continues, "he comes back!"

"Conn Smythe?" asks Graham.

"Not comes back exactly, but he opens a side door at the clubhouse and waves at me saying: 'Psst! Hey Moe! Pssst! Come into the clubhouse for a second.'

"So, I do, of course," continues Moe. "Did you want something, Mr. Smythe?" I said back to him. But he doesn't say anything at first. Doesn't say anything. Just hands me a piece of paper. Then I turn it over and see it's a cheque."

"'Here, Moe. Do me, your country and yourself, proud,' he says.

"I'm confused as I look down at the cheque. I could hardly believe my eyes! I looked at him and said, 'Three thousand dollars!? Three thousand dollars? Oooh boy! For me?'"

"You gotta be kidding me!" blurts out Graham.

"Not kidding at all! 'All yours,' he says to me. 'All yours.' I was so stunned I didn't know what to say. But I knew I couldn't take it.

"I started to hand it back to him and said, 'I don't know about this. I don't know how I can ever pay you back, Mr. Smythe. It's would take ten years! Ten years!' Then he put his arm around me, which was okay. That was okay for him to put his arm around me. It was Conn Smythe after all and said: 'First, my name is Connie. My friends, call me Connie. And secondly no, you don't have to pay me back. This is just a little present. Don't you worry, it's just between you and me.'"

"Incredible," coos Graham.

"Then he winked at me and whispered, 'Our little secret' and began to walk away.

"I yelled out to stop him, 'But Mr. Smythe!' I said, 'Mr. Smythe!...'

"He did stop but he didn't turn around. He just stood still for a second or two. When he did turn around he corrected me.

"'*Connie*. My name is *Connie*. I told you, all my friends call me that.' And before I could say another word he put his finger to his lips and said, 'It's *our* little secret.' He came closer again one more time, patted me on the back, gave me a wink and left. Just left. Not one more word was spoken, and he was gone."

"What did you do then?" a wide-eyed Graham wonders aloud.

"I just stood there. Shaking. Shaking like a leaf. Like a *Maple* Leaf!"

Graham lets out a hearty laugh, enjoying the joke and turns a little more serious. "That's odd to hear you say that because few people back then had nice things to say about him. Everyone seemed to dislike him."

"Oh true! True! Seems everyone called Connie a jerk back then. But he sure was great to me. He just saw me, saw me for who I was. A little skinny kid, a little different than the rest and liked the way I played the game. The way I hit the ball. Said I had colour! Said I had colour! It was a life-changer for me. A life changer. For the first time, I had the cash to be able to compete for ten months of the year. No strings attached. I wouldn't have to stop playing golf for the winter months to save up money anymore. Oh no! For the first time, for ten months, I'd have meals, travel and entry fees already paid for. I could just focus on golf. For the first time! Just focus on my game. On me and my swing, me and my swing!"

Moe recollects further, "Oooh, then...then! Hoo! Guess what?"

"What?" Graham responds with great anticipation, thinking about how could there possibly be more to the story.

"Connie gave me another three thousand the next year! Another three! I don't know if I could have kept playing if it wasn't for him. I know he kept my future as an amateur in golf going. Gave me the chance. Sure. Gave me the chance. Oooh! It was hard not being able to tell anyone too. Let me tell you, real hard. I mean Connie, *my* friend!? Connie Smythe believing in Moe Norman!? But I had to keep that quiet because I was still an amateur. Technically, taking the money was breaking the rules. Didn't matter that all the other rich kids out there were getting money from their parents to get an advantage. Didn't matter. So, oh boy, are you kidding? I had to keep that quiet. Sure."

Graham's eyes are now bulging even more wide open with surprise and excitement than they have been through this entire story.

"Wait a second! *You're* Moe Norman?!"

"Sure am!" replies Moe. "Why?"

Graham rambles as he is taken off guard by this off-handed revelation. "Holy smokes! Moe Norman? For real? I mean...I don't know you, know you, but I've sure heard stories about you! No shit!? *You're* Moe Norman?"

Graham stands in awe for a second before getting up the courage, "Can you hit a ball for me? Please!?"

And with that simple request, Graham had just found the teeny-weeny, well-hidden, sliver of a crack, that lead directly to Moe's heart.

15

JUST WATCH

"THERE YOU GO, THAT'S FIFTY! FIFTY RIGHT AT THE TARGET. Right at the target every time," boasts Moe as he finishes hitting the last ball out of the first bucket and as Graham continues watching in complete mesmerized rapture with what he is witnessing.

"Amazing!" raves Graham. "I've never seen anything like it! You're everything I've heard you're to be."

I suspect it doesn't come as any surprise when I say nothing makes Moe happier than someone watching him hit a ball. And, once they heap on the praise nice and thick like that, you can bet all that you own that Moe would do this all day and night for Graham if he could. As he's about to grab another bucket to prove it, a golf cart comes racing up to them and it brings Moe to a cautious halt. One near-miss by a golf cart is plenty for one day.

"Graham what are you doing? We tee off in like fifteen minutes! Grab your clubs and get in the cart!" shouts out the driver.

"Sorry, I completely lost track of the time. I've been watching Moe here, hit some balls. Moe Norman!"

"Who?"

"Moe Norman!"

The guy studies Moe with absolutely no recognition as to who he is nor his name.

"*Moe Norman!*" Graham repeats with great intensity.

"Okay, whatever, but we need to get going. As in NOW! Get your clubs and hop in!"

Graham wants to stay but knows he has a tee time commitment too.

"How can you call yourself a golfer if you don't know who Moe Norman is?" Graham admonishes his buddy.

Moe quietly interjects, "Maybe you know me as Moe the Shmoe or the Clown Prince of Golf?"

"Sorry pal, no offence, but I've never heard of you before," adding impatiently to Graham, "We really need to get going!"

"Not before you see this guy hit," stalls Graham.

"Seriously?" his buddy contests.

"Yes Pat, you need to see this for real. Can you hit one for him please?"

"Sure thing. Sure thing. Which marker do you want me to go for?" Moe asks.

"The two-fifty," suggests Graham, pointing out to the yardage marker.

Moe goes over to a fresh bucket of balls and brings it to the driving tee. He picks one up, places it on a tee and with no practice swing or hesitation he hits the ball in one fluid motion. The ball flies to within a few feet of the two-fifty marker and rolls no more than three feet past.

"Great shot," Pat says with his arms still crossed in impatient frustration. "Can we go now?"

"Hit another one, please," Graham begs.

Moe is more than happy to oblige, "Of course, of course."

Moe picks another ball from the bucket, places it on a tee and once again, with no practice swing or hesitation, he hits the ball in one fluid motion to within a few feet of the two-fifty marker.

"Wow, nice shot again," Pat praises, with a bit more meaning this time.

"Moe, hit another, please."

Pat begins to lose the little patience he has. "C'mon Graham! The guy has a good shot, I get it. But we need to get going!"

"Hoo! I don't want to make you late for your tee-off time. Don't want to do that. Let me speed this up. Let me speed this up."

Moe quickly runs to his golf bag and grabs a handful of tees, goes to the bucket of balls and pulls out five of them. He tees up all five balls in a direct line.

"You boys ready?" Moe grins.

He addresses the first ball and without hesitation, he strikes it. The second he makes contact with the first ball he moves up to the next one and he hits it too. He rapidly does the same with the third, fourth, and fifth balls as well. He is so quick, that the balls are all practically in the air at the same time at one point and all the balls land within a few feet of each other by the two-fifty marker. A few even clang into each other on the ground. As they land, Moe looks at Pat and Graham with that unforgettable impish grin that will always win anyone's heart.

"You'll notice the tees," points out Moe as he gestures towards them on the ground. "Not one has moved an inch from where I set them up. Picked them clean off each one. Picked them clean off."

While Graham has some reason to expect this could happen, he is still immensely impressed. Pat, on the other hand, is incredulous. They turn and look at each other with a what-the-f***-just-happened look on their faces, neither able to find the words to express what they just observed.

Moe is eating this all up, of course. There's nothing better than pleasing the disciples and silencing the skeptics. Knowing he has nothing more to prove to Pat and that he's already added him to his ever slowly growing fan base, he sets them on their way.

"Go on now, Graham. You and Pat get out on the course. The driving range is a beautiful place to be but it's the golf course where you'll find real heaven. That's where you'll find real heaven! It was nice to meet you both."

Pat too has now lost his enthusiasm to leave but knows they must. "That was crazy. I'd love to take more time to see you hit." Then turning to Graham, "But he's right, we've got to get going. Like, right now!"

Graham grabs his clubs and hastily straps his bag onto the cart. Just before he hops in he turns to Moe.

"That was amazing. *You* are amazing. Thanks for the shots and the stories. I'll never forget this day. I'm being completely honest when I say you're one of a kind. That's the best I've ever seen anyone hit a ball."

As Graham jumps in and the cart lurches forward and races off, Moe yells, "You're welcome! You're welcome. Have a good game. Have a good game!"

As they drive off you can hear Pat ask Graham, as he hands him a cold beer, "*What* was *that*? Who is this Moe guy again? And what's with all the watches on his arms?"

16

DOUBLE KETCHUP, DOUBLE MUSTARD

IT'S A BIT LATER IN THE DAY NOW, WELL PAST LUNCHTIME, AND I arrive back at the driving range in a great mood. I'm relieved to have gotten several crucial tasks checked off my to-do list and it's time for me to take a breather. I'm also keenly aware that with six buckets of balls in front of Moe, the likelihood of him having stopped to get something to eat would be one-million-to-one.

"Hey, Moe," I call out. "I brought you some hot dogs!"

"Oh! Thanks, Nick, thanks! My stomach was getting the grumbles. Double ketchup, double mustard?"

"Double ketchup, double mustard."

"Excellent, excellent," he calls back happily.

I pick a spot on the ground under a tree, pat the grass beside me, and suggest, "Why don't you come sit over here and eat."

"Just let me hit these last two from this bucket. Just these last two. You can watch!"

Moe tees up the first shot and it lands within a foot or two of the two-hundred-and-fifty-yard marker. He grabs another one, and with no practice swing or hesitation he hits the ball, and it lands within inches of the last shot and kisses the ball he just struck. While I fully realize the repetitive nature of my shot descriptions may be becoming a little redundant by now, I can assure you that if you ever get to see it for yourself you would not be bored. Most likely, you would be begging for more.

In fact, as if to prove my point, just as I sit down, and Moe finishes his last shot from that bucket, a foursome of guys are in the process of leaving. As they do one of them turns to Moe and says, "I've been watching you hit. That's a pretty amazing shot you have there. Very impressive."

Then one of his playing partners turns to me, "Have you seen this guy hit the ball? The guy is like a machine." Then he turns to Moe and adds, "Nice shooting."

"Thanks," Moe says. "Enjoy your round."

With that, the four of them continue off to the first tee for their round.

I look at Moe, "Quietly going about your day impressing the masses are you?" as I grin.

"What can I say? Just doing my thing. Doing my thing. Four hundred and fifty. See that? Four hundred and fifty, right at the target of my choosing. Only another hundred and fifty to go."

Moe grabs the now empty third bucket and neatly stacks it on top of the first two empty ones, puts down his club and comes over to sit beside me. I'm somewhat concerned as he's looking red and flushed in the face.

"Are you wearing any sunscreen?"

"I meant to, but then I got to hitting balls and forgot. Totally forgot."

I point towards his golf bag. "Before you eat, go get some and put it on your face then. No hotdogs until you put some lotion on."

Fortunately, I didn't have to tell him to rub lotion anywhere else on his body since, despite the rising heat, he was still fully covered by his trademark long pants and a turtleneck. It never matters how hot it got outside; a full set of clothes stayed on. I don't think I've ever seen him in a pair of shorts and a t-shirt or even a short-sleeved collared shirt. Just looking at him practically makes you sweat yourself.

"Now that I'm thinking of it, it wouldn't hurt for you to throw on your visor too, while you're at it," I add.

Moe dutifully goes to his bag, pulls out some lotion and slathers a ton of it all over his face. He also, much to my surprise, dons the visor as advised. Sweet! You always enjoy the little easy-win victories like this with Moe.

"Thanks for throwing the hat on for me but you could go a little easier on the lotion, don't you think?" I chuckle as he looks like Casper the Friendly Ghost now.

"Oh, can't let them call me the clown prince of golf for nothing," he fires back. "Gotta put some whiteface on now and then for them don't I? Play the part? Play the part."

Moe reaches out to grab a hotdog, but I stop him. "Gross! Wipe your hands first. They're still covered in lotion!"

As I hand him a napkin, he is already wiping it off, all over his pants. Dutifully he stops and takes the napkin and wipes whatever is remaining on his hands into it. Once finished he shows me both sides are clean and grabs a hotdog. In a matter of a few quick bites, it's gone. He's every bit as ravenous as I thought he would be.

"Geez, Moe. Slow down. Did you even taste that? You're worse than my dog eating a piece of cheese!" I tease.

Patting his belly, "If you're going to put in a hard day's work, you've gotta feed the fire. Gotta feed the fire."

He grabs another one, eating it quickly too but with at least a modicum of my advice adhered to. We both enjoy the silence and our hotdogs for a few minutes. When the time feels right, I inquire about what I primarily came to find out.

"I know I'm beginning to sound like a broken record, but have you worked on what you're going to say? Do you want to show me something?"

Moe leaps to his feet. "Sure, I'll tee one up!"

"NO! Not show me a golf shot! Show me what you're going to say later tonight. Nice try."

Sounding a bit deflated, "Oh...not yet. I'm still thinking. Still thinking."

I glance over his shoulder and can't help but see that the suit hasn't been touched other than being pushed further away to the side. As hard as I try not to, this starts to make me more than slightly annoyed.

"And don't forget about the suit, shirt, and tie...and the shoes and socks, either!"

"Sure. Sure. I'm still thinking about it. And I won't. I promise. A deal is a deal."

"I'm serious!" trying to make the point as big as I can.

"I know. I know," he mumbles back. "A deal is a deal."

With that firmly pointed out, I get up, gather all the hotdog wrapping remains, ready to head back to the clubhouse.

"Wait, let me hit some for you before you leave! Let me hit some! You can watch!"

I give him a strong look that suggests he already knows I can't and that I don't want to have to tell him why again.

Sheepishly Moe responds, "I know, you have lots to do. I know. Lots to do. Sorry. It's okay. I'll see you later. See you later."

"And when I come back I expect you cleaned up, with the new clothes on, and something written down. A deal is a deal. And I don't want to find that you're exhausted from doing too much in this heat!"

"Understood. A deal is a deal," he repeats to himself as he watches me heading back to the clubhouse.

"A deal is a deal."

17

MISTER SANDMAN

As I continue on my mission back to the clubhouse, the unthinkable happens. Instead of Moe going right back to hitting golf balls, not only does he finally stop and start to think about what he is going to say later today but he even makes a concerted effort to look towards the suit that is taunting him.

It's a long contemplative moment from afar. And it's not an appreciative look, not by a long shot. He eyes it as if it was a straight jacket for the terminally insane rather than the gorgeous suit it is. Keeping a great distance from it seems to be his ultimate priority before eventually relenting and going in for a closer inspection. He examines it intently, getting close enough to get a whiff of its newish, never-laundered-yet smell, but still steadfastly refuses to touch it again. Looking and smelling will do for now.

With no hint of embarrassment or humility towards the few golfers hitting at the driving range, Moe removes his turtleneck sweater, revealing a white, sweat-soaked sleeveless undershirt underneath. While carefully avoiding brushing up against the suit without even so much as a fingertip, he takes the dress shirt off of its hanger and throws the dress shirt over the bar. He retrieves the same hanger and uses it to hang the moist turtleneck back up in its place. Taking one more studied look at the suit he gingerly grabs the one item under consideration for the moment -- the checkered dress shirt -- and puts it on. He does the buttons right to the top but doesn't tuck it into his pants. He steps back from the rest of the items and looks down at the shirt, already missing the weight of his familiar soggy friend like a child would their favourite blanket. He runs his hands across it although I'm not even sure he could feel the high-count cotton thread through those weathered palms and calloused fingers. It's not that he altogether hates it, but it's not his turtleneck. For now, this lone item is as far as Moe is willing to go with the new wardrobe.

Baby steps I say, baby steps.

Decked out in his old plaid pants and his freshly ironed new checkered shirt, Moe goes to one of his golf bags, pulls out three golf balls, and sticks them in his pocket. His plan is to continue practicing by going to the putting green and sand bunker area. He grabs the three balls because he prefers the feel of real golf balls to practice his putting and sand trap shots, rather than the driving range kind of balls. He doesn't overly relish heading over to this area as he's not a fan of this type of practice, but he knows he has to do at least a little of these kinds of shots now and then, and now is as good a time as any.

Leaving the rest of his belongings behind unattended -- knowing it's a safe thing to do on this golf course -- he trots off with a fresh unopened can of Coke in one hand, the three extra balls in his pocket, and a putter and a sand-wedge gripped in the other hand.

When he arrives, another golfer is already in the trap practicing his bunker extraction techniques and Moe watches in amusement. The other guy takes three attempts, kicking up more sand than a sea turtle laying eggs before he blasts a ball out. And when I say out, I mean barely.

"Dammit!" swears the golfer, frustrated not only with the result but from the dry and choking assault of all the sand, blasting into his face following it.

As I have mentioned earlier, in general, Moe is not the type to talk to someone he doesn't know; but if he can offer a tip or two on how to improve your golf swing, that's altogether different. In that case, he may momentarily find it hard to bite his tongue.

"You know the key to a good sand trap shot?" Moe asks as the guy continues to try and get sand out of his mouth and eyes. "The key to a good sand trap shot is to try and not be a hero. No sir. If you get in one, you take your lumps. You take your lumps. Don't be a hero. You put it in there, so just get it out."

Moe puts down his unopened Coke, tosses his putter into the grass, grabs a ball from his pocket and tosses it into the trap. "Let me show you. Let me show you."

The golfer – saying nothing and still spitting a few last granular remnants from his mouth – stands aside. Moe addresses the ball, swings, and hits the ball out. Not a phenomenal shot but certainly not a bad one either.

"See? Just swing easy and focus on the next shot. Get it done and move forward."

As you can imagine, the golfer having received this unsolicited advice from a guy with wild hair, in an untucked checkered formal dress shirt, colourful plaid pants and a sad pair of worn-out golf shoes, quickly deduces that it's time to extract himself from this situation before it gets as complicated as his last bunker shot.

"Great advice! Thanks," the golfer says as he begins to exit the sand trap, trying to keep any interaction as short and sweet as possible.

Ignoring the attempt to leave, Moe stops him.

"I don't practice these shots much. Why not you wonder? Because I'm not one to hit it in a sand trap! It's not my target. If I'm in a sand trap, it's usually only by choice. Only by choice. It's only all you other guys who keep finding them. Finding them because of your bad shots."

Erroneously sensing he has the golfer's attention; Moe persists in sharing more.

"One time, I was in the Saskatchewan Open and I was up by three going into the last hole, and I thought I'd make it more interesting. You know, make it entertaining for everyone and give me some variety. I was on in two, putting for birdie and then I purposely putted across the entire green and into a tough sand trap. That's right! Putted right into the trap! Right on into it! I wanted to see if I could get it up and down and still win. Hoo! You should have seen everyone's faces! Wondering what the heck I was doing."

"Mhm," the golfer reluctantly offers, not caring about the story, focusing more on trying to spot the fastest escape route possible.

"I did it. Still won by two. Won by two. No risk, no reward, right?"

"Uh, right. Good for you. Great story." Looking at his watch, "Wow. Look at that, I have to run. Enjoy your day."

The golfer scrambles out of the sand trap, quickly clutches the few clubs he had lying in the grass and makes a quick exit without looking back. He is just short of running. I suspect he wishes he was running but he is being polite, trying to make it not look too obvious how much he wants to be rid of Moe.

Moe watches him scurry off before he himself climbs out of the sand trap, noticing the golfers' last sand shot still lying in the grass.

"Hey, you forgot your ball!" Moe yells back at the fleeing golfer, far off in the distance now. "Don't you want your ball?!"

Realizing the guy is out of earshot, Moe bends down and picks the ball up. "Hmm, nice! A brand new Titleist. Nice!" as he slides it into his pocket. "Finders keepers, finders keepers."

Looking up at the blazing sun, Moe can no longer ignore that he was starting to feel the ramping up of the midday humid heat. He pulls out a handkerchief and wipes his increasingly wet and dripping brow and eyes. His eyes were even starting to sting a little as the abundant sun lotion applied earlier, starts to have its consequences.

"Hoo! Starting to get a bit toasty out here. A bit toasty," he says out loud to himself. "Maybe it's not a good time to hit bunker shots.

Maybe, it's time to take a little break. But just a little one. Just a little one."

Moe grabs the ball he shot earlier out of the trap and puts it back in his pocket. As well, he picks up the Coke he had placed on the ground when he arrived and opens it. He takes a good long swig, all the while eyeing the sand trap with a hint of mischief in his eyes.

For Moe, a sand trap was not just a sand trap. It was also a convenient place to take a nap.

You see, back in the early days of his career, Moe spent more nights *sleeping* in a sand trap than he ever did *playing* out of them during the day. Often, it was because he had no other choice. He barely had any money back then and sometimes the only money he had was for the entry fees to the tournaments and nothing else. So, if that meant there were nights he had to sleep outside to save money...well, then that's what he did. Usually, he could get a room at some cheap motel but sometimes it just wasn't in the cards and a sand trap was his go-to solution.

Succumbing to his need for a little lie-down, Moe climbs back into the sand trap, gets on his hands and knees, and pushes some of the sand together to form a small mound. As he does so, he continues to talk out loud to himself.

"One of the best things about a sand trap is that you can always make yourself a good pillow. Perfect for whenever you want to make yourself a great sand bed. Oh yes! A nice comfy sand pillow, just like this one!"

Once it's a perfect size he lies down, with the newly formed mound under his head, and closes his eyes. He lays there for a moment, with his arms across his chest, eerily reminiscent of someone lying in a coffin, and effortlessly drifts off to sleep.

18

THE PERFECT MARRIAGE

MOE GETS NO MORE THAN FIFTEEN MINUTES INTO HIS SAND NAP before he's stumbled upon by Karl -- the same employee who turns off the driving range lights I mentioned earlier. Needless to say at first, Karl is unsure of what is going on. Finding a seemingly unconscious body lying in a sand trap on his rounds is not exactly an everyday occurrence. As he jumps out of his truck and runs towards the trap he initially fears the worst. But as he approaches, a loud snore suddenly erupts from Moe, and he quickly realizes that as odd as this sight is, it won't have an unhappy ending.

Karl kneels beside Moe and gives him a firm shake. "Hey, Moe! Moe! Are you alright? Wake up."

Moe bolts upwards with a jerk, momentarily confused and unaware of his surroundings. By instinct, he starts brushing at his leg and determinedly flicks his foot hard into the air almost kicking Karl, and screams, "Get away! Get away from me!"

Not needing any more warning, Karl quickly gets up and takes a few steps back. "Hey Moe, it's me, Karl. Take it easy. Everything is okay!" he assures.

Quickly realizing where he is, Moe starts to laugh at himself.

"Hoo, look at me! Look at me! What a silly old fool I am. Still worrying about waking up to a snake. Worried about waking up to a little old snake. Sorry about that Karl. Hope I didn't scare you."

"What do you mean snake? What snake?!" asks Karl inquisitively as he looks around with a slight sense of trepidation.

"Oooh! There is no snake. It's just my muscle memory. Just my muscle memory.

"Oh good," relaxes Karl.

"I can remember more than one morning in the past when I woke up with a snake wrapped across my legs in one of these sand traps. Hoo! Sure can. Happened more than once! It wasn't ever trying to bite me or anything. Oh no, the poor bugger was just trying to keep warm too. It got damn cold in there at night! Sure! Usually, I'd just move my leg to get rid of it or just wait patiently until it slithered away. Depended on the size and how fast I wanted it gone!"

Moe clarifies further with a hearty chuckle, "Guess I wanted this imaginary one gone fast!"

"You've slept in sand traps? At night?" Karl questions skeptically.

"Oh sure! It was a long time ago now, but sure. Not that I miss it though. Oh no. It sure wasn't my favourite thing to do. Oh, no sir. It was cold in a sand trap at night! Damn cold!"

Giving his head a good shake, loosening the tendrils of his sand nap cobwebs, Moe rubs his eyes and gently gets up to dust himself off. He struggles a bit as he attempts to fully straighten his stiffened back. It wasn't like the old days anymore when he could take a sand trap nap and jump out and get back at it like a limber cat. Slowly climbing out of the bunker he grabs the trap rake and starts smoothing out the indentations in the sand to ensure it's pristine for the next golfer.

"I always say, the number one rule in golf with sand traps is to always leave them better than you found them," Moe tells Karl.

"I couldn't agree more," nods Karl back. "But I can guarantee you, not enough golfers know and follow that rule. Here, let me help you," as he picks up another rake.

"Are you sure?" asks Moe.

"No problem. I was coming over here to do just this anyway."

As they both rake to get the trap back to pristine condition, Karl is still intrigued by this sleeping in sand traps admission. "I have to ask you...why would you ever want to sleep in a sand trap?"

"Want? Oh! It was never really a case of want. More a case of I had to. I did what I had to do. That was the price I had to pay to play, back then. I couldn't always afford a place to sleep, so that was the choice. No shame in that. No sir. No shame. Besides, I was all alone anyway. It didn't matter where I slept. It wasn't like I had a lady friend or wife to worry about or go back to."

Abruptly halting his raking, Moe looks down towards his feet. He wiggles his toes inside his shoes and notices there is a weird feeling inside one shoe. Sand has got in from the large opening in the front toe. Delicately sitting on the side of the bank of the trap Moe pulls the shoe off without unlacing it, exposing a sock that has a hole in the heel much bigger than the one in the toe of the shoe. Realizing sand got inside the sock too, he removes that as well and gives it a good shake before slinging it over his shoulder. Turning the shoe upside down, the grains begin to pour out. Who knew so much sand could get through that one hole! It reminds him of sand falling through a glass timer and that time is ticking and he needs to get back to work! Once it seems to have all drained out, he bangs the shoe against the rake a few times to get every last granule out. Satisfied that he's resolved the problem, the sock goes back on, followed by the shoe.

"I liked that though," Moe continues. "I liked not having to have a lady friend. Liked not having to worry about anyone but me. I guess I decided to fall in love with my clubs. That's what I married I guess. My clubs. And who can blame me? I only went on three dates in my whole life."

"C'mon, you're not serious. You've only been on three dates?" a taken aback Karl questions.

"Oh, yes, only three. And three too many at that! Terrifying disasters! I had no idea what to do or say. No idea! Hoo! I don't know how you guys and gals can sit around and chit chat and make all googly eyes at each other for hours on end. Hours and hours on end. What a waste of time! Always turning into a bunch of mushy kissy fools. Hoo! No thanks! Hoo! No thanks. So yeah, I married my clubs and it worked out great! I go to sleep every night knowing they'll hit a good shot for me today and another good shot tomorrow. Every time."

Moe finishes raking and leans on the rake grinning, "And they never talk back to me or tell me what to do either! Sure! Not a bad word ever! Let's see all of them married folks try and beat that! Hoo! Let's see them try and beat that!"

Karl laughs out loud in response. "Ha, I hear ya. Trust me, from experience, I hear ya!"

Finally finished with their raking, they both stand back and scrutinize the sand trap closely.

"As perfect as a smooth wind-swept drift on a Mojave Desert dune," Karl declares. "Just how I like them."

Moe nods with approval and his mind immediately shifts to more important things.

"Well, I better get back it. Still have a hundred and fifty shots to go. One hundred and fifty to complete a full day's work."

Moe glances at the adjacent putting green and gives it a brief moment of consideration before declaring, "That practice green can wait for another day though. Wait for another day," as he tosses the rake to the side, grabs his coke and clubs, and marches off.

"See you later, Karl. Thanks for the wake-up call."

Karl chuckles back, "No problem. But if you ever need a nap again, come find me. We have a cot in the employees' locker room. Enjoy the rest of your day."

19

IF THE SHOE FITS

As Moe commences his walk back to the driving range an annoyed expression slowly creeps across his forehead with each advancing step. It doesn't take long before he stops and looks down at the same shoe that was giving him grief in the sand trap. Despite having emptied it earlier he can still feel sand in it, and it's becoming increasingly irritating. It occurs to him that it would have been smarter to wait until he was done raking the trap before emptying his shoe, as more sand must have gotten back in through the toe hole. While we are not talking about a situation quite as bad as the princess and the pea scenario, it's close enough. Moe does not like anything amiss. Particularly when it comes to the things that he can control in his golf world. Golf shoes included.

He takes a few more steps and stops again.

"Darn it!" he says to himself out loud. "I hate when my shoes aren't feeling just right. They have to fit like a glove when I'm hitting. Have to feel like they aren't even there. That's why these old ones are usually always the best! They fit me like a glove and are full of memories of perfectly hit shots that lead to more."

He removes the beat-up shoe and turns it upside down again.

After banging hard on the heel a few times, a small amount of sand drops out. Not nearly as much as before, so the perplexed expression magnifies on his face. He expected much more sand than that and wonders how that little amount could have felt so bothersome. Shrugging his shoulders he puts it back on, starts waking and immediately stops again.

"That's still not right!" he says out loud to himself and takes off the problematic golf shoe once more. He puts his hand deep inside and rummages around until he finds the answer.

"Aha!" he triumphantly exclaims as he pulls out a small stone. "I knew there was something more," as he tosses the rock into the perfectly manicured lawn by the path, disappearing forever into the lush blades of grass never to bother anyone ever again.

With the problem finally resolved, the shoe goes back on, and his journey continues. But not for long. He stops again and looks down exasperated, talking to his shoe.

"Darn thing! Still not right. Still not right. I guess you need a good cleaning now. A good cleaning that I don't have the time for! I have balls to hit!"

Instantly he abruptly changes his destination in mind and begrudgingly bolts off towards the direction of the parking lot to exchange this pair of shoes for another that are stored in his car. Once he locates his car he stops and admires it for a few seconds. Despite his compelling desire to get back to the range as quickly as possible, his precious wheels deserve a moment of his appreciation. He loves, loves, loves his car. He was right when he said that his clubs were what he married, but if that's the case, then it's his cars that he had his affairs with.

Moe only purchased one kind of automobile in his entire life: Cadillacs. And he always bought them when they were only one year old. This way they were still in pristine condition and retained that unmistakable new car smell but didn't come with the same sticker shock. He is a huge fan of their luxurious smooth ride but even more so of the roomy size of the interior and the massive trunk. It is these last two characteristics in particular that made them incomparable for him over any other make or model.

While it's completely true Moe spent more than a few nights in his early golfing career sleeping in a sand trap, the rest of the evenings were not always necessarily spent in a cheap motel. No, the truth is, he spent many a night sleeping in his cars when money was extra tight. Often living out of it for days and days at a stretch. So, it made sense that a roomy interior to accommodate a good night's sleep and a huge trunk to hold his belongings were vital considerations.

Outside of these two factors, there was one more critical reason for wanting to have a car for himself. A reason that overrode the brand, size, and driving requirements. If he had his own car he wouldn't have to hitchhike anymore.

For the longest time, Moe never had a car. He couldn't afford it. And he was far too shy to ask anyone for a lift to get to the next tournament. Or even worse, get a lift, and then be put in the paralyzing position of trying to make conversation with other players for hours on end in an enclosed six-foot space. He would rather have died than have to talk for hours with golfers who he was supposed to know – but didn't -- with no escape. So, since he didn't have a car, he chose to hitchhike from tournament to tournament.

I remember saying to him that it must have been terrifying at times, but he said it wasn't. He said that people and times were different back then. That while it was a risk, it wasn't as big a one as I may think. Far more people did it back then than they do now.

He told me, "Luckily, most people who were kind enough to give me a ride didn't need to talk too much after the first few minutes, so that worked out well. Usually, they'd turn on the radio and we'd just listen to the music. I especially loved it when I got a lift from someone in a pickup truck. That way I didn't have to sit in the front cab with the kind driver. Oh, no! If it was a truck I could ride out in the back and enjoy the breeze and the scenery rather than trying to make up some silly conversation up front in the cab. I'd even prefer sitting back there if it was raining out. Oh sure! I'd take wet silence over dry talk any day."

Most people always thought hitchhiking was a crazy thing for him to do but nothing was going to stop him from getting to those tournaments. And when he couldn't afford to own a car, hitchhiking it was. And best of all, by not taking rides from fellow players, when he finally did get his car, he didn't have to worry about returning any favours. He could drive to the tournaments all by myself, just how he liked it.

Moe always says, "I can talk to myself all day. There's no better company than yourself."

I always loved the story of Moe buying his first car. As usual, it was a story with a twist. There's never anything plain and simple when it comes to my lovable pal Moe.

20

DREAMS REALLY DO COME TRUE

It was in 1958 in Brantford, Ontario when a twenty-six-year-old Moe bought his very first car. His eyes had been peeled on one car in particular at a local dealership. Every time he went to look at it he arrived with a pent-up excitement that was bookended with an ever-increasing sense of trepidation. Because he had to take his time to save up the money to buy it, there was a deep-down lingering fear that he would arrive one day, only to find out that some other lucky soul bought it out from under him. It may have been nothing more than an inanimate object to you and me, but for Moe, it was much more than that. He had fallen head over heels in love. The thought of losing it to someone else was slowly driving him crazy. Chinese water torture may have been easier to handle.

When Moe first laid eyes on the precious cargo, it was proudly perched in the front row of the dealership on a special ramp reserved for the newest inventory. This way the car stood out above all the other vehicles on the lot, signifying this was "the one" you wanted to own or rather, the one you *needed* to own. And it captured Moe hook, line, and sinker upon first sight.

It was freshly washed and waxed, as beautiful as the day it left the production line and was ready and raring to be driven home by the first lucky guy to grab it. Although it was an unnecessary bonus lure for Moe, it had a big "Own Your Dream Car Today!" sign painted on the front windshield, and a big red bow fastened across the hood. The sun bounced off it like a prism. It stood like a work of art. It was painted a deep blue, with massive chrome bumpers on the front and back, perfectly balanced with a spectacularly detailed chrome grill. It was flawlessly complemented with abundant chrome meticulously flowing down both sides. Each hubcap was like a brooch of glistening silver, with a red Cadillac emblem smack in the middle of each, mounted on pristine whitewall tires. On either side of the trunk, the body design created the illusion of two fins or wings that gave it that unmistakable Cadillac signature look. Inside, white tufted leather seats beckoned and a long blue dashboard with a huge, mostly chrome, steering wheel dared you to take her out for the fastest ride of your life. The odometer was long and massive as it read out your speed horizontally from zero to one hundred and twenty miles per hour. It was perfection.

Luckily for Moe, after a few weeks of loving it from afar as it teasingly sat for all to see on its preferential presentational perch, it didn't sell. It came down off the showcase ramp, replaced by another piece of new automobile bling, and was now parked amongst the other cars for sale in the front row. After another few weeks passed, it went into the second row, then to the third until it eventually found the back row. Every time it moved further back he had a small heart attack. When he couldn't immediately find it in its last parking spot he was punched in the gut with the realization that someone else may have claimed it. But that wasn't to be the case. Fate was on his side. Finally, after a few torturous months of antagonizing anticipation, yearning, and saving, the time had come to claim his first love. This was easily going to be the biggest transaction and commitment he had ever made in his life.

"Is Allan here? Where's Allan? I need to see Allan!" bellowed

Moe as he excitedly burst through the dealership doors with a worried sweat beading up on his anxious temples.

A nice guy in his fifties, slightly overweight and balding, in the predictable used car dealer kind of bad plaid suit, made his way over to attend to him. Moe spotted him immediately and rushed towards him.

"Hey, Allan! Told you I'd be back! Told you I'd be back!"

I should point out that this did not get Allan overly excited. Normally when a customer returns like this it would be a momentous opportunity for any salesperson. Target locked on and torpedoes ready to fire. But Moe was not a usual customer. You see, Moe didn't just spend the last few months admiring the car from afar. At least once a week – if not twice – he would come onto the lot and take a look at it closer up. Sometimes he would even ask to sit in it. But he would never ask to take it out for a test drive. Not ever. And every salesperson knows that if you can't get the prospective client into the car and have them go take a test drive, you're dealing with a looky-loo and not a serious buyer.

"Hey, Moe! What can I do you for?" responded Allan politely but not over-enthusiastically.

"Still have the '57 Coupe De Ville Cadillac I was looking at?" knowing full well it was there.

"Sure thing," Allan replied and, being a slow day, strategically changed his usual tactic.

Instead of letting Moe wander off and go take yet another unsupervised look, he suggested, "Tell ya what. Lemme bring her around for ya, why don't I?"

Much to his surprise, Moe gushed, "I was just going to suggest the same thing!"

Sensing a seismic shift from the normal Moe visits and the ever so slight scent in the air of a sale, Allan quickly went to a large pegboard behind the reception desk that was full of car keys and fobs, ran his fingers along a few rows, before he came across the set he was looking for.

"Bingo! Excellent! Just give me a minute or two and I'll be right back with her!" as he vanished quickly out the door.

A few minutes passed and Allan pulled up to the front of the dealership where Moe impatiently paced. He waved and gave Moe's dream car horn a heavenly honk.

"Oh, there she is! There she is!" Moe oozed, looking at it as if it were the most precious thing on earth.

The red bow was now long gone and pinned to another competitive newer arrival and the sign had been washed off the windshield. Moe slid his hand along the side of the car, feeling the hot metal, radiating heat from sitting out in the summer sun. The exterior metal was hot enough that you and I may have pulled our hand back right away, but Moe didn't have to due to his tough weathered skin and deep calluses. What an amazing feeling it was, being able to admit to himself this was all real and this was soon going to be his!

Like a tiger surveying his prey and sensing this could be the chance he had been looking for, Allan immediately went in for the sales kill.

"Whad'ya say, Moe? Hop in and take the wheel. Let's take her for a test drive!" as he started to open the driver's side door so Moe could assume the driver's seat.

But instead of taking the driver's seat, Moe pushed the driver-side car door closed – locking Allan back inside and just barely giving him time to get his foot back in before losing a few toes – and went over to the passenger side. He opened the front passenger door and plopped himself into the seat. With a huge grin, Moe ran his hands across the huge dashboard in front of him and opened the glove box for a quick peek. Once finished looking in the box he shut it and adjusted his seat to recline mode, letting it go as far back as it could go. He peacefully closed his eyes, enjoying the warm leather of the bucket seat enveloping his body. Then suddenly, as if electrified by the seat, he gymnastically climbed over the front seat into the back seat and lay fully prostrate. As he lay there, he took long deep breaths, inhaling that unforgettable newer car scent, letting out a resounding "Hoo, Hoo!" of satisfaction.

It's fair to say that Allan wasn't quite sure how to take all this in, as it was unlike any other car inspection he had ever encountered. Usually, the first thing most guys want to see is under the hood and to go take her for a ride. Preferably a ride alone so they could see what it felt like as the massive odometer got past eighty miles per hour at the very least.

"Can I see that trunk again, one more time?" Moe begged.

"Umm, of course, but don't you want to take her out for a --"

Before Allan could even finish his sentence Moe was out the door, waiting for the popping sound of the trunk being opened. By the time Allan deployed the switch and got to the back of the car, half of Moe was already inside the trunk, checking out every square inch of it, sizing up what he could put where. At this point, Allan's enthusiasm began to deflate as he started to get that here-we-go-again feeling.

But Moe surprised him.

"Twenty-six hundred dollars, right? Twenty-six hundred?"

Suddenly sensing that he may finally be making a deal after all, he pitched back, "And not a penny more! A heck of a deal at that!"

"Then I'm buying it! I'm buying it! Twenty-six it is."

Allan was a bit stunned at first that there appeared to be no negotiations to be had and that Moe was ready to pay the full sticker price. He could hardly believe that, just maybe, all of these months of patiently dealing with looky-loo-Moe were going to pay off handsomely after all.

"Wise choice Moe! Looks like she's been waiting all this time just for you. Guess it was fate! So, how you gonna go abouts paying for her?"

"With money, of course," Moe deadpanned.

"I know that. I mean how? Do you want to finance it?"

"Finance it?"

"Yeah, you know, pay it bit by bit over time on credit."

"Hoo! Heck no! Heck no!" Moe chastised back, as he quickly dug into his pocket producing a wad of one-hundred-dollar bills. "I pay with cash. I don't have a credit card or a bank account! Hoo! No way. No way! I pay with cash."

Moe started to count them out loud, one at a time, as he laid them into Allan's palm. "One, two, three, four...(and eventually)...twenty-six! There you go, twenty-six hundred dollars. I've saved for this for a long time. You only buy what you can pay for. Only buy what you can pay for."

With the transaction completed, Allan held up the set of car keys, which were every bit as spectacular as the car, with the fancy chrome Cadillac key fob catching the sun as it dangled before Moe like a sparkler.

"Excellent Moe! These babies are all yours then. Congratulations!" as he offered him the keys.

"Oh, no, you can keep those, for now. I don't need them," as Moe put out his hands in a stop motion, steadfastly refusing them.

"Keep them?" responded Allan with a bewildered look.

"Yeah, I don't need them."

"Moe, you need them to drive the car."

"Oh no, I can't! I can't drive it! I can't drive at all! I've never even tried! I still need to get my license. So, no, I don't need them. Don't need them at all just yet. I do need to leave the car here until I get my license though. I'll let you know when I do! Hope that's okay? It's okay isn't it?"

"Um, ok. Uh, yeah. Sure. Let me know then. The keys and the car will be here waiting for you when you need them," still taken aback by this new wrinkle.

"Great! Thanks, Allan, thanks! Let's go park her then shall we? And let's put her way in the back where nobody can touch her. Is it okay if I ride along?"

"It's your car Moe, of course. And once we're done, let's go in and finish up the paperwork."

They both slid back into the car and, with a still bewildered

Allan in the driver's seat, and an enraptured Moe once again lying prostrate in the back seat, off they went to park the first in a line of Moe's dream cars.

And to complete what would easily be one of the oddest sales of Allan's career.

21

THE PEN IS MIGHTIER THAN THE SWORD

BACK AT THE GOLF COURSE PARKING LOT, HAVING GIVEN HIS CAR its proper due, Moe promptly opens up the trunk. It's jam-packed and bursting to the brim with golf-related items. It's so tightly cramped that it's shocking things don't come flying out like a jack-in-the-box. There are boxes and boxes full of golf balls, including some old bowling ball bags with "The Strand" logo on them, stuffed full as well.

And I should point out, only Titleist golf balls. They are the only ones he will ever hit on a golf course. His golf balls are like his cars in that he is unwaveringly loyal to the brand that works for him.

Amidst the hoards of golf balls are a few sets of golf clubs, rolls of lead tape, numerous easy access turtlenecks, pants, other assorted clothing items, and several pairs of golf shoes in varying states of wear. In all the madness, specifically stuffed to the top on one side, are stacks of magazines and newspapers that mostly contain stories on the tournaments he performed well in. Strategically placed on the other side are self-motivation articles, books, and cassette tapes, predominantly by his favourite speaker, Tony Robbins.

He looks to the side where his golf shoes are usually kept but doesn't see the pair he particularly has in mind, to replace these troublesome ones. Puzzled by their absence and stubbornly determined to find them, he starts taking items out of the trunk one by one, placing them on the ground around his car, as he looks. As luck would have it he finally finds the pair he wants resting under almost everything else. With his latest mission accomplished, he takes the soiled shoes off, tosses them in the trunk, and slips on the fresh pair.

"Much better!" he thinks to himself. "Problem solved."

To anyone passing by and seeing all the various items piled up around his car now, they would likely assume it will be impossible for him to ever get it all back in. But Moe has unpacked and repacked his car a thousand times and knows the organizational science to get it all back in. As he picks up the stack of newspapers – the last of the items to go back in -- and shoves them into their preferred resting place, he takes a moment to leaf through some, enjoying the stories and memories from the past. It never ceases to feel good to be reminded about one's accomplishments now and then and read how others witnessed your wins.

After sufficiently filling his memory bank with good memories, he's about to close the trunk when one article, in particular, grabs his eye. The headline on it reads: **Moe Norman: Rare Athlete or Idiot Savant?**

Moe studies it, not reading it through as he has thousands of times before but just focusing on the title. The longer he looks, the more his stare intensifies, and you can see the wheels turning in his head. He puts the article down and begins to rummage around in the back of the trunk again, keenly focused on looking for something else. Finally, he finds what he is looking for. A pen.

Moe picks up the article, studies the heading one more time and clicks the ballpoint pen open. In one simple confident flourish, Moe crosses out the word "idiot".

He puts the pen away and places the article back on top of the pile, flattening it out with his hands as he does. He carefully studies the now revised article headline and the smallest of grins forms at the corners of his mouth. He closes the trunk and pats it gently with his hand.

And maybe, just maybe, at this moment, he has just started a new journey towards closing the door to many things from the past.

22

THE CANADIAN AMATEUR

FITTED WITH HIS NEWISH PAIR OF SHOES, MOE EAGERLY STRIDES back to the driving range. Just as he embarks, he notices a young dad and his young son carrying their clubs directly ahead of him, deep in conversation. It's obvious the young boy wasn't going to be able to carry his clubs too far at his age but that he would have likely had insisted that "I can do it myself! I'm big enough now!" and the father acquiesced. At least until they get to their golf cart, that is.

Moe had always secretly dreamed about shooting a round of golf with his father but sadly, it never came to fruition. He never had the forever cherished memories of being told how to hold a club or having his dad see him hit his first good drive or get his first par – or better yet his first birdie. He'd never have those special recollections of simply shooting a game of golf with his father and talking about life and loves, as they ambled along the fairways together. Never getting to experience that irreplaceable pleasure of just hanging out, being with dad for the day, all by himself, sharing an equally beloved passion.

Moe's relationship with his father wasn't the best. His father was a very stern, no-nonsense and emotionally unavailable kind of man.

Critically destructive to their relationship, he had no use for the game of golf and even less for the kinds of people who played it. His father said golf was for people who had too much money and thought they were better than everyone else. He also thought that it was a game for sissies and that real men played real sports like hockey. He despised the game so much that he never invested a penny of his hard-earned money or a minute of his own free time in encouraging, supporting or sharing Moe's fixation.

When Moe first wanted to try golf as a kid, there wasn't a chance in hell his father would buy him any clubs. For the first few years that Moe taught himself to golf, he resorted to using a branch off of a tree, shaped like a golf club. And even then, I kid you not, with a tree branch he could hit the ball with some accuracy. When a club member at the golf club he caddied for as a young boy gave him his first club – a used five iron -- there was no looking back. When Moe finally was able to cobble himself together a full set of clubs, instead of being able to proudly show off his prized possessions, he had to hide them from his father under the front step in a crawlspace that was too narrow for his father to crawl through. Either that or his father would have taken them and sold them, or worse yet, break them one by one and throw them out. And the punishment would have likely extended beyond that as well.

Moe himself never had any children. Since he was never married and with him being paralyzingly terrified of women -- or any form of relationship -- I suppose that's not any surprise. But seeing he had no real connection with his father I suspect that could have played a role in it as well. But in any event, not having kids was okay with Moe.

All that being said, he loved kids. I mean *really* loved them. Moe may not have ever been willing to give the time of day to most adults, but he would always have the time to stop and chat and enjoy interactions with almost any child who crossed his path. And they loved him equally back. They were drawn to him like moths to a flame. Whenever he saw a child he'd throw a golf ball towards them to catch right away, using it as a tactic to instantly engage them. It immediately

established interaction and communication that rapidly blossome
into much more.

As the boy and his dad walk in front of Moe he can overhear their conversation more clearly as he gets closer. Rather than hearing the excitement and witnessing the father/son comradery he is expecting, Moe is saddened at the dialogue going on between them. The father is offering a torrent of pre-game advice like, "remember to keep your head down," "don't rush your swing," "remember to do this" or "remember to do that." It goes on and on and dismays Moe to no end. Not that he is against giving advice, not at all, as you have experienced already in this story. But not once does the dad say, "and most of all have fun!" It doesn't take a fortune teller to deduce that the round ahead is not going to be very enjoyable. Not for either of them. The longer the dad goes on with his advice, the more Moe can see the excitement leave the poor kid's eyes and the heavy burden of all the expectations begin to weigh down on his tiny little shoulders, even more than the heavy bag of clubs he is already being challenged by.

It takes everything within Moe to not interrupt and yell out to the young lad, "Don't worry what your dad or other people are doing or telling you to do kid! Do what works for you! Do what works for you."

As the lecture continues ahead of him, Moe starts to slow down his usual torrid pace. He can't bear to hear the berating of the boy anymore, letting the two get further and further ahead until they are out of earshot.

"Just believe in you and dare to follow through kid. Then you are set for success. Then you are set for success," he thinks to himself, all the while trying to telepathically mind project those same thoughts into the boy's head. How he wishes he could run up ahead right now and tell him that simple lesson. To save him from having to learn it himself. Or even more specifically, to save him from his father. But he knows that isn't his job. Life's important lessons occur at their own pace.

Seeing this young boy, his relationship with his dad, and knowing he importance of confidence stirs a strong memory up for Moe. As it does for me.

It's from the 1955 Canadian Amateur in Calgary. It was a big tournament for Moe and one that changed his life in many ways. No Canadian had won it since 1951 and the pressure to remedy that was fierce. Bad things happen in three's they say, and everyone was praying the Canadian losing streak was over and not going to go to four.

Moe had breezed through the early rounds and beat the number one seed – a fellow named Bajus -- seven up with six holes to go in the semi-final.

In the finals, it looked like it was going to be another easy win for Moe against another skillful player, Lyle Crawford. Moe birdied three of the first four holes and everyone began to think it was going to be a cakewalk. But Crawford was no slouch. By the time they got to the tenth hole, they were all even again. It went back and forth for the rest of the back nine and by the time they were finished the first eighteen holes of the thirty-six-hole matchplay final, they both needed the well-deserved lunch break.

At most professional golf tournaments there are always sponsors and big money involved but not so much for the amateur ones. However, when it comes to a national amateur title, the big sponsorship money shows up. As a player, you're definitely more coddled, but you're also more on display.

When it was time for lunch, there was a special player's tent set up where the competing players went to eat. While these tents would mostly be off-limits to the general public, those with the right amount of pull could find a way in and rub shoulders with those earning a reputation on the circuit or with those who were in contention over the week. The exclusive eating areas were large white tents stocked with food of all types to satiate almost any player's needs. It was a sanctuary for the golfers. A suitable place to step away from the pressure, get out of the sun, grab a bite to eat, recharge, and best of all, connect a little with your fellow players who understood what you were going through.

No one understands the pressure you're under in a golf tournament better than those who have been through it themselves. If you are a golfer, you know full well how the mind can infiltrate your swing in a nanosecond. How quickly you can go from being full-on confident and sticking it close to the pin on every green, to being unable to hit the ball without a massive hook or slice. For me, it's with the putter. It never fails to baffle me that when I start to get nervous I get the "yips." It seems every putt I hit is always just short of the hole. My caddie could be screaming "never up, never in!" at the top of his lungs, but when the nerves get jangled every putt is always just short of the hole and there seems to be nothing I can do about it. It's as if there's an invisible force field in front of every cup. Being around the guys in the player's tent, who understand and can commiserate with what you're going through, can go a long way to help clear your head between rounds.

While most golfers made a beeline to the tent to be with their fellow players, Moe did the exact opposite. Rather, I have to take that back; he did make a beeline to the tent but it was only so he could grab -- as quickly as humanly possible -- a handful of hotdogs and a stash of Coca-Cola and get the heck out of there. He didn't want to run into anyone that he would have to politely chat with or, just as worse, be stuck at a table with the other players, having to chat and interact and expend all that energy trying to be "one of the boys". And he most certainly didn't want to get cornered by some business type with the necessary pull to get into the tent -- who odds are, had a few too many drinks already -- wanting the prestige of talking to one of the finalists. He knew that the reason for this break was for him to recharge. He needed to rest, recover, and get ready for the final eighteen. The last thing he needed right now was to be surrounded by people he didn't know, expend energy trying to get to know them and completely stress out and feel like a duck out of water. No, what he needed was some one-on-one Moe time.

Heading directly to the barbecue area at the back of the tent he grabbed himself five hotdogs and placed them into a bag he had at the ready. Next, he grabbed two massive fistfuls of mustard and ketchup packets that he buried into his back pant pockets. Once he had those, he fished out another bag and went to the coolers, full of a variety of cold drinks, and placed six Coca-Cola into it. Eyeing some bags of chips on another table, he snapped up a couple of the barbecue flavoured ones and held them in his teeth. Fully armed with his favourite food and drink in both hands, and desert held in his teeth, he attempted to escape from the tent. As he was trying to leave, one of the tournament officials stopped him.

"Mr. Norman, you can eat here in the tent you know. There are plenty of places to go and sit and enjoy the attention you're attracting. That was one heck of a front eighteen! You're surprising a lot of people this week."

Moe would have none of it.

He politely responded to the official, without taking the time to remove the two bags of potato chip bags still clenched in his teeth, "Ooh, yesh. I know. Shank you. Shank you. I jusht need to go and grab shomething firsht. I'll be back shoon. Real shoon," as he pushed past the well-meaning official without looking back.

This of course was a lie. He had no intention of returning to the tent nor coming back "real shoon."

Finally free of the lunch area, Moe could invoke his game plan. Having golfed at this course a few times before, he was familiar with the layout. Luckily, because of that, he knew of a great secluded spot along the Bow River that snaked itself through the course where he could escape from everyone. Carrying his yummy hot dogs, chips, and Coca-Cola banquet, he glanced over his shoulder to make sure that no one was watching and slickly darted and disappeared down an obscure little path that wound its way through some bushes off of one of the holes. As he walked down the narrow twisting and turning path he could hear the increasing roar of rushing water. After about a minute on the secluded path, it suddenly opened up and revealed a

gorgeous clearing that overlooked the powerful river. The food ‹
may have been a sanctuary for the rest of the players, but not f‹
Moe. This was his sanctuary. A quiet spot away from everyone with
the hypnotic white noise roar of the water rushing by and a soon-to-
be mouthful of hot dog, barbecue chips and a Coke.

Upon arriving at the river, Moe went to the edge and placed his
food on a large outcrop of huge rocks. Before starting to eat he sat
down to take off his shoes and socks. As he sat down he heard a
squirting noise and instantly felt wetness forming on his behind. He
quickly jumped up and looked down to see what that was. On the
rock where he sat was a big wet blotch of red and yellow. He placed
his hand on the seat of his pants and when he pulled his hand back
he saw it too was covered in a swirl of red and yellow.

"Ohhh no!" he shrieked, realizing he had just sat on the mustard
and ketchup packets that were in his back pockets.

Pulling them all out and dumping them on the rock, he saw that
of the twenty or so that he had jammed in there, fortunately, only
three of them had burst open – one mustard and two ketchup – but
that was more than enough to still do quite a bit of damage. Despite
the colourful pattern of the plaid pants he was wearing today, there
would be no mistaking the mess on his butt.

Not giving up, he quickly took the pants off and went to the
water's edge to try and wash the stain out. Unfortunately, it was
mustard and ketchup and you and I both know that stain wasn't going
anywhere without some strong detergent to help. Nonetheless, he
gave it the good old college try and attempted to get some of the stains
out, but mostly he just smeared it around even more and the blotch
just got larger and larger until it turned a yucky brown. As a bonus
level to the fiasco at hand, the seat of his pants was now soaked. Frustrated, he looked at the mess he made of his pants and with no other
options possible, regretfully pulled them back on. He grimaced as his
skin met the moist polyester fabric and his nether regions felt clingy,
wet, and sticky. Tasty too, I guess, for any passing animal that might
have come his way. Once they were on he comically tried a few phys-

origami positions on himself to try and get a good look at his behind to no real success.

"Oh, what the heck. What the heck," he resignedly said to himself. "Just one more thing for them to laugh at. Oh yes, one more thing to laugh at."

Accepting that there was nothing more he could do to resolve the situation and that time was quickly ticking away for him to get back for the final round, he went back to removing his shoes and socks. Once removed he placed them to the side and stuck both his feet into the frigid cold mountain water.

"Ooooh, that's cold! So cold! Feels so good!" he emitted with pleasure, closing his eyes for a moment and enjoying the liquid cool swirling around his feet and through his toes.

Not before long, the grumbling in his belly could no longer be denied. He snatched a hotdog, opened two each of the still-sealed condiment packets, squirted them on and devoured the first hot dog in two bites. He grabbed his bottle opener and cracked open a cold Coke to help wash it down.

"Ooh! Won't this make everyone mad!" he couldn't help but think to himself. "They expect me to eat with everyone else. Sure! Make me sit in there with the rest of the herd of cattle. Sure! I'll never understand why everyone wants a part of you all the time and can't just let you, enjoy yourself. Geez, they've been watching me all morning. Heck, they've been watching me all week! Why not let me have a little of me to myself!?"

He opened another Coca-Cola, took a sip and slowly demolished the rest of his hot dogs, with some intermittent barbecue chips tossed in for good measure. As he ate he was blissfully silent, letting the white noise of the rushing water hypnotically soothe his mind as much as it did to his hot tired feet. If he could bottle these seconds in time and sell them he would be a very rich man.

As he sat back in his blissful reverie a young twelve-year-old boy appeared at the end of the path. He was in bare feet, his shoes held in his hands. He wore rolled-up blue jean overalls, a white t-shirt, and sported a blue hat with a Winnipeg Jets logo on the front. The boy was surprised to come across someone in this secluded spot and it stopped him in his tracks. He quietly eyed Moe. It didn't take long for it to dawn on him who this guy with his feet in the water, and a blank stare on his face, looking out over the river was.

"Mr. Norman?" the boy shyly squeaked out.

Moe was too deep off in his thoughts to hear him.

"Mr. Norman? Is that you?" he asked again louder.

Hearing him this time, surprised, and caught off guard, Moe whirled around quickly. The movement was so sudden that the boy took a step backwards in trepidation.

"Oh! Hey kid. You surprised me! How are you doing?"

There was a slight beat as the boy determined whether this was safe or not and then said, "Umm, they're all looking for you."

"Who is?" questioned Moe back.

With a shrug of his shoulders, "Everyone."

"They are, are they? Looking for me? Hoo! I'm right here!" he laughed.

Still a little bit unsure of the situation the young boy continued, "Well yeah, but they don't know you're here Mr. Norman. That's why they're all looking for you. At least, that's what I'm guessing."

"Part of the plan, my boy. Part of the plan," Moe mumbled to himself.

Moe pulled a ball out of his pocket and tossed it.

"Here catch!"

The boy caught the ball.

"Great catch! You'd make a good baseball player."

This immediately helped set the boy a little more at ease.

"I only found you because you're here. This is my private place," explained the boy.

"Your private place?"

"Yeah. I like it here. I come here a lot. It's quiet, except for the sound of the river."

"Well, if you've been here before, you got the rights to it then.

vate places are special. Finders-keepers. Finders-keepers. Do you want me to leave?"

The boy shrugged, "If you want to."

Moe began to get up and the boy stopped him as he offered, "But I'd be happy to share it with you if you want..."

Moe reached over into his bag. "Coca-Cola, kid?"

With enthusiasm, the boy accepted. "Thanks!"

"Have a seat. Have a seat," Moe offered as he opened the Coke and patted his hand on the rock beside him.

The boy took Moe up on his offer, accepted the opened Coke, and sat down beside him. He let his feet dangle over the edge and set them into the liquid cool.

"Oh! I love how it's always so cold on my feet at first! It's freezing but it's so good!" the boy expressed with glee.

Moe took an instant shine to the boy.

"I know what you mean. Know what you mean. I thought the same thing!"

Moe held up his Coca-Cola. "Cheers, kid!"

"Cheers, Mr. Norman!" he offered back with a wide smile that was missing a front tooth.

They clinked bottles and both took a good guzzle of their similarly preferred nectar of the gods.

"You know you're supposed to look someone in the eyes when you do a cheers, right?" said the boy. "You looked at the bottle instead of me. My dad says you're supposed to cheer the person, not the drink and that not enough people know that. He says that if people don't do it right, be sure to tell them. That they would want to know. It makes doing a cheers way better."

"I never heard that! Never heard that before. We better do that again then!" as he offered his bottle for a re-do clink.

I cannot express enough how rare and monumental this moment was. As I have stated earlier, Moe hates to look people in the eyes unless he knows you very, very well. Even then, when it does happen, it is often only fleeting if not completely accidental. But here Moe was, willingly offering to look the boy who was a complete stranger, directly in the eye. This was something.

The kid reached out his bottle, their eyes met and without the usual excruciating need to look away, Moe comfortably held the stare, and they clinked.

"Cheers!" they both said in unison.

Within seconds Moe let out a loud burp, which is instantly echoed with aplomb by the young boy. They both smiled. Moe let another one rip, and the young boy heartily took up the challenge and gave a huge "burrrrrp" right back. They both broke out into cheerful laughter together. Once their hilarity subsided, they both sat in silence, looking out at the torrents of water streaming past, enjoying the almost deafening roar passing by their now almost numb feet. Neither of them was uncomfortable with the silence nor felt the urge to break it. Both were blissfully unaware that when they took another sip of their Cokes, they did so at the same time, and then in unison, they wiped their mouth afterwards the exact same way.

Another beat passed and Moe finally broke the silence.

"My friends, by the way, call me Moe."

"I'm Nicholas," the boy countered.

"Please to meet you, Nicholas, pleased to meet you."

They clinked their Coca-Cola's, eyes meeting once again, and each took a sip. Moe saw the boy had already finished his. "You want another?"

It was easy to tell the boy did. "I probably shouldn't. My dad would say one is enough."

"Well now, don't get me wrong, you should listen to your parents, but...your parents aren't here and I'm not the kind of guy to spill the beans...so....," as he pulled another one out of the bag and dangled it up for the taking.

There was a moment of hesitation on the part of Nicholas and Moe made it look like he was going to throw the Coke in the river.

"Oh well, then maybe them fishes are thirsty!"

"No!" blurted out the boy. "Fish can't be thirsty! They live in the water. They can drink all they want whenever they want!"

"You're probably right. You know what? You're as smart as you look! As smart as you look! Well then, better not make me waste it on them then," as he offered it to the boy again.

"Thanks, Moe."

Moe clicked off the bottle cap and handed the bottle to him.

"My pleasure! And don't worry. It's our secret. It's a double Coke kinda day. A double Coke kind of day. Just like it's a double eighteen holes kinda day."

As the boy took a sip Moe asked, "Are you liking the match?"

"Yes, sir! You're really good. My dad says you're someone to watch. He says you're a clown too, but I don't really know what he means by that."

"He does, does he?"

"He says he knows you're going to win."

Moe grinned back at him. "Not bad for a clown huh?"

"Yeah!" Nicholas giggled back in agreement.

"This is a great private place you've got, Nicholas. You chose well. You chose well."

"Right? It's the best! My dad teaches at the golf course, so it's easy for me to sneak out and get here. He always has lots of people around him, teaching them to golf and stuff. He teaches me too. Says I have lots of potentials. But sometimes...sometimes I just like to come here instead. To just be by myself. I love hearing the water whoosh by. How it drowns everything else out."

"I know what you mean kid. Know what you mean," nodded Moe back.

"But then, I always seem to end up getting in trouble for it. My dad says I need to 'socialize' more and play with the other boys. But I like being alone sometimes. I think I just like watching people rather than being with them sometimes, is all."

Moe didn't need to say a word in response as he could not agree more. Another comfortable silence came over them both while they both took sips of their Coca-Cola's, once again in an unknown unison.

"You must like being watched. There sure are lots of people out there today watching you!"

"Oh! Sometimes. Sometimes. But just by people on the golf course. Nowhere else, nowhere else. I don't ever really like talking to any of them anywhere else either. I like people seeing me on the course but as soon as I'm off it, I don't like being seen so much anymore. I don't want to talk to anyone."

Nicholas took it personally and the shift showed on his face.

Moe picked up on it and clarified with a smile, "But not you. You seem okay, kid. You seem okay."

This affirmation thrilled Nicholas to no end.

"Usually, the golf course is the only place I feel comfortable with when there are other people around."

"Why?" wondered Nicholas.

"I don't know. When I'm away from the course, it isn't my world. I always feel everyone is smarter than me. That everyone thinks I'm dumb. I only went to grade nine."

This little factoid made Nicholas incredulous. "Only grade nine?! Wow! That's only two more than me!"

"Yeah. Only grade nine. I was good at math though, really good. A prodigy they said. I could add and subtract and multiply numbers in my head real easily. I never had to write things down on a piece of paper to figure them out. Didn't need it. If you asked me to add or multiply something I could do it for you in a second. Right in my head. Right in my head. Go ahead, ask me a multiple question."

"Now?"

"Sure! Go for it!"

Nicholas methodically thought and threw out, "What's...sixteen times twelve?"

"One hundred and ninety-two," Moe replied without hesitation.

"How about, twenty-one times forty-four?"

"Nine hundred and twenty-four. Ask me something harder. Ask me something harder."

"Umm...what's...ninety-eight times four hundred and twenty?"

"Forty-one thousand, one hundred and sixty."

Nicholas giggled at the answer.

"What?" Moe asked, confident he is correct.

"Nothing," Nicholas smiled back, "I just don't have any idea if any of those answers were right. How would I know?"

They both laughed.

"Well, you can bet your life they were correct answers. Bet you're life on it."

"Don't worry, I believe you. That's neat you can do that."

"I wish I met kids like you when I was growing up, Nicholas. Back then, people always made fun of me because I could do all that math stuff in my head. The kids at school were always teasing me for stuff like that. And I didn't like the rest of the things we did at school either or having to be around the other kids. Not at all. Besides, I was always playing hooky from school to play golf, so it made sense for me to quit in the end. Just made the most sense. My parents didn't care either, so I quit."

"Wow, you were so lucky!"

Moe was moment by moment becoming even more of a rock star to Nicholas.

While Moe was thoroughly enjoying Nicholas's enthusiasm, he was also aware that he didn't want the boy to get the wrong idea either.

"Maybe. Maybe...but school is a good thing too! Knowledge is important. One of the most important things of all."

"I'd rather be better in golf than being in school getting smarter, that's for sure. My dad never seems to care much about how smart I am. But he sure wants me to golf better. To reach my full potentials."

"When I'm on the course I feel like I'm the smart one. Smartest of them all. But the second you take a club out of my hand, every-thing changes. I feel stupid. It makes me want to disappear."

"Kinda sounds like the golf course is your special private place," concluded Nicholas.

Moe smiled but didn't say anything. They both luxuriated in another harmonious moment of silence.

"Sounds like you're a pretty smart guy, Nicholas. A pretty good golfer too. That's a pretty good combo. Pretty good combo. I'd love to see you hit the ball sometimes."

"Yeah, that'd be neat."

All of a sudden Nicholas cocked his head, stood up on the rock, and looked towards the golf course. "I think I can hear them calling for you Moe. We better head back. The back eighteen is gonna start soon."

Moe knew he was right and was resigned to the reality that he had to get back. Although on so many levels, chatting with Nicholas seemed a much better option.

"Guess you're right, guess you're right."

As Nicholas quickly slipped into his sneakers, "I better go find my dad. I hope you win!"

Moe dug into his pocket and threw him another ball. "Here kid!"

"Gee, thanks!"

"Hoo! Another good catch. Looks like you have a good backup plan as a shortstop if the golf doesn't work out. Tell ya what, if I win, you can have my putter too."

Nicholas's eyes opened wide with anticipation and excitement, "Really? My dad says you're gonna!"

"Tell ya what. Let's meet back at your private place if I do, after the match."

"Okay! Deal! See you, Moe!" hollered Nicholas as he started to run off. But before getting too far, Nicholas stopped and turned. "And hey, Moe. It's *ours*! It's *our* private place now!"

And with that Nicholas bolted off disappearing down the path, back to the first tee where his dad waited to watch the rest of the match with him and all the other golf fans. Moe knew it was time to head back as well but waited for a few more precious moments before going back. Trying to extend the quiet quality 'Moe-time' just a little bit longer.

The tournament organizers however were having no part of it and soon descended. They found where he was and dragged him back for the remaining eighteen.

And what a back eighteen it was.

At first, as you can well imagine, there were more than a few wisecracks from the gallery over Moe's freshly christened ketchup and mustard bottom pants as he stepped up for his first drive. Many of the comments were along the crude lines of, "You got Norman where you want him now Lyle, he's crapping his pants!" and so on. I'll just leave it at that. There were other quips far worse than that which aren't worth repeating. Fortunately, most people who watch golf tournaments are gentlemanly and polite, but you could spot right away there were going to be a couple of well-lubricated yahoos who were more than happy to show their darker side.

The heckles came fast and furious over the first few holes and it looked like the teasing may come into play, in Lyle's favour. To his credit, Lyle coldly stared down more than one of the guys shouting their vulgarities to try and silence them, but he didn't do much more than that. He had his own game to focus on, after all.

Moe bogeyed the first hole and then the second as well. It was quickly looking to become a rout, but the other way around this time. But after those first two holes, Moe found a way to shut it all out. He played with a focus and a purpose that was impenetrable as the match wore on. The better he played, the more irrelevant the comments became, and eventually, they drifted away altogether. By the time they both got to the 36th hole they were tied. They knotted the 37th and 38th holes as well. On the 39th Moe hit a great drive right down the middle and hit his second to within eight feet of the pin. You could just sense that he knew that putt was going in. He couldn't wait to hit it!

Crawford was just off the green and had a lengthy chip shot. It was still very sinkable and the silence in the air was thick as he took more than a few calculated practice swings, trying to feel just the right amount of momentum for his swing and to read the correct break. In the end, he decided to have it land about ten feet from the cup and let gravity take over, letting it roll the rest of the way, to break hard to the left at the end. The pitch was well struck, rolled right to the cup on the line he had planned but took a bit harder break to the left than anticipated. It rolled past leaving him with an easy uphill two-foot tap in for par.

But before his shot even hardly had the chance to stop, Moe was up to his ball and ready to putt. People must have thought he was insane to not take the proper amount of time and make sure he had a solid read on the possible game-winning putt. You could tell it would break just before the hole and while it was only an eight-footer it was extremely downhill and would break hard and run far past without the ideal weight. The proper speed would be everything. If it were me and I was having a case of the yips, even I would be hard-pressed to leave it short.

There were one of two lessons about to be learned. One: Take your time and get a good read before you putt, or two: Just trust your instincts and hit it.

Thankfully rule number two prevailed. It was perfection! Right into the middle of the cup!

And just like that Moe was the Canadian Amateur champ for the first time in his career. Pure vindication of him and his swing at long last. And better yet, a footnote as the winner of the longest match ever.

To put an exclamation point on the vindication, he would win the next year as well.

23

THE PASSING OF THE BATON

YOU WOULD THINK THAT ONCE THAT PERFECT SEEING-EYE-PUTT dropped into the cup, and Moe felt the addictive rush from the appreciative tumultuous roar that instantly followed, he'd want to eagerly eat up the adulation and attention that he'd been denied for so long. With this title, he became an instant star on the amateur stage. Hopefully, it was also going to put an abrupt end to a lot of the nay-sayers and their endless critical banter about his swing and more. Sadly, that was not to be the case as Moe quickly found himself right back into hot water with the authorities.

Right after any tournament win, the protocol is for the winner to immediately head over to the presentation area to receive the winning trophy, followed by having your photo taken for the national and local newspapers and then interviews with television media. Finally, you meet with the press gallery and the adoring crowd that awaits you, your win and newfound fame.

Moe however had a completely different plan for after the match. He vanished. He was nowhere to be found.

Eventually, the officials angrily gave up looking for him and one of the fellow golfers who had at least some kind of friendship with Moe accepted the trophy on his behalf and shared a few words.

As you can imagine, the leadership of the amateur golf association was not impressed and believe me, they had memories like elephants. There would be a price to pay for his no-show effort after that otherwise dramatic victory and for his disappointing of the well-heeled fans.

After the win, Moe snuck back to the secret place by the Bow River and had more Coca-Colas and more "Moe-time". Nicholas showed up shortly afterwards too. He came racing down the path, running out of breath from the race over.

"You did it, Moe! You did it! Congratulations. You're the Canadian Amateur Champion. That's so cool!"

"Hoo! Thank you, Nicholas. Thank you!"

"I never doubted you. Not for a second! My dad didn't either!"

"Hoo. Not bad for a clown! Not bad for a clown. Be sure to tell your dad that!"

"A friend of my dad said you're the Clown Prince of Golf now. So, I guess your something royal now too. Very cool, don't you think?!" not comprehending the sentiment behind the statement.

Moe knew what the comment meant and instantly felt the gravity of it. It was the first time he heard the "clown prince" nickname for him, but it certainly wouldn't be the last. It tore at him that even with such a momentous win, the desire to make fun of him never seemed to abate. But he was not going to let it get him down. Not today. Not now anyway. This was a victory he was going to savour.

"Oh, by the way, they're all looking for you again too!" Nicholas warned him.

"Hoo! I bet they are. I bet they are. Them big wigs want to put me on display now, like a prize poodle in a dog show. Oooh! I don't want that. No sir. I just wanted to win the tournament and be done with it. The title is all I want. All I ever wanted. I don't need some trophy and a bunch of attention. And most of all I don't want to have to talk to all those people! Hoo! No way! People I don't even know fawning over me like they're suddenly my pals. No thanks!"

"But you gotta go back, you gotta! They want to get your picture with the trophy. That's one of the best parts of winning! You get your picture up on this big wall with all these other guys who won. Some of them are really famous too! I don't think you'll have to say anything though. Another guy got up and said a bunch of stuff for you. But the trophy is still just sitting there."

"Ooh! Did someone now?"

"Yeah! So, come on come back. Come get your picture taken with it! Maybe I can get one with you too even!"

While his impulse was to stay, Moe could tell how much it would mean to Nicholas.

"All right. For you, I will. For you, I will."

"Yay, let's go then," he urged. "We can always come back here later."

"Okay," he agreed. "Ooh! I almost forgot. Here, this is yours," extending his putter out to Nicholas.

"For real?!" he questioned, before reaching out for it.

"You bet! A deal is a deal. A deal is a deal!"

Nicholas took the putter and held it preciously as if it were made of gold. It may not have been fit for a king, but it was for a prince at least. A clown prince, anyway.

"Maybe you can use it when you win this thing yourself, in a few years," Moe joked.

"Nah, I'll never be as good as you."

"You never know Nicholas, you never know. Don't ever count yourself out. Not ever."

24

BY INVITATION ONLY

Winning the Canadian Amateur was a dream come true and to be the golfer that ended the three-year drought for Canadians was the cherry on top. It was a championship victory that Moe had always wanted and now no one could ever take that away from him. He even had a picture with him holding the trophy as undeniable proof. With this feat accomplished there was still one important thing left for him to gain from it. Something that would surpass all other dreams that may dare to dance in his head from time to time.

But for now, that dream would have to be put on hold.

Now that the summer tournament season was over it was time for Moe to go back to toiling at The Strand and the leather factory to make money, biding time until next year. Each day that he would have to wait was to be every bit as agonizing as it was waiting to buy that first Cadillac. Perhaps even worse.

In late January of 1956, while Moe was in the midst of his world of wait, he was having one of those kinds of days at work that he would rather forget.

It was a gruelling day of setting pins at The Strand where not only had a stray flying pin hit him twice, but he had also bashed his head trying to avoid a bowling ball that some fool threw too quickly when he was still getting out of the way. He had an ever-reddening huge goose egg of a welt growing on his forehead from the steel beam it struck full-on, as he narrowly escaped the oncoming bowling ball. When he left work with his growing headache it was so cold outside that he almost chose to expose his forehead to the elements in the hope it would stop its throbbing growth. His tight toque and parka hood pressing on it wasn't helping either. To add to the misery, Moe had forgotten his gloves at home, so his hands were already frozen cold in no time, even though they were in his pockets, and his fingers were going numb. Worse yet, he had to walk backwards for most of the trek, tripping more than once, as the stiff winter wind sandblasted his face with snow pellets whenever he walked directly into its full force.

Once he arrived home and before he could even get his parka and boots off and have a chance to thaw out, his sister who was sitting and waiting on the stairs said, "What took you so long to get home! Don't worry about taking all your stuff off and come upstairs. Now!" as she scampered to the top of the stairs and vanished out of sight.

Knowing they rarely shared more than a few sentences, he knew something serious must be up. Moe kicked off his boots and dutifully refrained from taking the rest of his winter clothes off and followed her up as ordered. When he got to the top of the stairs he instinctively assumed she had gone to her room and walked down the hall to where she should be. Her door was closed, so he knocked on it before entering.

"Marie are you in here?!" he bellowed, not at all interested in a game of hide and seek.

Instead of her opening the door and letting him in he could hear her down the hall.

"Shhhh! I'm over here. Not so loud. Get in here," she quietly said as she poked her head in and out of his room, like a carnival whack-a-mole game target.

Moe trudged back down the hall towards his room. While he was admittedly a little bit intrigued, he was mostly annoyed by all the secrecy. He stood in his bedroom doorway wanting the nonsense to come to an immediate end.

"What's this all about Marie! I've had a crappy enough day today. I have a huge headache and I just want to eat something and go to bed."

"Get in and close the door," said Marie.

"Just tell me what this is all about," he repeated without moving.

"Just get in and close the door why don't you!"

"Fine!" he countered, fully entering the room and closing the door behind him. He crossed his arms and glared, "What? This better be good. This better be good."

"You owe me, you know? You owe me big time."

"Why? Why would I owe you?"

"Keep talking like that and maybe I'm going to change my mind and not show you" she taunted with a grin.

Moe's eyes narrowed, "Show me what?"

From behind her back, Marie held up an envelope with a grin that grew even more pronounced on her face.

"Show you this. I intercepted it and made sure Mom or Dad didn't see it. It came in the mail today. Special delivery."

Seeing the letter more clearly, Moe's mouth dropped open and his eyes bugged out so much that he looked like a caricature of Wile E. Coyote when he gets to within inches of finally catching the Roadrunner.

"Seems to have come from someplace in Augusta, Georgia..." she teased further as she read the address. "Thought it may be important..." as she started waving it in the air.

"Gimme that!" he barely managed to utter out loud. But he was so caught up in the excitement of the moment that he didn't make any effort to reach for it.

Marie waved the envelope closer in front of him.

"If Dad had got it first, he probably would have torn it up into a million billion pieces and never even told you. You know that right? So, you owe me. Big time."

If Marie were being completely honest – and not just being a bratty sister at that moment – she would have admitted that he didn't owe her a thing. She was truly glad to have been able to be there when the letter arrived and to make sure that Moe got it safely and intact. She would never outright admit that she was immensely proud of her brother right now, but she was.

Marie held out the letter. "Go on then! Open it! Let's see if it was worth me risking getting in trouble over."

Moe reached out his trembling hand and took the envelope. He held it like it was as precious as the first edition of the Bible and examined both sides carefully. He knew instantly where the return address was from and the postmark over the stamp. He could hardly believe his eyes that it was addressed to him and only him: Mr. Murray Norman.

"For heaven's sake open it!" blurted Marie, no longer able to hide her impatience.

Moe tried to gingerly open the envelope, but his still semi-frozen hands were not fully cooperating. Not to mention those huge thick paws of his weren't exactly designed for opening something this delicate.

"Let me!" demanded Marie, as she held out her hand, tiring even more of the slow pace of things.

He handed it to her and warned, "Be careful though, Marie. Don't rip it. Don't rip it. I want to keep it. Keep it forever."

Marie grabbed the envelope and carefully opened it without tearing it even the slightest bit. She handed it back to him so that he could do the rest. Moe opened up the flap and pulled out the folded letter inside.

Before reading it, he sniffed the paper, giving it a deep inhale as if there were to be some sort of special scent that went with it. Finally, satisfied with whatever real or imagined olfactory reward there was, Moe unfolded the letter. He was shaking as he read it to himself. Not from being cold any longer but from the celebration of what his eyes were embracing.

Marie watched in silence until he stopped. Then he did something that he had never done before or since. He hugged his sister. Being as completely out of practice with such an intimate gesture as he was, she clumsily raised her arms back and returned it the best she could.

As they awkwardly stood in this once-in-a-lifetime embrace Moe whispered to her, "I did it, Marie! I did it. I'm going!"

"Read it to me!" she pleaded as she released her part of the clumsy hug.

Moe took a deep breath, cleared his throat, and read it to her. As he read he realized that by saying all of the words out loud for the first time, it was as if it was being officially confirmed. It was real. It was going to happen.

"Dear Mr. Murray Norman:

The Board of Governors of the Augusta National Golf Club respectfully requests the honour of your presence at the Nineteen Hundred and Fifty-Six Masters Tournament to be held at Augusta, Georgia.

Signed, Robert Tyre Jones Jr., President "

He looked at her, still shaking and letting it all set in.

"Well, smell you, mister big shot," Marie grinned.

25

THE MASTERS

WHILE IT WAS ONLY GOING TO BE A THREE-MONTH WAIT FOR
The Masters to happen once Moe opened that letter in January of
1956, it may as well have been a lifetime. Staring him in the face
would be a seemingly endless long string of dark winter days leading
up to the brilliant bright one. It was like putting a full pot of water on
the stove and being forced to watch it boil over and over again, all the
while you had to paint the kitchen it was boiling in and watch the
paint dry too.

As the date got closer, it became even more agonizing, and the
last few weeks in particular were excruciating. Having all those
watches on each arm didn't help either. It was as if they only existed
to remind him of not only every hour that passed but how many more
were still needed to. He was chomping at the bit to get out on the golf
course and prove his worth, knowing in the end – that no matter what
– soon on his resume there would always be a record of him playing
in The Masters. Only the most elite golfers in the sport are ever able
to boast of that.

For those of you reading along that are unaware of The Masters
and its magical allure and historical significance, let me take a

moment to fill you in a bit on what it's all about. The tournament is special and unique in so many ways.

It was started by one of the most famous amateur players of all time, Bobby Jones. He built the course in 1930 along with an investment banker named Clifford Roberts and a well-established course architect, Alister MacKenzie. The first time the tournament was played was in 1934. Because it's an invitational event, the field is smaller than most PGA tour events and the likelihood of being able to compete in it during a career is therefore made even more difficult. As well, once you win the tournament, you have an invite to play in it for the rest of your life.

Since 1949 the winner has been awarded the infamous "green jacket" in addition to a trophy. Immediately following their victory, the winner goes to Butler Cabin – a historic building on the grounds – to don his new jacket and be interviewed on TV. When you win you're allowed to take the jacket away with you for the year of your reign and proudly show it off all you want. But at the start of the tournament in the following year, you must bring it back to the Augusta National course where it is permanently stored. The jacket is forever the property of the winner, but it is stowed with the jackets of other previous winners in a specially designed cloakroom on the golf club grounds. Going forward, you will only wear it when you are at the golf course. If you are fortunate enough to win the tournament more than once, you don't get another green jacket. The first one is your only and forever one unless the jacket has become too big or small and needs to be re-fitted. As you can imagine, it's a tiny group of players who have earned this honour in the history of the game.

Another unique perk for winning the tournament – outside of the huge cash prize in the millions of dollars going to the best score – is that the winner gets to choose the meal for the Champions Dinner the following year. It's held on the Tuesday of the tournament week and is solely for past champions and select board members of the Augusta National Golf Club. Wouldn't it be something to see the faces of the organizers if Moe won? Hotdogs, barbecue potato chips, and Cokes for everyone!

One of the much-loved traditions for the tournament is the honourary tee shot on the morning of the first round. It's a special moment that began in 1963, honouring the past, and has included many legends from the game of golf. From 1981 to 1999 the usuals taking the first shots were Gene Sarazan, Sam Snead, and Byron Nelson with a few others tossed in for good measure. After they became incapable of playing any longer due to ageing health or death – the last being Sam Snead in 2002 – the tradition was shelved for the next four years. In 2007 arguably the most loved golfer of them all, Arnold Palmer, whose followers were a massive fan base called "Arnie's Army", became the sole golfer to take the first ceremonial shot. Years later Jack Nicklaus and Gary Player were added to the mix and the three of them hit the first shots for the thrill of the crowds for the next decade. It was a highlight moment every year for golf fans, watching these legendary veterans of the links still hit the ball very well and see the obvious fun, friendship, and camaraderie that still existed between them. After Palmer's death in late 2016 only Nicklaus and Player took the ceremonial shots until they were joined by Lee Elder in 2021, who was the first African American to ever compete in the Masters back in 1975. Sadly, it was the only time he would take such a shot as Elder died the following year. In 2022 another huge fan favourite of the golfing world Tom Watson will join Nicklaus and Player.

In addition to the actual tournament itself, there is a special bonus mini-tournament played on the par-three course on Wednesday, the day before the championship starts. The small executive course exists in addition to the championship course on the clubs' grounds. It's designed more like a social event for the players, not taken very seriously score-wise, and it's a chance to let off some of the ever-increasing stress that builds in anticipation of the four days lying ahead. Quite often the players will have their children be their caddies or have family members play along with them. Interestingly, no player has won the par-three course tournament and won The Masters in the same year.

On top of all this history and tradition that The Masters is dripping in, there is one other characteristic that helps set this tournament apart from all others. That is the gorgeous Augusta National Golf Course itself.

When not hosting The Masters, the course is set up so that from the regular tee-off boxes a medium or high handicap golfer would have a playable game. But don't get too excited that you are ever going to get a chance to play it, as it is a private golf course, with an extremely limited number of members. The truth is the chance of you ever playing it is nonexistent, which of course just adds to the allure. Once the tournament begins and the golfers tee off from the back tees it instantly becomes a whole other golf course, one that would test any professional golfer to the highest of degree. To make matters worse – or better depending on whether you are a player or a viewer – they usually tweak two holes a year following the tournament, to make them more difficult in the years to come. It's an ever-evolving test for the best.

There are many famous pieces to the course that are attributed to it as well. These include Rea's Creek which is the watery hazard that runs through the course, eagerly gobbling up many a golf ball and the bridges that cross it. Within the course, three bridges go over the creek and they have been named in honour of three players who were particularly spectacular in their play on it over the years.

There is a Hogan Bridge (named after Ben Hogan's lowest score on 72 holes that lasted for decades), Nelson Bridge (commemorating his birdie on the 12th and eagle on the 13th, to solidify his win in 1937) and Sarazen Bridge (commemorating his eagle on the 15th that enabled him to tie Craig Wood and win in the only 36-hole playoff the next day. A shot referred to as the "shot heard round the world.") It was also the home of Eisenhower Tree which was found on the 17th hole (until an ice storm claimed it a few years back) that President Eisenhower advocated many times be chopped down as it always got in the way of his golf shot.

Throughout this breathtaking course, you'll find some of the fastest greens in golf. But before you reach them, you must traverse spectacular fairways, lined by some of the most majestic of trees which included Azaleas, Dogwoods, and Redbuds. There is also the renowned "Amen Corner" – the extremely challenging 11th, 12th, and 13th holes – where many a championship dream has died and a stretch of holes that Arnold Palmer was known to play in a most amazing fashion, better than any of his contemporaries. Amen Corner is probably the most famous part of the course to be sure, but there is no denying that Magnolia Lane is a close second.

Magnolia Lane is not part of the playing course but it's rather the three-hundred-and-thirty-yard drive you have in your car as you arrive at the golf course. A narrow road flanked by stunning, towering rows of magnolia trees on both sides. It would be hard to have created a more majestic and dramatic approach to the clubhouse than this. Any golfer would have chills as they drove down this tunnel of history meandering towards the historic old clubhouse beckoning to them in the distance. As Gary Player once said, *"The Masters is the only tournament I ever knew where you choke when you drive through the front gate."*

Once you piece all of this together, I bet you can imagine the range of emotions that must have been running through Moe's veins late that evening on the Sunday before the tournament. What he must have been feeling as he arrived and stood looking up Magnolia Lane for the first time in his life. The reality dawning on him that it was at last no longer an image put together in his mind's eye, but that it was the real thing. That he could finally see it, feel it, hear it, smell it, and taste it for himself. All of its renowned history and beauty, combined with the unmistakable pressure building up within him for the days ahead, were as intoxicating as any drug ever could be. Best of all, it was probably the first time in his life that he felt his accomplishments were going to finally be recognized.

26

THE TREASURE CHEST

A FEW HOURS HAVE NOW PASSED SINCE MY HOTDOG DROP-OFF TO Moe, and I sense it's about time for another check-in with him, to make sure things are progressing as they should. I also need to grab a couple of things from my car and so I figure this would be as good a time as any to do it.

As I get to my car and open the trunk to access what I need, I notice a flickering flash of light coming from below me. I'm startled at first, not knowing what's causing it, and I realize it's just the sun bouncing off of something metallic lying on the ground, beside and partly under, the car next to me. However, I quickly realize that this may not be just "a something" but rather an *everything*. It looked like the brass box that contained all of Moe's Masters' mementos! I bend down and pick it up and open it to confirm my suspicions. Sure enough, inside were numerous items including his Masters' invitations, his player tags, a dried Magnolia flower, his scorecards, and numerous other important related cherished paraphernalia.

"What on earth is this doing here?" I ask out loud to myself, knowing there is no way this should be lying here unattended.

One thing that I know for sure is that Moe would protect this box, and all the items contained in it, with his life. I couldn't think of anything more valuable to him than this box. Moe's Masters appearances were probably the most career-defining events for him – memorable in so many ways. Very few people know of the incredible Masters stories attached to the items that lay inside. They were not only extraordinary tales, but they also went a long way to defining Moe and who he is. There is no way he would be this careless with it on purpose.

While I am now somewhat extra concerned, ready to find Moe immediately and clarify how this got to where it is, I also take a selfish moment to go through the contents. Moe was always willing to show off what was inside this box, but it was extremely rare that he would actually let you touch any of it. So, I am going to take advantage of this golden opportunity.

As I explore the box's familiar contents the events of Moe's 1956 Masters, as explained to me in detail by Moe on numerous occasions over the years, come flooding back, starting with the dried up Magnolia flower.

I put it up to my nose expecting to catch its scent, but sadly the years have robbed it of any. I suspect, however, that Moe would say differently. I'm sure it would be a safe bet to say the memories of picking up this flower and smelling it would emit an aroma to him as powerful today as it was the day it was plucked. He always said that stepping out of his car and arriving at Augusta national was no less profound than a Christian going to the Holy Land.

Oh yes, the 1956 Masters is a story indeed and this box holds volumes more than meets the eye. That tournament was a game-changer for Moe in many ways.

I'll do my best to explain it to you in full.

27

JUST BREATHE

Moe arrived at Augusta on the Sunday evening before
the tournament started. All players were allowed to practice on
Monday, Tuesday, and Wednesday before the tournament officially
started on Thursday, and he planned on using all three days to practice non-stop. He wanted to get there on the Sunday so he could try
and fit in a good night's sleep and then be well-rested and ready to go,
for the first practice round to come the following morning.

Upon stepping out of the car and feeling his feet crunch onto the
sacred ground below, the first thing Moe did upon arriving at
Augusta National, was to close his eyes. Close them and take a slow,
determined, deep and full breath. He was instantly consumed by the
bold, sugary-sweet, intoxicating scent of the full blooming magnolia
trees permeating the spot in which he too was now rooted. A scent
that would grow even stronger with each step he took forward
amongst them. The trees towering above him looked down on him as
if they were candy shop owners and he was a little boy in their store
for the first time, both wary and pleased with his arrival. In no time
their irresistible succulent scent would lead him onto the hallowed
grounds before him, as if their perfume was a long finger, beckoning

for him to keep coming forward until it safely brought him to the stately clubhouse and rolling expansive green heaven beyond it.

The overpowering fragrance welcomed everyone in the same way. Just like the perfume or cologne does of the sexiest person you had ever met as they opened up a door in front of you and you had no choice but to bolt through and embrace them. Had there ever been a better aroma, he had not experienced it.

The first deep breath was followed by a second, and then a third, before he opened his eyes, letting them add their perception to this banquet of history and sensory delights spread out endlessly before him.

"You okay, Moe?" asked Irving, a long-time friend and fellow amateur golfer who had been one of a small group of players playing with Moe throughout the spring tournament season. Irving was kind enough to drive him to Augusta as this was not a time to be hitchhiking. As a reward, he was going to watch Moe play in the tournament as his guest.

Moe's reaction to Irving's voice was surprisingly aggressive. He put up his hand like a stop sign, preventing Irving from saying anything further. It was as if Irving had just shouted at the top of his lungs rather than had asked a simple question. The thing was, Moe didn't want this transformational moment of reverie to be interrupted or to ever end, and Irving's voice cut into him like a knife and risked doing just that. At this exact second, it was fully dawning on Moe that he was being welcomed for the very first time into a very special and unique club of golf heroes. A select club that few were invited to experience. Best of all he had been given the chance to belong in it for the rest of his life if all went as planned.

"I'm fine, Irv! I'm fine!" he dismissed, unaware of his uncalled-for tone of voice.

As Moe lowered his hand and continued letting himself be engulfed in this enchanted state, Irving also began to realize how special this moment was and chose to join him, letting the magic wash over him as well. The second Irving stepped out of the car and took in the beauty and majesty of this once-in-a-lifetime opportunity, the scented spell of Augusta National fell over him. The tiredness he had been feeling from the long drive only seconds ago, instantly evaporated. He may not be playing in the tournament, but it was a dream for him to at least watch it once -- in person.

Normally the only way to see The Masters live and in person is to be a player, be a member or a close friend of a member, be a friend of a participant, or be lucky to have your name drawn in an audience lottery that's held every year and entered into by the many thousands. They say getting a ticket to The Masters is the second hardest ticket to obtain in sport, second only to the Super Bowl. And here he was, in the flesh. His lifelong dream to walk the grounds of Augusta National was going to come true. And he was going to be able to watch his friend fulfill his dream of playing in it, at the same time. An incredibly special moment, of which the gravity of its importance had begun to set in for both of them.

They each stood still for a good minute or so, in the middle of the road, spellbound and trying to comprehend the waterfall of words that raced through their minds should they have had to try and explain what they were feeling. They stood together but apart. Each with their own previously imagined thoughts of what they would see, starting to find their new true reality. Both of them were firmly held in the powerful grip of history and the tantalizing what-ifs of the future four tournament days that lay ahead. Had it been their choice they could have stood there for hours – and they may have – if not for the loud blaring honk of a car horn from directly behind them that erased the moment and made them both practically jump out of their shoes.

"Hey fellas, sorry to scare ya! I know it's a pretty sight, but can you move on out of the way so's I can get by, please and thank you!" came from a head leaning out an open window of a car.

"Sorry about that!" apologized Irving. "Let me move my car out of the way for you."

Irving quickly fished in his pocket for his car keys but couldn't find them. After a slight panic, he remembered he left them in the ignition and hopped into his car, moving it onto the shoulder. Moe moved himself to the opposite shoulder as well, giving the driver ample room to get between them.

Once the car was moved, Irving immediately came out of his car and back onto the road.

"Thanks, guys!" waved the driver politely.

"Thanks for being patient! We just had to stop and take a good look," Irving explained into the rolled-down window of the well-dressed gentleman.

"No worries fellas! I get it. Enjoy your evening!" as he waved and drove on.

Both Irving and Moe were immediately magnetically pulled back into their original spot in the middle of the road, watching the car as it drove down the lane away from them. They watched as its taillights grew smaller and smaller, speeding off into the distance. Not a word was exchanged between them until the car turned at the end of the road and vanished.

"Was that...?" Irving fumbled, unable to get the words completely out.

"It was. It was," Moe said, finishing Irving's sentence for him. "That was Ben Hogan. Ben Hogan!!"

They both looked at each other, with expressions on their faces like kids coming down the stairs on Christmas morning. This was truly going to be the week of a lifetime, wasn't it?

28

YES, YOU CAN

Sufficiently stirred, energized, and ready to experience more, Irving started to walk back to the car, encouraging Moe to do the same.

"C'mon, let's get to the clubhouse and drop off you and your things. This here is only the beginning. This here isn't even the icing on the cake. Heck, this is just the plate the cake is served on!"

Moe isn't quite yet ready to move on, however, and he still needed another minute or two for himself.

"Just give me a sec, Irv. Just give me a sec," he said as he wandered over to a huge painted sign that was permanently installed by the road.

The large sign had a white background with a map of the continental United States on it. On the right middle-ish side of the map there was a golf hole, and a golf pin with a red flag, strategically placed in the spot where you would find the state of Georgia. In green lettering, it reads: AUGUSTA NATIONAL GOLF CLUB: MEMBERS ONLY

Moe reached up and gingerly touched the sign as if it was so delicate it might break if he wasn't careful. He methodically ran his fingers along the wood grain, feeling each letter, tracing each one out with his finger. Finally, he rose on his tiptoes, and he gave the spot where the flag goes into the hole a gentle kiss. A kiss so full of love and adoration that no woman had ever received such from him; but if they had, it would have made them swoon and blush a bright red, right on the spot. It's fair to say that it may even have made them faint.

"Hooo! Here I am," thought Moe to himself. "Here I am. Moe Norman, at The Masters. *Playing* in The Masters. Moe the Shmoe! The clown prince of golf playing in The Masters! The most prestigious tournament in the world. No one can take this away from me."

Moe turned to Irving, suddenly as giddy as a kid on his first day at Disneyland and his loss for words became a distant memory.

"Oooh boy, Irv! It's a whole different world out here, isn't it? A whole different world! You hear stories about Augusta, sure! Lots of fluffy stories about how green it is, the magnolias, the big white clubhouse, the azaleas...the history. But when you're here, actually here. Oooh! There's nothing fluffy about it. Nothing fluffy at all. No sir. It's real. It's all real! And the players who are gonna be here! Oooh! Sam Snead, Tommy Bolt, Gene Littler, Arnold Palmer, Byron Nelson, Gene Sarazen, Stan Leonard, Al Balding...and we've already met the best of them all! Ben Hogan! BEN HOGAN! I can't wait to get out there and practice tomorrow morning. Can't wait!"

"But you won't be doing any practicing unless we get you settled in for the night, now will you?" cautioned Irving.

"Yes, you're right! You're right! Let's follow the way Mr. Hogan went. Let's go! Let's go!"

As he opened the car door and jumped into the front passenger seat, "Maybe we can catch up to him!"

Like a shadow, Irving followed right behind him. He turned the key in the ignition, started up the car and they began the final leg of their long pilgrimage.

"Don't go too fast though, Irv! Not too fast!" Moe cautioned. "I want to count how many Magnolias line the road on the way up. I want to count each one. I want to remember each one. I want to remember this forever."

While the sun continued a lazy descent and the tall shadows of the trees ever increased their darkness on the landscape, the two of them couldn't have wiped the huge smiles off their faces if they tried. All that was left before them now was another three hundred yards and this part of The Masters voyage – the last part that they would take together -- would be completed.

The rest of it, the most critical part of it, would have to be taken by Moe alone.

Moe started counting the trees on either side of the road as they pressed onwards, trying to imprint them on his brain forever. "One, two, three, four, five, six..."

29

SEPARATION ANXIETY

"Fifty-eight, fifty-nine, sixty and sixty-one!" Moe finished up, as they took the same turn in the road as Ben Hogan, learning that it wasn't so much of a turn as it was a continuation of a circle drive. As they followed it, it took them to the entrance of the grand-looking, but not ostentatious white clubhouse. As soon as the car came to a halt the weight of the tournament instantly started to creep heavier on Moe's shoulders.

"Are you sure I can't just stay back at the motel with you tonight, Irv? Do I really have to stay here? All by myself? I'm not gonna know anyone. Not gonna know anyone at all. I'd rather stay with you. Stay with you."

"Sorry, but they want you bunked in the Crows Nest, pal. It's where all the amateur players stay. I'm sure you'll find someone you'll hit it off with no problem."

"You know that's not true. Not true at all," Moe complained, starting to dig in his heels.

While Irving did know full well that the odds of Moe striking up a quick friendship with someone was remote, he also knew he had to keep him here and that he wasn't coming back to the motel to stay with him.

"It's tradition, Moe. All the amateur players stay in the Crows Nest. You can't come to The Masters and start messing with tradition. Geez, I'd kill to be staying in there with you!"

"But --," Moe tried to argue back.

"No but's. Its tradition."

Without allowing any room for further discussion, Irving got out of the car and opened the back trunk where Moe's one suitcase and his golf clubs rested. He pulled them out and put them both out on the curb. Moe made no effort to help and sat stubbornly sulking in the passenger seat.

"I'm happy to get these out for you, Moe. But that's it. You're on your own from here. I'm not carrying these to your room."

Just as Moe begrudgingly opened his passenger door and stepped out of the car, a uniformed man emerged from the clubhouse. He quickly trotted down the one front step and short walkway that leads out to the roadway and went directly to Irving.

"Welcome to Augusta National. How may I help you gentlemen?" he politely inquired.

"We're here for The Masters Tournament. We're playing in it," proudly stated Irving. "Well, he is rather, I'm just dropping him off. He's playing and I'm going to watch."

Realizing he chose the wrong person to give his full attention to, the attendant quickly turned to Moe.

With professional aplomb, the attendant effectively concealed his inner reaction to the comical if not frightful sight, standing before him. Moe was always something to behold and today was no exception, fully decked out in his usual bright plaid pants, colourful turtleneck, scattered blonde hair, and a huge crooked toothed alligator smile.

"I sure am! I'm here to play! Hoo! Hopefully here to win too! Hoo, Hoo! Get me a green jacket!" squealed a fully beaming Moe.

The attendant barely moved a muscle as he took in the sight before him. He gave Moe a quick studied look over, as efficient as any border guard official would do at an embassy front door, to someone with a knapsack on his back, looking for possible troublesome tell-tale issues before letting him into the secure landlocked world of Augusta National.

"This is Moe, Moe Norman," Irving clarified further.

The attendant instantly kicked into action.

"Ah yes, Mr. Norman. The Canadian Amateur Champion. Welcome to Augusta National. We've been expecting you. We're so happy to have you. My name is Marc, and I will be here in the club-house for you should you need anything."

"Hoo! Did you hear that Irv? They're expecting me. Happy to have me! Hoo! How about that? I even have my own guy here in the clubhouse for help!"

Moe leaned in and looked at Marc's name tag, spelling it out loud, "M-a-r-c. That's an interesting way of spelling it. Mark usually has a "k" on the end. Not a 'c'."

"Yes, that's often true. This is the French spelling of it."

"Hoo! Well, we have tons of Frenchie's up in Canada. I bet you and I are going to be a good fit! A good fit!"

"I am sure we will," he responded, forcing a smile. "Now, this must have been a long day for you both. I hope you had a pleasant drive. How about we get you to your room, get you a good meal and let you settle in for the evening?"

Marc pointed to the suitcase and the golf bag, "Is that everything of yours then?"

"That's it!" said Irving as he went to pick up the suitcase, and as Moe rushed to grab his clubs.

Marc instantly stopped them both.

"Please, don't worry about those! The suitcase will be taken directly to your room Mr. Norman and your clubs will be taken to the pro shop to be stored and cleaned up for your practice round tomorrow morning. How about you let me take you directly to your room so you can freshen up before your dinner."

The panic on Moe's face began to increase as he realized this was it. He was going to be on his own from now on. "Maybe it's okay if my friend Irv here hangs around for a bit? Just for a little while?"

"I'm sorry but it's just players only from here on, Mr. Norman." He turned to Irving with an apologetic smile, "No offence intended."

"None taken," replied Irving. "I completely understand."

"Mr. Norman then, this way please, after you...," said Marc as he held out his arm, gesturing towards the walkway and the single step that led into the clubhouse.

It may be only one step, but it looked to Moe as if it were as high as Mount Everest.

Moe looked again to Irving with an expression that pleaded for him to stay or to at least take him back to the motel with him. The obvious panic was escalating as each second ticked by.

"You'll be fine," Irving reassured him. "You're clearly in good hands here with Marc. Have yourself a good dinner, get a good night's sleep and I'll see you in the morning. I need to check into my motel too you know. Like this fine gentleman said, it's been a long day and I for one am ready to go relax and settle in for the night. I'll see you tomorrow."

Irving jumped back in the car, gave a quick wave to Moe, and drove off. Moe watched, praying that somehow the brake lights would turn a brighter red and Irving would suddenly lurch to a stop, turn around, and show mercy on him by inviting him to stay at the motel after all. But as the red taillights of the car grew smaller and smaller into the distance it was clear that was not going to be the case.

Feeling abandoned, Moe turned to Marc, unsure of what to do next.

Marc's arm was still gesturing to Moe, and his smile was unwavering, "This way Mr. Norman, this way, please. Let's get you to your room." Pointing to the ground in front of him, "And please, watch for the step up as you enter."

And just like that, the first of more than a few uphill climbs for the week had begun. And this one single step was a huge one.

30

NESTLED IN FOR THE NIGHT

As soon as they entered through the front door, Moe's trepidation instantly vanished and the kid inside of him took over. He was like a whirling dervish as he attempted to take in everything around him all at once. He knew full well that few people ever got this far into Augusta National, and he wasn't going to waste this opportunity. As Moe feverishly imprinted everything into his memory bank, Marc took a moment and stopped and reached behind the entrance desk where a humidor was conveniently hidden for the members.

"Could I interest you in a cigar, Mr. Norman? To take back to your room perhaps if you wish?"

"Hoo! Oh, heavens no! Heavens no! I've never smoked in all my life. Never had a drink either. Why would I want to do that? Why would I want to dull my senses? Why now? Hoo! I want to be alert. I want my senses alive and focused! My mind is the generator, and my body is the motor. I don't want anything getting in the way of clogging it all up or to do anything that would get in the way of experiencing all this. Hoo! No way! Thanks, but you can put those away! Put those away!"

Marc dutifully placed the humidor back into its hiding place and as he does Moe escaped, bounding into the room before him. Inwardly Moe was like a kid in a toy store but on the outside to Marc, he looked more like a bull in a china shop. Moe peered into the dining area, which also doubled as the Trophy Room, and saw there were portraits on the wall of the founders Bobby Jones, Clifford Roberts, and member, President Eisenhower. He entered the room – not knowing whether he was supposed to or not -- and took a close look at a set of clubs and a golf ball that was mounted on the wall and read the plaque secured beneath it.

"Hoo! These are the clubs used by Bobby Jones? And the ball used by Sarazen when he made his double eagle in '35? Hoo! Isn't that something! Isn't that something!"

Before Marc could even comment, Moe's radar spotted more rooms off of this one and eyed there was a bed in one. He made a beeline down the hallway towards it.

"Is this where I'm staying?" he exclaimed as he scurried off to investigate further.

Marc recognized he had his hands full and quickly intercepted Moe, which stopped him from proceeding any further. "No, your room is upstairs in the Crows Nest. Let me take you there. Please, follow me."

Making sure that Moe was within arms reach, Marc directed him to the main staircase where they proceeded to the second floor.

"Hoo, will you look at that!" Moe gushed as they reached the top.

He saw there were doorways to a Library, a Members Locker room, and to the Champions Locker Room. Of course, Moe chose to go towards the Champions Locker Room, the one room that he was not allowed inside.

A quick learner, Marc was at the ready to stop him, having antici-pated such a move.

"That is the Champions Locker Room, Mr. Norman. You are not allowed in there, sorry."

"Well, not yet anyway," grinned Moe with his best devilish grin. "Not yet!"

"Right," Marc politely responded with another fake smile.

"We need to go up one more level to get to the Crows Nest," Marc continued, pointing to a set of vertical stairs that may as well have been called a ladder. "After you, Mr. Norman."

"You know you can just call me Moe. Everyone does. Moe, is fine."

"Thank you, Mr. Norman," not willing to be that formal. "Again, after you," pointing to the steep climb.

When Moe reached the top he emerged upon a small sitting area with four windows, one on each wall. There were five beds and one bathroom. This was the original dormitory for the clubhouse and the first onsite housing the club had. While it was certainly nothing fancy or luxurious, it may as well have been The Taj Mahal to Moe.

"Ohhh, look at this. Look at this! How wonderful!" Moe praised.

However, it quickly dawned on him that there were five beds. Four too many. He was not going to be alone.

"Ohhh..."

Unaware of Moe's' rising anxiety, Marc pointed to the bed assigned to Moe, and in doing so, confirmed Moe's worst fears.

"This is your bed for your stay Mr. Norman. There will be four other amateur players staying up here as well. As you can see, lying on top of your pillow is your Masters player pin for you to keep and wear, as well as your bag tag. You are player number twenty-seven."

Like a well-oiled machine, having been through this introduction process a thousand times before, Marc continued, "There are more towels and bedding here in the closet should you need more than these provided for you on your bed. There is a shower in the washroom for your convenience as well, should you want to have one before dinner. Speaking of which, when shall we expect you in the dining room?"

Just like anywhere else, the thought of eating in the dining room, where others would be present, was not to his liking at all.

"I was wondering...I was wondering if I could eat up here instead? Rather than going downstairs?"

"Of course, Mr. Norman. Not a problem at all. We would be happy to bring something up for you."

With one crisis averted Moe relaxed. "Great! Thank you. Thanks so much!"

Marc went over to a table in the small sitting room, picked up a menu resting on top of it, and handed it to Moe. He pointed to a phone perched on another small side table and instructed, "Have a look through this and give us a call when you are ready to eat. Someone will be happy to bring your meal up to you. Now, is there anything else I can answer or get for you then?"

"I don't think so. Oh, wait, my suitcase. What about my suitcase?"

"It should be here any moment. In fact, if you would kindly allow me, I'll go check for you right away."

Marc climbed down the stairs and disappeared.

Left standing alone in the middle of the Crows Nest, feeling like a fish out of water, Moe proceeded over to his bed. He gently stroked the bed cover with his hand and sat down on it. He also poked the pillow to test its firmness. He glanced around the room to make sure he was alone, bounced up and down gently on the bed a few times and thought to himself, "Hmmm, not bad. Not bad at all. Certainly better than any cheap motel or sand trap that's for sure."

Moe lay down on the bed and instantly recognized that he hadn't taken his shoes off. He sheepishly kicked them off, thankful that no one was around to see that. He closed his eyes briefly, just for a few seconds, before the grumbling in his belly got the best of him, and he started to look at the menu still clutched in his hand.

There was surprisingly not much to it. The options included a shrimp cocktail as an appetizer and a soup-of-the-day. The main choices consisted of steak, broiled fish, fried chicken, or macaroni and cheese with any side of green beans, squash, or cornbread. For dessert, there were two options, ice cream or a peach cobbler.

While the steak sounded yummy he was astounded he did not see a hamburger or a hotdog on the menu. Even worse? No french fries!? (Bobby Jones thought they were unhealthy and would not allow them on the clubhouse menu and it has stayed that way until this day.) Moe was in dire need of comfort food, and he was disappointed he couldn't have it.

"Maybe I should sneak out and get something," he thought to himself. But that wasn't a realistic option, and he knew it. He didn't have the money to go out and be ordering food. He was lucky they were feeding him as it was. So, steak it would be. And cornbread. He had heard about cornbread before, that people down here loved it, and it sounded good too, so he was going to try it. He was also going to have the Peach Cobbler *and* ice cream if they would let him have both.

He picked up the phone and politely gave the person on the other end his order. When he hung up he lay back down on his bed and tried to close his eyes again. But they wouldn't stay closed. He stared for what seemed forever at the ceiling, as his heart increasingly pounded harder and harder in his chest as the reality of everything settled in further. The realizations kept coming to him in waves. He was here. This was happening. He was playing in the 1956 Masters.

Just as he managed to talk down the rising fears and started to chill out a little, another head popped up into the room from atop the steep ladder-like stairs, which made Moe practically fly out of his bed.

A voice boomed out, "Hey there! Hope I didn't wake you!"

Immediately following behind the intruder was Marc.

"This is one of your fellow roommates for the week, Mr. Norman. This is Ken Venturi. Mr. Venturi, meet Moe Norman."

"Please to meet you, Moe," said Ken as he went over to Moe and offered his hand.

"This is the last player for the day. The others will be arriving at various times tomorrow," added Marc.

With this new arrival -- and complication -- Moe's thundering heart practically pounded out of his chest. He was no longer alone in what he was hoping would be his sanctuary for the night. Now there was nowhere to run to get away from others. This out-of-the-way space wasn't destined to become his private secluded spot as he had hoped after all -- like beside the Bow River was – if only for one night. Furthermore, the finders keepers rule won't have a hope in hell of holding up here.

There wasn't any turning back now. He would have to shake Ken's hand and try to get used to shaking many more over the coming days. As he reciprocated Ken's outstretched greeting he knew there was no way he was to be getting a minute of sleep tonight.

31

PRACTICE MAKES PERFECT

As HE LAY THERE, TRYING TO KEEP HIS EYES CLOSED FOR A WEE bit longer like a little boy scared that if he opened them too early and spotted Santa Claus all the gifts would disappear, Moe's mind raced with thoughts. "Is it okay to get up now? Can I get up before the sun rises? Is there a certain time I have to wait to go out and practice and hit some balls? Time is wasting away just lying here doing nothing. Is someone else out there already? Before me? Putting in a hard day's work while I lay here, doing nothing? Why didn't I ask Marc?!"

Ultimately caving into his insatiable desire, Moe opened up his eyes once and for all and sat upright. Between the volcanic rising anticipation of today's practice round and Ken's intermittent snoring that would have challenged the decibels of any jet engine, there wasn't very much sleep to have been had anyway. It didn't matter though as the lack of sleep hadn't affected Moe in the slightest, and he was chomping at the bit to get out there. Adrenaline alone would get him through this day with no problem.

Very quietly, he put on a fresh pair of plaid pants and a bright green turtleneck. Instead of putting on his shoes, he carried them; gingerly moving across the room, as he tiptoed in his stocking feet to the opening at the top of the stairs. Had he been wearing a hat with ear flaps on it he would have looked eerily reminiscent of Elmer Fudd as he approached Bugs Bunny's rabbit hole as he chased that "wasskily-wabbit." Once he got to the opening he accidentally dropped one of his shoes and it tumbled to the floor below with a loud thud. "Uh-oh!" he thought to himself, as his head snapped towards Ken, fearing the worst. Luckily, other than a few grunts as he rolled over onto his side, Ken was unperturbed. With the coast clear he scurried down the stairs and disappeared below like a successful thief in the middle of the night.

When he got to the second floor, he put his shoes on and took another fleeting glance towards the Champions locker room. This time it held less of an allure. Not so much because of the warning he had earlier from Marc, but because Moe's desire to get out on the course and strike some golf balls surpassed it. When he landed on the main floor he was relieved to see that the coast continued to be clear. There was not a soul in sight to stop him or ask what he was doing up so early and he slipped noiselessly through the front door, out into the still dark, dawning morning.

As he ventured about, he quickly surveyed there were several permanent buildings on the grounds near the main clubhouse, each serving its purpose in the daily operations of Augusta National. Today however and for the rest of the week, there were also various temporarily added structures specifically for the big tournament. Moe's eyes were peeled for the one location that would store every player's golf clubs. As soon as he found his clubs he intended to head out onto the course whether there was enough daylight yet or not. He had decided that until he was told no, everything he wanted to accomplish this morning was going to be a yes. It was time to get at it!

Every building around him was the opposite of the still sleepy and silent main clubhouse. The buildings were already fully awake, swarming with staff scurrying everywhere, preparing for this first practice round day and the eagerly anticipated arrival of the majority of the players. Everything had to be simply perfect and a man in a blue suit looked to have everything firmly under control. His army of men was like a well-oiled machine, buzzing about with their scheduled tasks. In the distance, Moe spotted a growing lineup of golf clubs being set up outside of one of the temporary buildings and went over to look and see if his were there. Sure enough, there it was with a tag on it that read: Player Number 27. He quickly looked around, pleased to see that fate seemed to be on his side once again and that no one was there to stop him, and hastily scooped up his bag, heading off at his usual torrid pace towards the first tee.

Of course, it would be more helpful if he knew where the first tee was. Having never been to Augusta before, Moe had no idea. Fortuitously, there were enough signs throughout the grounds to direct him.

By the time he found the correct signage and knew that he was headed in the right direction, the first light of the day was just becoming evident as the sun came closer and closer to peeking onto the horizon. It would blast out a pinpoint of light any minute now. If you were a fisher, you knew this was the perfect time in the morning to bait your hook and send out your first cast. That this is when the fish would start to bite. And for Moe, this was the same moment. But for him, he was the fish, and it was time to take his first big bite out of the golf course.

When he got to the first tee he put his clubs down and stared out at the lush fairway beckoning before him. Each hole was named after a tree and this first hole was called Tea Olive. It was a four hundred and twenty-five-yard par four. Never had he experienced goosebumps like this before. His whole body tingled as he rubbed his two meaty palms together getting ready to grab his driver and take that first shot. There was just enough light now that he knew he could hit the ball and find it and so he was ready to go. There was no way he was going to wait until there was better morning light like most of the other lazy golfers would. No way. They let you play and practice as much as you wanted in the three days leading up to the Thursday tournament start, and he had planned on using up every single minute of it. Every single second! If he had his way he'll be teeing up every day before the sun rises and well after it sets.

Right now he was experiencing the same feeling and intention he had as he was about to shake Ken's hand the night before: No looking back. Game on.

Now he would shake hands with the golf course.

32

CLIFFORD ROBERTS

LIKE A ROBOT, MOE WENT TO HIS BAG, PULLED OUT A BALL, grabbed a tee, and chose his driver. It was a momentous moment, this being his first-ever golf shot at Augusta, and he knew it. It was no different than an actor saying their first line or singing their first note at their first rehearsal for their first Broadway play. He told himself that despite the significance, he was to hit this shot as if it was any other shot he had ever made. Trust the work put in, trust the process, and believe.

Taking a deep breath to start, he exhaled it, and without any change to his routine -- including no practice swing even though this was his first strike of the day -- he teed up the ball, addressed it and made his attempt. That glorious sound of the club cleanly hitting the ball first thing in the morning was always his type of crack. His drug. Today was no exception as the sound filled his veins and rose the cadence of his heartbeat, as the sensation reverberated in the still air around him and throughout his soul.

The ball flew right down the middle of the fairway to exactly where he intended.

"Like falling off a log for me," he proudly praised himself as he picked up the tee that had not moved a millimetre. "Like falling off a log."

He put the driver back in his bag, grabbed his clubs, threw them over his shoulder and with a determined and steadfast gait he set forth on his first-ever round of golf at Augusta National. Life was perfect.

Once he arrived at his ball he was very pleased with the result and chose a club from his bag for his approach shot to the green. He looked once at the green, decided where it should land, and struck it. It was another nice hit. The ball landed on the putting surface, took the appropriate slope, and stopped about fifteen feet from the pin.

"Not bad," Moe acknowledged to himself, "Not bad at all."

He tossed the club into his bag, fully at peace knowing everything was finally reduced back to just him and his ball now. Nothing else mattered and nothing else could interfere. The rest was all just unimportant background noise. Just how he liked it.

Until he heard the sound of a golf cart running at full throttle from behind him, that is.

Moe spun around and saw the same guy in the blue suit from earlier. He was waving his arms frantically in the air to get Moe's attention. He guessed there must not be a horn on the cart because he was sure the guy would be pressing it incessantly if it had. It seemed his bad luck with people in golf carts started exceedingly early in life. At some point, you had to wonder if the reason Moe refrained from riding in golf carts was really because he hit the ball so straight or rather because of the memories he had from meeting odd people in awkward situations driving them.

As Moe watched the cart get closer and closer he began to get flustered, becoming increasingly concerned that he had done something wrong without realizing it. Had he come out too early after all? Was it wrong to have just taken his clubs without asking? The last thing he wanted to do was cause any sort of commotion or worse, bring attention to himself. But there he was, and there came the speeding cart with the extremely unhappy-looking man in the blue suit with a look on his face that would make anyone stop in their tracks.

As the cart came to an abrupt halt a few feet away, the driver climbed out, smoothed down his blue suit with his hands, adjusted his tie and determinately licked one hand which then went up to slick down his hair that had got tussled during the sprint across the fairway. He was laser-focused on Moe.

"You sure are an early riser. The sun is barely even up yet," he pointed out, conveniently not sharing that he too had been up for a few hours himself already.

"Hoo! You know it!" beamed Moe, masking his internal worry. "You have to get up good and early if you want to be able to put in a good day's work! Hoo! Real early! Good hard work takes time! From dawn to dusk!"

"Couldn't agree more! I'm Clifford Roberts," the man said with a well-rehearsed politically polite smile, extending his hand as he did so. "I run the tournament."

"Hoo! I know who you are. Hoo! I know who you are," replied Moe, his hand extended back. "I'm Moe. Moe Norman. Player twenty-seven. Pleased to meet you!"

"Pleased to meet you too, Mr. Norman. You're the Canadian right?"

Moe beamed back, "I sure am, Mr. Roberts, I sure am!" thrilled that someone as important as this knew who he was.

During this exchange, poor Clifford did his best to avoid showing any outward reaction to the enormously strong handshake Moe gave him. Nor to his repulsion as he saw that everything he had heard about Moe's fashion sense was instantly confirmed. Including that one-of-a-kind crooked mass of a Moe Norman smile. Not only was it beaming brightly into his face, but it had grown exponentially in size by the second. It took him everything to not lose his cool and chastise his displeasure with the less than traditional golfing attire Moe chose to wear for his first go-around at Augusta.

Interestingly, on a side note, Clifford had more in common with

Moe in respect to what he was wearing than he would ever know. While Moe was always known to be golfing in his signature plaid pants and loud turtlenecks, it was widely known that Clifford always wore a slight variation of the same blue suit every day and that he had twenty-four identical ties to go with them. He always said – much like Moe – that life was far too short to be worrying about what to wear.

What Moe was unaware of, was that Clifford Roberts was the ultimate traditionalist and he had quite a reputation for it. Not all of it was good. He was a stickler for enforcing all rules and regulations to the exact letter of the law. Without exception. You did things his way or you would be shown the highway. He was also an absolute control freak who took immense pride in it and would go to any lengths to make sure he knew everything about every player. Which meant, he had heard much about Moe. Some of it was good and more than some of it, not so good. Clifford did not like to have any wild cards in his playing deck, and he did not like surprises. Therefore he knew in advance that Moe was one of the players he would have to keep his eye on this week.

All of these tenacious qualities he possessed in many ways led to The Masters being what it is today. For him and for those who were in his employ The Masters was not to be about money. It was to be about an arduous four-day battle on one of the most difficult courses on the planet, contested by the best in the world, to win the rarest of all prizes: the Green Jacket. It was also to be steeped in tradition and be revered second to none.

Much of the prestige of the tournament came about because of Clifford's control. With the advent of TV, he quickly envisioned there was a way to make sure he could shape the historic story going forward. This 1956 edition of The Masters was to be the first time the final two rounds were to get national TV coverage and so the stakes were remarkably high. He was to rule this inaugural, and every subsequent broadcast, with an iron fist. He had complete control as to what a broadcast would look like and how it was to be run. Including who could do it. Of all the major networks only CBS has had the rights to broadcast The Masters on TV and they are only given the contract for only one year at a time. That way, should they not do as commanded, it could be taken away from them, with the knowledge that NBC or ABC (and now ESPN) were sitting in the wings drooling at getting their chance. He also had the power to choose who could advertise during the broadcast, the fee that each advertiser would pay, and how much time commercials could take up.

The Masters has four minutes of advertising per hour while other majors like the US Open have over eight minutes per hour. Weekly tournaments on the PGA can have as many as fifteen minutes per hour! Unlike other tournaments that milk all the money and profits that they can from a broadcast, the goal of The Masters is to only make as much as it can to help pay for the tournament and nothing more.

Now that the world was watching, Clifford would do everything and anything to make sure that his battlefield and its warriors were exactly what he wanted them to be. It was going to be a carbon copy of what he had envisioned in his head. Including what players were to look like, how they would behave, and what ideals they were to represent and uphold.

No exceptions.

And right now, directly in front of him, stood good 'ol nobody, Moe the Shmoe from Kitchener, Ontario, Canada. The poster boy for *not* checking off even *one* of Clifford's precious little boxes.

Moe was grinning ear to ear like there wasn't a worry in the world for him. All the while, Clifford stood purse-lipped and stone-faced as Moe was easily one of the biggest accidents waiting to happen this week and he sensed it. If he wasn't careful, this Canadian guy could be a problem.

Well, not on his watch, Clifford promised to himself. Not on his watch.

33

THE RULES ARE THE RULES

"I HAVE TO ASK YOU A QUESTION," STATED CLIFFORD, GETTING right down to business. "Where is your caddie? No one goes out on the golf course without a caddie. No one. Those are the rules."

Upon hearing this Moe's smile was instantaneously wiped from his face, feeling like a trap door has just been pulled open from under him. He didn't want a caddie. He hated them. All they did was get in the way. Despite being one himself at one point, as a kid. They slowed him down, they talked too much, and he had no desire for someone else to be touching his ball. Even more importantly, he didn't have the money to pay for one.

"Ohhh, well...Mr. Roberts...I...well, you see...you see, I don't need a caddie. I'm quite happy to carry my clubs by myself. I can do that on my own. Hoo! Oh, sure. I'm fine to do that on my own."

"These are the rules, Mr. Norman. Each player will have a caddie and each caddie will be chosen from the tournament pool. No one can bring their caddie with them," he continued, without any attempt to understand Moe's reasoning. "And the rules are the rules."

(This rule, by the way, was repealed in 1982.)

"Ohhh, well sure. I see what you mean, but I really don't need one. I don't want to be a bother to anyone. Oh no, don't want to be a bother. And please, call me Moe. Call me Moe. Everyone does."

In a very matter-of-fact and unwavering tone, Clifford patiently clarified, "This isn't a request – Moe – you will need to have a caddie if you want to practice on the golf course. Full stop. End of discussion."

Moe was at a complete loss. Of course, *if he had to*, he would have given in and got a caddie. He wasn't that stubborn or stupid. Nothing was going to keep him from being out there. But he had no way to pay for one. No way on earth.

"But...." Moe continued, trying to find a way out of this perilous predicament.

"No buts, Moe. Please put your bag in the back of the cart and we will go back and get you a caddie. Then you can restart your practice round," instructed Clifford as he walked back to his golf cart, the discussion permanently closed.

Moe didn't move a muscle. What in heaven was he going to do?

Clifford turned and saw that Moe hadn't moved. "C'mon then. Let's get going. I have plenty of other more important things to be attending to and I am sure you want to get back out here on the course."

Moe still didn't budge. He couldn't see any way out of this other than the truth, which would be utterly humiliating.

"Moe?" repeated Clifford, with a tinge of annoyance in his voice. "Is there something wrong? Something more you would like to say?"

"Ohhh, no. Nothing is wrong. Nothing at all. Why don't I just leave my clubs here and come back and get them?" Moe strategized, trying to stall as he tried to come up with a solution. He needed more time to figure this one out.

"Please put your clubs in the back and let's get going! I have better things to be doing than arguing with you over the rules."

Realizing there was no way around it, Moe got his clubs, solemnly putting them in the back of the cart and dutifully came around the side and sat in the passenger seat. Before his behind could even fully land on the seat, they both lurched backwards as Clifford put the pedal to the metal and the cart lunged forward. In an instant, the two of them were hurtling full steam back to the area where the caddies were waiting to be assigned their players. During the dash both of them were completely silent, looking directly ahead as if each other never existed. Clifford was furious he was having to deal with such a ridiculous situation and Moe was mortified that he was, as of yet, unable to find his way out of it.

The ride took merely a minute but to Moe, it felt like an hour. Endless scenarios kept looping through his mind, trying to find one that would get him out of this dilemma without having to admit the reality that he was poor and unable to pay for a caddie. Ultimately admitting to Clifford and everyone else that he did not belong there after all.

As they approached near their destination Moe finally established the courage to tackle the situation head-on. He cleared his dry throat, "Please, can you stop here, Mr. Roberts. Stop right here."

"What's that? Why? We aren't there yet," he continued, without slowing down.

"Yes, I know. I know. But can you please stop here anyway? I have something to tell you."

Dripping with annoyance, Clifford brought the cart to a sudden halt and glanced at his watch. "Alright then, what's so important that we need to stop."

"It's about the caddie --," Moe began.

Clifford cut him off, exasperated that the discussion was even continuing. "Of course, it's about the caddie! You are using a caddie, Mr. Norman. This is not up for discussion!"

"The thing is, I can't. I can't use one."

"What in God's green earth are you talking about you can't use a caddie? That is ridiculous!"

"I can't," Moe pleaded one more time. "I just can't. I wish I could. But I can't."

With borderline fury in his voice, "Well then, you aren't playing today! It is as simple as that! I don't know what else to say. Spend the day on the putting green for all I care but you are not going out onto my golf course without a caddie!"

Moe's entire world had now spiralled and fallen apart. Not go out on the course today?! You may as well shoot Moe in the head then and be done with it. Put him out of his misery!

Just as Clifford was about to step on the gas again, and with no other option, Moe blurted out his truth, losing all of his self-respect in the same instant.

"I can't have a caddie, Mr. Roberts...I can't...I can't because... because I can't afford one. I can't afford one. I don't have any money for something like that. I've spent all the money I have just to get here."

Having finally spoken his truth Moe sat broken, as he stared down at his feet. As broken down looking as his golf shoes.

Clifford had never encountered anything like this in all of his life. Who couldn't pay for a caddie? Even more ridiculous? Who thought it was even possible to play a round of golf without one?

Clifford stared at Moe for a good thirty seconds, as his tongue inside his mouth swirled on his inner cheeks, as he surmised what to do. Moe continued gazing at his feet, not daring to look up. He wished he could just crawl into the hole in his shoe and disappear forever.

Breaking the silence, Clifford finally spoke up. "The rules say you need a caddie and come hell or high water you will have one. Augusta National will be happy to provide one for you, for both practice rounds and the tournament, free of charge."

"Ohh...," responded Moe, not sure what to say. "Ohh...you don't have to do that..."

"Do you want to play, Mr. Norman, or not?" Clifford asked sternly, at the end of his rope.

"Oh, sure. Sure! You know I do! Of course!"

"Then let's find you a caddie and you can be on your way. The rules are the rules," as he pressed his foot full on the gas pedal, thrusting them both into their seats again, steering towards the assembled caddies eagerly waiting to see which pro they were to be assigned to.

In a nanosecond, all the weight of the world fell off of Moe's shoulders. It was a huge relief to have that crisis averted and to know that he would soon be back onto the golf course.

But you did have to feel a bit sorry for the caddie assigned to him. Not because he was assigned to someone like Moe, but because the poor guy had to carry Moe's clubs. And by that, I mean for fifty-four holes on the first day of practice and forty-five holes on each of the Tuesday and Wednesday following!

34

THE WARMUP

THE BIG DAY HAD FINALLY ARRIVED. SUNRISE ON THURSDAY morning, the first day of the four-day Masters tournament. Unlike on Monday, Moe was not found rising from his bed just before sunrise. He quickly learned that as long as he followed the rules, he could get up and hit balls whenever he wanted. There was no rule about that. A tragic loophole learned by his caddie as well. Best of all, the kitchen opened up extra early on the day of the tournament to accommodate the early tee-off times. So, Moe was already up, well-fed, and preparing for his long-awaited tee-off hours ago.

The first day of the tournament was everything Moe anticipated it to be. Good and bad. It was exhilarating to be around the best golfers in the world but at the same time, it was cripplingly intimidating. It was interesting for him to see how everyone at this level had the same goal – to shoot a great opening round of golf – but that the way they went about preparing for it was so uniquely different. Everyone had their own routines, and everyone was careful to respect them. There was no right or wrong way of doing things. Some of the players talked to each other while they practiced, while others completely ignored everything and anyone around them. Each trying to find their competitive zone, space, and game face. Some would spend hours at the range, some would spend more time on the practice greens, and some spent most of their time doing nothing – knowing they did not tee off until later in the day – instead, simply hanging about and soaking up being a part of it all as they waited for their rightful turn.

Perhaps the most unnerving wrinkle in all of this for Moe was him being on the inside of the ropes at something of this great magnitude; instead of being on the other side looking in. It would take an adjustment period for anyone to get used to it, even seasoned professionals. It's probably why only three players have ever won the tournament on their first try. In the inaugural tournament in 1934 by Horton Smith, in 1935 by Gene Sarazen and lastly in 1979 by Fuzzy Zoeller. There were so many golf fans everywhere! No matter where you looked there they were, clamouring to see a player, shouting out some form of praise or encouragement to get their attention. Or, best of all, achieve the holy grail of all fan accomplishments: getting a scrap of paper, a hat or a golf ball autographed by their idol of choice.

When it came to Moe, he was glossed over by the majority of the fans. He was only ever noticed because, among all these well-known, well-dressed, and athletic players, he stood out of place. The odd-looking little man, in colourful mismatched clothes with the craziest of swings. I'm sure more than one of the officials panicked and had to double-check to make sure he was supposed to be on the player side of the ropes. When he did get noticed it was usually snickers of disrespect or pointing fingers of judgement that were cast his way. And he was cognizant of every single person that evaluated him that way. Normally, Moe would have garnered even more attention for his bizarre look and form but today he was surrounded by the greatest players in golf, and that easily took precedence for the fans. Moe was but a footnote for most of them.

After having hit a ton of balls at the range, well off to the side so that he did not have to talk or interact with any other players or draw the attention of the fans watching, Moe eventually found himself at one of the practice greens. As he would readily admit, putting was not his favourite thing to practice, but at Augusta the greens would kill you if you were not dialled in perfectly. It wouldn't matter how precise you were on the fairways if you couldn't complete the feat on the greens.

It always intrigued – and often irritated -- Moe as to how much time his fellow golfers spent on the greens practicing their putting strokes. It seemed like they were always trying to change something in their stroke rather than finding the precise way to replicate what worked. They were implementing this grip or that grip, trying to place the ball closer or farther, their stance wider or thinner, hold their hands firm or loose, up the shaft or down the shaft. It was endless! As far as Moe was concerned you just grab the putter like any club, look towards the hole, keep your head down, keep it still, and hit it. Easy-peasy. The problem with that theory though, many would say afterwards, was that if Moe had spent a little more time perfecting his putting stroke, his chance to become a star would have increased substantially. It may even be fair to go as far as to say it would have been undeniable.

As Moe begrudgingly continued his half-hearted practice putting, where watching the other players took precedence over his own preparation, he was suddenly interrupted as his caddie came bolting up to him and pleaded, "There you are! I know you said you didn't want me to bother you until it was right before tee-off time... well, you're up next! We need to get you to the first tee! NOW!"

Looking down at his watches, Moe saw his caddie was right. His tee-off time was next! He'd been unfair to his caddie, making him wait until the last minute like this and he had been hanging around the greens for way too long, spending too much time quietly being a fan himself. It was officially time for him to get out there and prove his worth. To prove that he belonged to be among the best and that he was worthy of much more than just being able to watch his peers practice up close. His knees wobbled under him as the full realization settled in.

Moe's caddie quickly snatched up his bag and took charge of the situation. "Follow me!" and started briskly walking, leading the way towards the first tee. A brisk walk Moe could easily match.

Surprisingly, Moe turned and ran away in the opposite direction.

Would it all be too much for him after all? Was he giving up?

"Moe, where are you going? The tee is this way! We can't be even one second late or you'll be disqualified!" his caddie warned.

"I know, I know," shouted back Moe as he sprinted onto the putting green, rudely invading the other player's practice routines. "I have to grab my golf ball. Grab my ball! These cost a dollar twenty-five each you know! A dollar twenty-five! I can't be leaving it behind!"

What the caddie was naively unaware of was that there were only three new golf balls in Moe's bag. He had planned to use that one ball that was now lying on the putting surface, for the entire game ahead. He had no intention of losing even one ball today or on any of the days. Not on the course and certainly not back there on the practice putting green.

Moe grabbed the ball, quickly caught back up to his caddie and they both scurried off.

"Hand me my driver please!" Moe shouted as they ran, "Hand me my driver. And a tee! I have my ball!" as they both instantly vanished, gobbled up by the masses devouring each group on the first tee ahead.

35

THE FIRST ROUND OF THE 1956 MASTERS

Teeing off at The Masters on the first day is a prestigious ritual unlike any other in sport. As mentioned earlier, it begins with the ultimate greats from the past hitting ceremonial shots. Once that's complete, the tournament officially commences with the first group. I always have mixed feelings for those players in the first group who have to hit first. On one hand, it would be inspiring to watch the ceremonial tee-off close up like that, but on the other hand, it would be unfortunate to have the added pressure of being the one having to hit a great shot after all that pomp and ceremony. It plays out as follows:

A player's name is announced as he steps up to the tee and the gallery robustly and politely applauds. While some players will receive a more thunderous ovation than others, every patron at The Masters is very well behaved and you will find yourself quickly removed if your conduct is not within the well-posted guidelines. You aren't even allowed to bring a cellphone nowadays so you can't be distracted or be the cause of one.

It's a ceremony every professional golfer dreams about. If you are ever lucky enough to find yourself in that position and you are unable to sense the overwhelming butterflies fluttering in your stomach when you hear your name announced, then you better have someone check your pulse and call an undertaker because you are already dead.

Every player reacts differently when they step up and hear their name announced. Some will politely acknowledge the crowd before getting on with it, while others will soak up every second, waving to everyone in the crowd, taking their time to tee it up so they can enjoy all the eyes on them and get pumped up by it. Alternatively, some will enjoy the moment for a second or two, showing their appreciation, before quickly following it up with a display of extreme seriousness as they contemplate their first swing, letting everyone know he is ready, and here to win. Just watch me! More often than not, what they do at the moment their name is announced, is a true tell of their personalities and of the pressure they are feeling in the moment.

Assigned to be playing with Moe during his first and second rounds was Harvey Ward. Like Moe, he was invited to play based on his amateur golf accomplishments. He was a highly regarded amateur golfer and in his career, he became one of only two players to win the British, USA and Canadian Amateur Championships. Mr. Ward was the first to tee it up. This was his eighth time at The Masters and so his first shot outwardly looked to be slightly easier on the nerves than for most players. But don't kid yourself. Only a little. Your first shot at The Masters never gets old nor does it ever get easy.

Mr. Ward went up onto the tee box, waved, and smiled at the crowd as he was slowly and regally announced to the patrons by the tournament announcer:

"Fore please! Harvey Ward, Jr., 1954 Canadian Amateur Champion and 1955 USGA Amateur Champion. Now driving!"

There was immediate applause from the crowd in response, and it was punctuated by a random shout of encouragement from a well-meaning friend in the audience. Mr. Ward took advantage of the opportunity to cut the tension by taking the time to acknowledge the comment from his pal. The crowd enjoyed the moment with him.

Instantly switching gears, he got right down to business as the assembled crowd dutifully became resolutely silent. You could hear a pin drop into the grass. He went over to his caddie, who pulled out his driver for him and handed it to him. He teed up his ball, stood behind it, and lined up the shot. He moved over to take a practice swing and then another, before finally addressing the ball and struck it. It was a good shot down the fairway and the patrons applauded their approval. He nodded his head with a polite thank you and stood back to give his driver to his caddie. In doing so, he stepped away and allowed his fellow competitor to now take his rightful turn.

A few seconds ticked by, and Moe was still nowhere to be seen. You could already sense the befuddlement in the crowd as the muffled whispers started to build.

Mr. Ward was beginning to look concerned as well. Everyone knew that without exception if you miss your tee-off time you are out of the tournament. Moe had under a minute to go.

As if on cue, Moe burst through the crowd behind the tee, with his ball and tee in one hand and his driver already pulled from his bag in the other.

As the announcer saw Moe, he began:

"Fore please! Murray Norman – "

But before the announcer could even finish Moe's introduction, in one fluid motion, Moe pushed past Mr. Ward and his caddie, ignoring everything and everyone around him, galloped up to the tee-off box, teed it up and without any hesitation or practice swing, he hit the ball. It was of course, straight down the middle. As it flew through the air, Moe immediately took off down the fairway following it, leaving his tee behind, and not even waiting for his ball to land.

The crowd was silent as the stunned announcer tried to finish:

"Uh... the 1955 Canadian Amateur Champion. Uhhh....already driven..."

Mr. Ward looked at Moe's caddie who shrugged back, "Sorry, I have to warn you, it's going to be an odd day, Mr. Ward. Prepare yourself," as he rushed off to keep up with Moe.

When he reached Moe, the caddie was momentarily at a loss for words as he was still processing – like everyone else – what just transpired back on the first tee.

"What was that all about?" exclaimed the caddie finally.

"Hoo! I just wanted that opening shot over with! I was shaking like a leaf. Shaking like a leaf! Boy oh boy, I just wanted that finished! Over and done with! Now let's play some golf, shall we! Give me my seven iron please," as he handed the driver back to the caddie. "Let's make two good ones in a row!"

Without even looking to see where Mr. Ward was or what he was doing, he went to hit the ball. His caddie was mortified, having to call out, "Wait! It's not your shot! Mr. Ward is first."

Moe looked back at Mr. Ward, rolled his eyes a bit and good-naturedly hollered, "C'mon! Let's pick it up, shall we! We don't have all day! Just trust your swing and hit it!"

Mr. Ward was not impressed with Moe's unnecessary commentary or his unsolicited advice, but being a gentleman and a professional, he refused to say anything and went about his routine and shot.

Moe's caddie quietly muttered to himself, "Gonna be an odd day, to say the very least, Mr. Ward. You have no idea..."

36

TWO DOWN AND TWO TO GO

AT THIS POINT IN MY MOE MASTERS STORY, WOULDN'T IT BE perfect if I were to now tell you that Moe hit his next shot onto the green and it went directly into the hole for an eagle to start his round? Talk about the ultimate opening to a tournament! Right? But that's not what happened. Both he and Mr. Ward both made par. Which, on the first hole at The Masters was something anyone would take. A great way to settle down the nerves.

In the end, the first two days of play were uneventful and held nothing special to share for either of them. Mr. Ward shot a four-over-par 76 on the first day and a two-over-par 72 on the second. Moe shot a 75 on the first day and a less than satisfying 78 on the second. It wasn't so much that Moe was playing badly but he was having an awful time on the greens. His fairway play was stellar, but the greens had been a disastrous roller coaster ride. As he walked off the course after the second round he wasn't at all happy with his score, but he wasn't beating himself up about it either.

Determined to do better and knowing that practice makes perfect, Moe headed directly to the driving range after his round. Looking at his scorecard, it probably would have been more constructive to go to the putting greens instead, but it was always his routine to hit the driving range first. While he may have been a whopping eighteen shots back of the surprising leader Ken Venturi by the end of the day -- yes, the same amateur he was sharing the Crow's Nest with – there was no quit in Moe. If anything, he was even feeling more driven than normal as he was thinking if any amateur should be leading this thing it should be him!

The great thing about how the tournament was played was that there was no cut after the first two rounds so Moe was determined to substantially improve on his last two rounds and finish much further up the ladder. As he headed off to the driving area he told himself he must try and leave some time for the putting green for later. It was very important to do so.

No guarantees though.

37

HOME, HOME ON THE RANGE

AFTER THE MASTERS SECOND ROUND, MOE WAS SECURELY BACK in his safety zone, off to the side, quietly hitting his bucket of balls, fine-tuning his long-range shots that didn't need tweaking. He was tranquilly thrilled to be amongst all of the other pros – many of them famous – going about their own golf business. On the driving range, everyone was each other's equal in many ways, just doing whatever they needed to do to get better, and he was finally beginning to get the sense that he was settling in. He was enjoying being surrounded by this elite fraternity of players who loved the game as much as he did, rather than being intimidated by them. It was as if they were slowly becoming his brotherhood. That, just maybe, he had started to fit in. It was calming to be around the few humans who categorically understood how hard it was to be this good at this elevated level and stay there. Most of all, whose passion for perfection could rival his. He was one of the elite now. Incredibly, a few of the players were even beginning to call him by his name!

Almost finished with his current bucket of balls, Moe leaned on his club and took a moment to pull a hankie out of his pocket to wipe his sweaty brow and watched his neighbouring competitors hit a few shots. Not willing to take too much of a break, he soon grabbed another bucket and went right back to teeing up another ball. He struck it and watched the perfect trajectory with a smile of satisfaction. Just as he bent over to grab another ball, he heard a voice from behind him.

"Nice shot."

Turning his head over his shoulder, Moe was gobsmacked to see the compliment was delivered by none other than the legendary Sam Snead. Knowing full well who Sam was -- the top player for almost four decades, winner of 82 PGA tournaments (the most in history) and easily one of the best players the game has ever seen -- Moe stood awe-struck, unable to vocally respond to the well-deserved accolade without much more than an "Oooh!".

Sam took a quick beat, taking the time to visually absorb all that Moe was and continued, "So, tell me. How is it you got into the tournament son?"

Finding the courage to speak words, his voice higher in pitch than normal due to his excitement, Moe cooed with a hint of embarrassment, "Oooh, I won the Canadian Amateur, sir."

"Oh yeah? Well, congratulations! Well done!"

Sam followed this up with what was music to Moe's ears. "I've heard some good things about you kid. I hear you hit the ball very well."

"Why thank you. Thank you for saying that!" Moe blushed.

If the world had ended at that moment, Moe would have been okay with it. Imagine that! Sam Snead knowing about him! Knowing about Moe the Shmoe!

"I also heard you had a bit of an interesting tee-off on the first hole yesterday," added Sam with a sly grin.

Moe was embarrassed, turning beet red. How would he know about that?

"Hoo! Yes. I may have been in a bit of a hurry. A bit of a hurry. I just wanted that shot done and over with. Hoo! Just wanted to get out there and play. Get out there and hit the ball when everyone wasn't so close up and everything. Get me some breathing room!"

"I hear ya son. That first tee, particularly on the first day, can be quite intimidating." He leaned in a bit closer and with a soft voice offered, "Want me to let you in on a little secret?"

Wow! Sam was going to share a secret with me, thought Moe. He couldn't believe what was happening. He even gave himself a pinch in the arm to make sure he wasn't dreaming.

"Ohhh, sure. Sure! Please tell me!" he begged.

"At the very least, always let them say your name. So's they all know who you are. If you play it right over a career, *who* you are can sometimes be more intimidating to your competitors than your game itself," throwing in a wink for good measure.

"I'm Sam Snead," he humbly offered as an introduction.

Vigorously shaking his hand back, "Oooh! I know who you are! Know who you are Mr. Snead! I'm Murray Norman. People call me Moe. Please, call me Moe."

There was a grimace on Sam's face as Moe's handshake enthusiasm was ratcheted up a notch more than normal.

"Whoa, that's quite the grip you have there, son! Careful!" as he quickly extracted his hand and looked to make sure that he hadn't broken any bones.

"Oh! I'm sorry, I'm so sorry!" exclaimed Moe panicking.

In jest, Sam warned back, "Good thing these are insured for millions!"

Moe took his jest as gospel and was worried that he had hurt him. "Oh, no! Mr. Snead, are you okay?"

"I'm just pulling your leg there, Moe. But that is quite the handshake, nonetheless. Tell you what, why don't you hit one for me?" Sam asked as he pointed to a ball.

Okay, remember when I just said a moment ago that if the world ended now, Moe would be okay with it? Now I *really* mean it! Moe could have died and gone to heaven on the spot. Sam Snead wanted to see *him* make a shot?! *He* gets to hit a ball for Sam Snead?!

"Hoo! Sure, Mr. Snead! SURE! Hoo, Hoo! Sure!" he squealed with delight, his vocal pitch hitting a level where he could almost shatter glass.

Almost tripping over himself to get a ball and a club he pleaded, "Is there anything you want to see? Anything in particular? How far? What club?"

"How about we start with the driver," Sam suggested. "That club is a little more unpredictable for most of us. No need to make this too easy right off the bat do we? Having heard how good you are, after all."

"Sure thing, Mr. Snead! Sure thing!"

Moe quickly grabbed his driver. "Any marker in particular?"

"I'm thinking the two-fifty. Have a go at it."

"Beside it, in front of it or past it?" Moe asked, without a hint of being cocky. He was so eager to please Sam he could taste it. If he were a dog his tail would be wagging a hundred miles per hour.

Sam liked the confidence Moe was showing. "Well...if you put it that way, why not hit three shots and do one of each? If you can, that is."

Moe beamed ear to ear. "If I can? If I can?! Hoo! Just watch Mr. Snead. Just watch!"

At this point, a number of the fellow golfers had picked up on the conversation, as had a few of the patrons, and a slight crowd was forming. Moe teed up three balls straight out in a row, inches from each other.

"Now son, I didn't mean do it all at once," as a few in the gathering crowd chuckled. "You can do them one at a time. Take your time."

"Oh, no worries Mr. Snead, no worries. This makes it harder. Just doing it slowly, one at a time, is like falling off a log for me. Like falling off a log."

Without any further discussion, he hit them one at a time, in rapid succession. Crack, crack, and crack!

As predictably as the sun comes up each day, one of the balls landed right before the marker, one beside it and one past it.

There was instant applause from the crowd. Sam, however, did not applaud. Even to a trained eye, it was not completely clear if Sam did not like having the spotlight taken away from him like Moe just had or whether he wasn't convinced with what Moe just did.

"Well, well. Let me see you do that again. Wouldn't want to walk away thinking you were just lucky now would we?"

"Hoo! No problem. Hoo! No problem," tossed Moe eagerly back.

Once again Moe lined up three balls and hit them in rapid succession. They were all carbon copy results of his first display of prowess. Once again, there was applause from the crowd. This time they were accompanied by five slow and measured claps from Sam.

Clap. Clap. Clap. Clap. Clap.

"Well done! You seem to be walking the talk. Good for you. How's about we try an iron now?"

Moe tossed the driver aside and eagerly asked, "Which one Mr. Snead? Which one?" looking every bit like a little puppy trying to please its new owner.

"Whichever you wish son." Then he corrected himself, "Try the three iron."

Moe grabbed the three iron. "Where to, Mr. Snead. Where to?"

"Wherever you like. Just hit one. I just want to see you hit it," he said without much challenge in his voice.

"The two hundred then," stated Moe with growing confidence. "The two hundred."

Moe struck the ball, and it landed beside the two hundred marker. It was followed by more applause.

This time though, nothing from Sam again. Just a cryptic "Ah" once the applause stopped.

Moe was confused by the comment.

"What do you mean by that Mr. Snead? Is there something wrong?"

"Hit another for me, please. If you will?" asked Sam as he folded his arms.

"Of course!" replied Moe as he hit another with the three iron with the same great result.

No applause from the crowd this time. They all looked to Sam.

"Aha. That's what I thought," he quipped.

"What, Mr. Snead? What is it?" pleaded Moe.

"Oh, nothing Moe. Nothing at all. Great shot."

Moe remained unconvinced. "But you said 'aha.' What does that mean? 'Aha'?"

"Nothing at all, Moe. Nice one. Great shot. Have a good rest of your practice. I probably should go hit a few myself."

Sam turned and began to walk away as a crestfallen Moe watched, feeling somehow that something had gone wrong. Even more so, he was saddened that this once-in-a-lifetime opportunity to hit balls for the legendary Sam Snead was becoming history.

Sam took a few more steps, stopped, and turned around, "Do you mind if I gave you a little bit of a tip, Moe?"

"Mind? MIND?! No sir! Not coming from you. No sir! Please!"

"It's just that you're coming down way too steep on the ball with your long irons. The secret to hitting a long iron is to hit them like fairway woods. Don't hit down or try to force it. Hit it like a nice three wood. Sweep it more."

Moe could not believe he was getting coaching from the one and only Sam Snead! It may as well have been coming from the Lord Almighty himself.

"Let me hit another for you then. Let me try that. Watch that I do it right."

Moe hit another and Sam dutifully watched. It's a good shot.

"There you go! You're a quick learner. You're getting there. Keep at it! Be sure to hit some more just like that."

Moe was over the moon, having pleased his master.

Sam began to leave again but just like before, he stopped, turned, and said, "Enjoy the tournament son. Augusta is a very special place.

Only the best of the best play at The Masters and everyone here is here for a good reason. So, you have fun and enjoy the experience. Go out and prove you belong."

With that final parting bit of advice, Sam was finally on his way.

Moe shouted out to him with great admiration, "Thank you, Mr. Snead. Thanks for your help! I really appreciate it! I'll put that tip to good use. Real good use! Have a good round tomorrow! I'll see you around!"

Sam said nothing in return but raised a hand back at him with a "your welcome" kind of gesture as he sauntered off.

Freshly invigorated from this incredible sage advice, Moe was practically frothing at the mouth in anticipation of applying this new tip. He immediately ran and took not one but two fresh buckets of balls. Once he set them down he returned for another two, as if golf balls were about to suddenly go on the extinction list. Not stopping there, he snatched two more. Now he was ready to implement his newfound guidance.

He looked pleasingly at the six buckets surrounding him, throwing his arms on his hips, "Three hundred balls. Under half a day of daylight left and half a day's work yet to be done. I better get at it."

Without wasting another second, Moe teed up a ball and hit it. Then another and then another and so on, as the buckets slowly emptied. Before each shot, you could hear Moe say out loud to himself, "Hit it like a three wood. Like a three wood. Sweep it...sweep it. Just like Sam says, sweep it."

38

RISE AND SHINE

It was early Saturday morning, the third round of The Masters. "Moving day" as they like to call it. Uncharacteristically, unlike every other morning since Monday, Moe had accidentally slept in. Nothing dramatic, of course. By sleeping in, I mean he woke up shortly after the sun rose rather than hours before it. He'd put in a solid day of extra practice following his round yesterday, trying to incorporate what Sam had suggested, and it had some residual effects. It took more energy out of him than he had anticipated.

As he sputtered awake, he felt the chill in the cool morning air of the room surrounding him. To help keep himself warm he grabbed the covers and pulled them up around his neck so he could snuggle in for just a little bit longer. As he reached for them a searing pain violently shot through his hands, travelling right up through his arms. It was as if they were being electrocuted or were on fire.

"Ow!" howled Moe, not caring if he were to wake anyone else up.

Fortunately, the other players were already long gone and off eating their breakfast.

"Owwwwww!" he screamed again, looking down at the source of the ferocious pain, finding it hard to comprehend what he was seeing.

Both of his hands looked like they were made of raw hamburger. The tough and rough skin was blistered and bruised. Many of the calluses that normally covered his hands were torn off and the raw skin below them was exposed and at risk of becoming infected. His fingers and joints were so swollen that he could barely move them. His one thumb looked like an entire new appendage altogether.

"Oh no!!! This can't be happening! Not today! Not today!" he hollered again in anguish, as he held his festering palms closer to his face.

He jumped out of bed, eternally thankful no one else was there to witness the scene and rushed into the washroom. He tried to turn on the tap to run ice-cold water over them in an attempt to soothe them but found his fingers were useless to him. Not to mention throbbing with even more pain by attempting such a manoeuvre. Tactfully, he used his wrists instead and got the cold water flowing. He thrusted them both under the tap, but the cold water did little to help the agony. It only added to it.

"Owwww!" he bellowed again as the searing pain increased in its intensity. "No! Nooo! Noooooo!" he wailed.

As he tried to keep his hands immersed, Moe deftly used his foot to slam the bathroom door closed behind him, to have complete privacy should someone return. No one can see this; he thought to himself. No one! How was he going to fix this?!

Looking down into the sink he watched as the water turned bright pink as his wounds bled into the fresh flowing water, pooling down the drain in front of him.

Moe could not remember the last time he cried.

Before now, that is.

39

MOVING DAY

WAITING ON THE FIRST TEE AND WARMING UP WAS VIC GHEZZI, Moe's assigned playing partner for the third round. He was a seasoned veteran having been around the professional game for many years and at forty-five years old he's now considered a veteran on the links. He had won eleven PGA tournaments in his career and one major: The PGA in 1941. Moe had been eager to meet him as they had something in common with each other. Vic had to beat the great Byron Nelson in a thirty-eight-hole playoff to get his most important victory just as Moe had to beat Lyle Crawford in thirty-nine holes for his first important win, the Canadian Amateur. They both knew how hard it was to get that first big win and had to play in extreme extra-hole playoffs to get it done.

At the same time Vic warmed up, Moe was making his way over to the first tee. As he walked he was blowing on his hands and fingers, trying to help cool them off with little success. Part of him wondered if wearing a golf glove – or two even, one on each hand – would help the situation. He normally never wore a golf glove since using it on his leathery hands would be pointless. It would be completely redundant. But today it would have at least assisted in covering his pitiful hands up so no one would notice them and maybe the compression could help with the swelling. But he doubted it worked that way, in reverse. He would have had to have been wearing them while he was practicing the night before and then slept with them on.

It was like when a hockey player takes a blistering shot in the foot during a hockey game. Normally if the player keeps the skate on, the boot helps keep the swelling in check. But as soon as it comes off, it can blow up like a balloon and then there's no way to get the skate back on until the swelling subsides. So, the player keeps it on between periods until the game is over. Besides, there was no glove in the world big enough to go over these hands right now anyway. So nix that theory.

When Moe arrived, Vic was bending over, giving one final stretch of his back. He looked up and greeted Moe in his strong New Jersey accent, continuing his warmup as he talked.

"G'mornin, Moe. How you doin? You're cutting it pretty close there fella, ya almost missed your tee-off time. That's not something you want to be making a habit of pal. Way better to get here good and early and get properly warmed up and sorted out, don't yas think?"

He let out a big hearty laugh and continued, "But hey, don't pay me no mind, I'm not the golf cops am I? Nah, I'm your playing partner for today's third round. Names Vic Ghezzi," as he extended his hand for a handshake.

Moe looked down at Vic's welcoming hand with dismay. It was bad enough he ever had to touch and shake anyone's hand, but today's sense of trepidation took it to a whole new level. Nonetheless, knowing he had no choice, Moe stuck out his hand and they shook.

"Pleased to meet ya, Moe! Have a good game."

"You too Mr. Ghezzi. You too," weakly smiled Moe.

Moe tried as hard as he could to keep a straight face as they shook hands, but he couldn't hide the agony for more than a second and noticeably winced.

"You alright?" asked Vic with concern.

Noticing Moe's hands, and being somewhat repulsed by them,

"Jeezus, Moe. What the blazes happened to your hands?! They look like a mess of disco fries!"

Moe apologetically fumbled out his response. "Mr. Snead...he gave me some advice last night on the range...after my round. Told me how to hit my long irons better."

"Criminy, Moe. How many did ya hit?!"

"I might have overdone it a bit. Just a bit," Moe confessed.

"How many is a bit?" Vic quizzed back.

"I don't know exactly. Not exactly. About eight hundred balls or so. Out on the range. About eight hundred."

"Moe, you crazy?" Vic exploded on him. "Eight hundred?! Look at your hands! You can't hit eight hundred practice balls in a day, not during a tournament ya bozo! How are ya even going to hold your club with those hands? Jeezus!"

"I know, I know. It wasn't very smart, wasn't smart," Moe apologized, practically inaudibly, on the verge of crying twice in a day.

Breaking the awkwardness of the moment, the voice of the announcer rang out:

"Introducing our third-round pairings. Fore please! Vic Ghezzi. 1941 PGA Champion. Now driving!"

Vic acknowledged the crowd and like a true veteran got right down to business. He teed up his ball, lined up the shot, took a couple of practice swings and hit the ball. He watched it keenly, his torso and arms twisting with body language afterwards, trying to will it to go straighter as it had a slight pull to the left and it ended up in the rough.

"Gawdammit!" he whisper-muttered to himself as he picked up his tee and brought his club back towards his caddie. But instead of handing it back to the caddie, he slammed it into the bag by himself in frustration.

Now it was Moe's turn.

"Fore please! Murray Norman. 1955 Canadian Amateur Champion. Now driving!"

True to form, acting as if nothing was wrong, Moe went to the tee-off box, teed up his ball and addressed it. If you were looking closely and paying attention, there was a clear grimace of discomfort on his face as he clutched the club tightly, which he must do, to make a good shot. There was a wince on his face upon ball contact as well and it was evident that it would be painful to hit the ball every time today. But pain or no pain, Moe was not to be stopped. He told himself he would work through the agony, he would complete the round, and he would do so by shooting a good score. No, a *great* score! Golfers do it all the time, shooting a great round when they're not feeling up to scratch. It usually makes them focus even harder. He was fully confident that this round was going to be one for the record books and they would all talk about it for ages afterwards.

He was right.

As he watched his ball in flight it was eerily reminiscent of Vic's shot. Unfortunately, Moe's ball was much more off-course than Vic's and it headed for the deeper rough. So far off course that it almost went out of bounds. On any other day, Moe would have stood there wondering what on earth just happened. His ball always goes straight off of the tee. It always goes exactly where he wants. The rough was not his target!

But today was not going to be just any other day. Not by a long shot.

After taking the shot Moe gingerly passed his driver to his caddie. He realized he was going to have to make substantial changes to his swing to counter the problems with his hands. As well as find a way to take into account the blood that was slightly dripping down his palms, making it harder to hold onto the club.

As the caddie took the driver and gave it a routine wipe down, he noticed the towel was instantly christened with speckles of crimson red.

Vic looked at Moe and then, at his own caddie. It was a combination of disgust, irritation, and pity. There was nothing more to be said as they headed off to see where their first wayward shots landed.

Fortunately for Vic, he found that his shot was completely

playable, and he had a nice lie. Moe's shot? Not so much. It was still in bounds, but it was deep into what they like to call the second cut. It wasn't as hard to play out of as it may on any US Open style of course, but it was still well enough buried that it would be a hard one to execute.

Moe was up first. He gingerly took an iron, wiped his hands against his pants, lined up the shot and hit it. In doing so he uncharacteristically took a divot that was much more a pork chop than a bacon strip. The ball's flight trajectory was extremely low -- as in barely off the ground low. It luckily cleared the rough and rolled perhaps a hundred yards further down the fairway. Two bad shots in a row. It was as if he had been suddenly transported into the twilight zone. It was the first time in his life that he felt like he wanted to slam his club into the ground in disgust. But Moe let the feeling pass and soldiered on. He was back on the fairway and that was all that mattered. Just like when you put it in a bunker, you take your medicine, get it out, and move on. All he needed to do was hit a great third shot to the green, make a good putt for par, and all would be well.

That's exactly what Vic did. His second shot went to about twenty yards from the pin and he made a two-putt for par.

Moe's third shot however was off track, hits the wrong slope in the green and was at least a forty-footer for par.

He three-putted and recorded a double bogey on the first hole.

"Trust yourself" Moe willed to himself as he walked to the second tee. "Trust the work, believe in the work. Believe in yourself. There's no bad on Moe's golf course. Only birdies and pars. Birdies and pars."

It seemed he was right, and the internal pep talk paid immediate dividends.

He hit a good drive on the second hole called Pink Dogwood and a great second as well. He hit a nice third into the green within eight feet of the pin, one-putted, and recorded a birdie. The only problem was that not one of the shots felt any less painful than the first. Even worse, the slight splatters of blood on the towel of the caddie quickly turned into streaks.

By the time Moe finished Yellow Jasmine, the par-five eighth hole and registered a par, it was clear this was indeed going to be a round for the ages. But for all the wrong reasons. He had already bogeyed the third and fourth holes, double-bogeyed the fifth, and bogeyed the six and seventh. Here on Carolina Cherry, the ninth hole, Moe no longer wondered about the twilight zone. He had concluded it was hell he had been transported to instead.

The round quickly became an absolute disaster with seemingly no way out of it. Still, to his credit, Moe got up to the tee and continued to hit the ball, acting as if it were any other day.

Then, the unthinkable happened.

As he swung the club it went flying out of his hands and into the gallery, just missing a patron. The club was so slick and covered in blood from his increasingly raw bleeding hands that it had become almost impossible to hold onto it. He took a moment and apologized profusely to the person it missed and he trudged on.

Normally, a golfer would have given the fan a golf ball for his trouble, but that was a buck twenty-five Moe wasn't willing to part with, even under these circumstances.

He tripled bogeyed the ninth hole.

As an exasperated and crushed Moe arrived at Camellia, the tenth hole, he looked down at his now unrecognizable hands. His right thumb had split wide open on the last hole and blood was gushing from it. There was no way the wound would be able to be closed without medical assistance. Maybe even stitches. He was terrified to swing the club now, worried it would fly out of his hands again and seriously hurt someone. He once again rubbed his hands on his pants to clean them off as best he could, but his pants were so wet with blood at this point that it offered little help. His caddie saw the problem and went to offer Moe his club cleaning towel which was now one hundred percent red itself. Hardly a solution.

Vic's caddie gave a concerned look towards Vic, holding up the towel he used to clean Vic's clubs. He wanted to give it to Moe to use but not without the permission of his boss. Vic nodded a silent yes and the caddie gave his towel to Moe's caddie, who then handed it to Moe.

"Oh! Thank you! Thank you! I promise we'll get it replaced after the round. Oh sure! Get you a new one. Thank you! Thank you!" Moe vowed.

Moe wiped his hand with the fresh towel and hit his ball. The club flew out of his hand again, luckily down the fairway this time and not into the crowd. It flew out not because it was too slippery but because he could no longer even hold onto it.

Vic stood stoically with his arms crossed, holding a stern glare out at the fairway, determined not to look at Moe. Meanwhile, his caddie was busily attending to fake tasks he had created for himself trying to avoid the moment altogether. The crowd was eerily silent as they watched the debacle unfold before them. Moe's poor caddie had the worst job of all, running down the fairway to retrieve the errant club.

Moe stood devasted and alone on the tee-off box, as he stared blankly out onto the fairway as if in a trance. He raised his hands and clasped them at the back of his head, bloodying his blond mop of hair in the process. He lowered himself into a squat position and continued to stare out, as blood dripped down his back and stained his turtleneck as well. At this point, there was practically no part of him that didn't have blood somewhere. Nothing seems to bleed more than a cut hand or a finger does it?

As he squatted, all of a sudden his eyes began to pour out as well. Not with blood but with tears. He couldn't believe what was happening. That he was crying and couldn't stop.

For the second time in his life and on the same day.

40

ON THE COUNT OF TEN, YOU'RE OUT

The ride home was a long and tough one. The last place Moe expected himself to be headed on the Saturday of a Masters tournament was back home, like this. And I don't mean back to his temporary home in the Crows Nest but all the way back to Canada.

For hours on end, Moe stared blankly out the car window, his head resting on the interior of the passenger door, hanging slightly out the open window, his hair tousled by the passing wind. When he wasn't in the front seat, he was curled up in a ball, in the fetal position, in the back. Both of his hands were wrapped in bandages, and you could see that blood had slightly seeped through them and that the dressing would need changing soon.

After they stopped to get something to eat and brought it back into the car, Moe chose the front seat again. Before pulling out of the rest stop and heading back out onto the highway, Irving watched Moe with pity as he tried to find a way to hold the hamburger in his ravaged hands and get them into his mouth.

"Can I help in some way?' asked Irving with deep concern.

Moe stubbornly shook his head no, as he strategically held the burger more in his palms than his fingers and took a big bite. He was ravenous. The condiments and juices from the burger flowed down his chin, onto his shirt, and into his bandages. Utterly frustrated he stared ahead, looking as if he was silently counting to ten before he started to silently chew again.

"I think we should eat here first before we go any further," decided Irving as he pulled his meal out of the takeout bag. "Once you're done eating we're going to have to clean you up. Those bandages are going to need to be replaced too. You need to keep those injuries clean so they can heal properly. The last thing you want is to get them infected."

Moe did not respond and kept chewing.

After they had eaten in silence and had gone back into the restaurant to get Moe properly washed up and the bandages replaced with new ones, they headed back out onto the road.

"Do you want to hear some music?" asked Irving as he turned on the radio.

Moe turned it off immediately without saying a word.

"Okay then...guess not."

A few tedious miles passed by, and Irving tried again, "Do you want to talk about all this? I'm a surprisingly good listener."

Moe gave nothing back and continued his woeful stare out the window.

Poor Irving nervously tapped his fingers on the steering wheel as they continued forward in more irritating silence. The silence was starting to eat at him big time. Another ten minutes passed by and it felt like an hour had been endured, for them both, just for different reasons. Finally, Irving gave it another go.

"Want to play a game of eye-spy?"

Success! He finally got Moe to look at him.

But it was not exactly the look for which he was hoping. The annoyed, disdain-ridden, eye-only delivered answer, was a resounding NO.

"Oh come on, Moe. We can't just sit here in silence for the next sixteen hours!" Irving responded with exasperation. "I'm just going to keep suggesting things until something gets through to you. I'm not kidding. Fair warning!"

A minute or so passed and Moe surprisingly responded, "I spy with my little eye, something that begins with 'L'."

"Hallelujah!" Irving rejoiced internally to himself.

"Licorice" he guessed first, as he looked down at the open bag of red Twizzlers between them that they had been snacking on.

"No," Moe answered in a monotone fashion.

"Lane!"

"No," in the same disinterested tone as before.

"Line! Like the one in the middle of the road."

"No."

"Leather!"

"No."

"Lake!" as he pointed to the body of water they were passing.

"That's a river. No."

"Lock! Like the one on the glove compartment."

"No."

"Leaves!"

"No."

"Oh, I know, license plate!"

"No."

"Lozenge!"

"No."

"Leg!"

"No."

"Limb!"

"Technically the same thing," Moe chastised. "No."

"L, L, L, L, L..." Irving repeated, the sound of the letter rolling on his tongue as he tried to spot something else.

"El-astic!" he guessed, saying it so it sounded like it started with the letter L.

"That starts with an E. No," replies Moe dryly with not a hint of appreciation at the attempt to make him smile.

"Tough audience," Irving grunted.

"That begins with a T. No," responded Moe without missing a beat.

Okay then, levity was out, thought Irving to himself. Better stick to the game.

"Lincoln!" as he saw another car pass by.

"Yuk. And no."

There was another moment of silence as Irving thought some more.

"You wanna give up then?" asked a hopeful Moe, so the stupid game could end.

"Not a chance. Not yet!"

Moe sighed. Let the torture continue.

"Light!"

"No."

"Landscape!"

"No."

"Lips!"

"No."

"Lid!"

"No."

"Litter!"

"No."

"Lungs!"

"You can see lungs, can you? Now you're being desperate. No. Give up?"

"Lever! Which incidentally, rhymes with never," he smiled back.

"NO," followed by an I've-almost-had-enough sigh.

"AHA! I've got it! Lightstone! My last name!" he shouted out, with a huge smile thinking he had cracked it.

"No."

"Darn, thought I had it."

"You're finally close though," Moe conceded.

"Close? How so?"

"It is someone's name."

"Hmmm....someone's name...someone's name...," he started to mull it over. A minute or two passed.

"Someone's name?" Irving asked again, completely stumped.

"Yup," said Moe.

Irving racked his brain for a few more minutes and as much as he hated to do it, "Okay, I give up, you win this round. What is it?"

"You sure?"

"Yes, I'm sure. You win. What is it?"

"Loser," answered Moe.

"Loser?" Irving asked back, completely lost.

"Yes, loser! ME! A big fat, pathetic, stupid, dumb LOSER!" as he repeatedly started smacking himself in the head, hurting not only his head but starting to reopen the wounds on his already throbbing hand. It quickly escalated into a full-blown tantrum.

"DUMMY, DUMMY, DUMMY! LOSER, LOSER, LOSER!"

Becoming very concerned with this meltdown, Irving quickly pulled over to the side of the road, coming to a complete stop and delivered a very pointed response.

"Stop that! You are NOT a loser Moe. Not by a long shot. You got to play in The Masters. Losers do not play in The Masters. You just made a difficult decision and had a bit of bad luck, nothing more. You're being completely unfair to yourself, and I won't just sit by and let you think that!"

"Losers stop. I stopped! Winners keep fighting. I'm a loser!"

"No!" shot Irving back. "You did not choose to stop, did you? You *had* to stop. You had no other choice. Am I wrong?"

"No, you're not wrong," he conceded. "By the tenth hole, I couldn't go any further. Just couldn't go. The blood was coming out like crazy. It wouldn't stop. It wouldn't stop! Sure! Hitting all those balls the night before did me in, they did. Did me in. My hands were so red and blistered I could barely hold the club. You saw! I even let my club go a couple of times! My left thumb was split wide open. I just couldn't go on. It was impossible. I couldn't go on. I coulda hurt someone. I told the official. He didn't want to accept my withdrawal, but he also said he understood. That he understood. But did he? Did he really? Does anyone?"

"Of course we do! That's what I'm telling you right now! I understand."

"Why do I do that? Why, Irv? Why do I try so hard to please everyone else and then hurt myself while I'm at it? Mr. Ghezzi thought I should finish the round. Said 'This is The Masters. You play on one leg if you have to!' But he didn't understand! Did he? No, he didn't! By the tenth, I couldn't even hold the club anymore!! Everyone thought I gave up. Mr. Ghezzi thought that I was giving up. That I quit. That I quit!"

A moment of silence engulfed the car and Irving decided not to interrupt it as he sensed Moe has more to say and he needed the time to formulate the words to say it.

"That I quit," he repeated. "That...I quit..." his lips trembling to form the words.

Moe started to fight back the tears again before he continued. He would NOT be crying three times in one day!

"Quit? QUIT? Getting to The Masters was my lifelong dream! There was no way I was quitting! Not on purpose! But I couldn't hold the club. I couldn't hit the ball. I had no choice! I had no choice. I got my dream and then I ruined it. Just tossed it away like a dummy! The biggest dummy of them all. Tossed it away like it was nothing! Just like a loser would."

He started to hit himself hard in the head each time he said his name. "Moe the Shmoe! Moe the Shmoe! Moe the Shmoe?! Moe the Shmoe the LOSER!"

Irving secured Moe's hands and forcefully held them down so he couldn't strike himself any further.

Moe began to weep once again.

Irving held him and let him cry.

41

SEVENTEEN OUT OF TWENTY-ONE

With Moe's brass treasure box full of Masters memento memories firmly clutched in my protective grip, I'm on my way to see if he's still at the driving range so I can give it back to him. I also want to solve the mystery as to why it was lying unattended on the ground in the first place. Moe was not the type to be careless with the few prized material possessions he owned and this one had to rank near the top.

As I arrive back at the driving range, I'm glad to find that Moe is still there. He's just finishing up another Coke from his already quickly diminishing, second stash of the day.

"Hey, Moe. How goes?"

"Goes good! Goes good! I'm even taking a little bit of a break. That should make you extra happy!" as he holds up his nearly empty can.

"I can't lie. That does indeed. Thank you."

As I get closer to Moe, his eyes spot what's held in my hands and his eyes quickly grow to the size of saucers. But before he can say anything, I hold it out and tease, "Look what I found. Throwing this away are you? I'd love to have some of this stuff if you don't want it anymore."

"Oh! My Masters box! Oh! Where did you get that? That's supposed to be locked up in my car. You shouldn't be touching that! Throw it away? Are you kidding?!" he exclaims as he reaches greedily for it with no less enthusiasm than Gollum would for his "precious".

As he quickly seizes it from my hands I explain, "I found it lying all alone on the ground by your car. I thought I should bring it to you, just in case you still wanted it," I wryly smile.

"In case I still wanted it? Still wanted it?! This box will be going into the ground with me when I die!" Moe clarifies.

Then, with a puzzling look on his face, "You found it by my car?"

"Yup. It was just sitting there in the open, on the ground behind it."

The puzzled look on Moe's face is quickly replaced by a look of recognition.

"Ohhh! Ohhh! I know what must have happened...I had to take a bunch of stuff out of the trunk when I was looking for something earlier. I must have forgotten to put it back in. You're a lifesaver, Nick. A real lifesaver. If I ever lost this I don't know what I would do."

Moe goes to a spot on the grass, sits down, opens the box, and starts to take inventory of all the items inside as he lays them delicately on the grass.

"I better make sure everything is still here. That nothing is missing." Then adds, "Not that I think you'd take anything. Oh no, I trust you. I trust you. But who knows who may have got their hands on it before you found it."

One by one he pulls out each item from inside the box, including his two golf bag tags from each of his Masters appearances, his duplicate playing scorecards, his scoring pencil, a menu, a hotel size small bar of soap and bottle of shampoo, the ball he used in the last round, three tees, a dried-up Magnolia flower, his two official invitations, a napkin and a small towel both with the Augusta logo on it, and the most precious of all: his two Masters player pins.

He picks up one of the pins and starts rubbing against it with his thumb. The same thumb he split wide open in his first Masters many years ago now. He enjoys the feel of the cool smooth metal against his leathery scarred appendage.

"Hoo! These two pins are my pride and joy. Oh yes, my pride and joy. These gotta be worth a million dollars. Each. And I'll never sell them. No matter what. Never."

"There sure are a lot of memories packed into that little box, aren't there?" I point out.

"Oh, you're not kidding! So many memories. Both good and bad. Good and bad. But I wouldn't change any of them, even if I could. No sir."

"Well, that's good to hear," I purposefully encourage. "Especially when you weren't necessarily able to be at your best like I know you would have wanted to be."

"Oooh boy, so true. So true. My performance in The Masters -- both times -- was sure not some of my best golf. Oh sure! Not my best. Not my best at all. Those fast greens just killed me. But I'll always be proud knowing I played in them. I mean, how many golfers can say that? Played in The Masters twice. Twice! How many golfers can say that? Kinda still bugs me though, that repeating as Canadian Amateur Champion in '56 got me another invite in '57, and then I went and missed the cut. Kinda bugs me even more that it was the first year they instituted a cut! And there I had to go and miss it by one stroke. One measly stroke. One measly stroke. Hoo!"

"Yeah, that was a bit of tough luck for sure," I agree.

Moe picks up the other player pin and holds one in each hand. They are identically the same. Both red and white, with the Augusta Golf Course logo on them. Only the date on each, 1956 and 1957, and the player number, being the difference. He transfers them both into one hand and makes two fists, holding them out in front of him, palms up. He looks at me as he lowers the one that has both pins in it as if his hands were a weigh scale.

"These carry a lot of weight these little guys do. A lot of weight. Not many people can say they earned a pair of these."

"I agree. It takes a lot of skill and hard work to get into the Masters and play against all the big guns. Once even, never mind twice. You should be proud."

"Oh for sure! Boy oh boy, it was something special to get a taste of the big leagues like that for the first time, instead of the amateur circuit. Oh sure! Lots more pressure and lots more weight on your shoulders in the big leagues! Hoo! Way more. But that pressure makes you better. Makes you tougher! When I came back from that first Masters and took time off for my hands to heal up, there was no stopping me. I was fearless after that."

"I remember that. Didn't you win something like seventeen out of the next twenty-one tournaments?"

"Sure did." Moe proudly confirms. "Including my second Canadian Amateur. And in two of them, the only reason I lost was because they kicked me out."

"They kicked you out?"

"Yup, they kicked me out. Kicked me out because they said I was playing too fast and was clowning around too much."

Moe shakes his head more in annoyance with that memory than in anger.

"Oh, boy! Hoo! Them amateur bigwigs sure seemed to have a thing in for me back then. And not in a good way. Not in a good way at all. I mean excuse me for not dilly-dallying and taking my sweet time out there when I'm playing! For hitting my ball straight and then wanting to go right up to it and hit it straight again. Again and again. Like it's my fault I play quickly because I hit it straight or to my target. One of the tournament officials of the Ontario Golf Association actually came up to me and told me that I had to start zigzagging when I was walking the course. Didn't matter where my ball was. Zigzag the course and take more time. And that wasn't all. They especially got their knickers in a knot when I'd give the crowd a little bit of fun and hit my drive off a six or eight-inch-long tee or better yet, off a Coke bottle after the game. Oh! The fans loved that! Loved it! Hooting and hollering, clapping like mad. Oh sure! I wasn't doing anything wrong as I see it. I was just trying to do my best to help fix what was turning into a long boring day with the other guys taking forever to hit a shot. I was helping not hindering. Sure! Helping not hindering!"

Moe opens his palm and gently puts each of the pins back in the tin box, giving each of them a kiss before placing them in.

"But it wasn't just my speed or having fun that what was bugging them either. I wish it was. Wish it was only that. And let's face it, not looking the same as everyone else wasn't helping matters either. Oh no! Not at all. But what really made them angry was that even though I was an amateur, I was making money off of playing golf. Not a lot, mind you. Hoo! Oh sure! Not a lot. Just enough to barely scrape by. But that was against the rules. That ticked them off big time. That was the tickle in the tushie for the bigwigs. They couldn't prove it of course and that just made them even angrier. They got so mad that they found a way to uninvite me from the 1956 America's Cup. I was already fitted for the team jacket, and we were booked to go. But just before it happened I find out I'm not going after all. No warning and no reason. Nothing. Just that I was to be replaced by another player. Later I got wind they heard that I may have been holding a little impromptu golf clinic now and then and I was passing the hat afterwards or selling prizes after a tournament win. Somehow word even got out about Connie too. But there was no way to prove it. That was a secret. Between him and me. But the way they saw it, if you're an amateur you cant make money from the game. Plain and simple they said. Though it was hardly simple was it? I was told later they were worried that word about it might get out during the international tournament. That I would be an embarrassment to Canadian amateur golf. A distraction and dark spot. But you have to remember, plenty of guys were doing it! Not just me. It was just me who was being singled out! We weren't all rich kids like so many of them were on the circuit you know. Hoo! Not by a long shot. Not by a long shot! Having mommy and daddy giving us money whenever we needed it to enter a tournament or to pay for travel, lodging and eating expenses. Oh no! The guys on the circuit with less had no choice but to bend the rules so they could compete. Had no choice at all! Sometimes it made me think my dad was right. Made me think that it was as if the game was only set up for all the rich people to succeed."

Moe closes up the brass box with a big "snap", and a wry smile forms on his lips.

"The biggest problem they had though? The biggest? Was that I had become a draw. I'd won seventeen of twenty-one tournaments. People were starting to pay to show up to see me play in the tournaments. They *expected* to see me. How do you go about getting rid of your best player, just because you don't like him? Hoo! When you can't prove why you may think he shouldn't be there? Hoo! But you know what? That started to make me think too. Oh sure! Sure did! Why do *I* want to be there? Why do *I* want to be around all this nonsense and backstabbing and hate from all them amateur bigwigs? And most of all? I mean...let's face it...if I was winning all the time, maybe it was time for me to turn pro after all. Time to play with the big boys. The problem for me was, you don't just decide you're going to the PGA. That's not how it works. And hardest of all, it took money. Money I didn't have.

"Luckily, late in 1957, I found out that there was a completely legal way to make some quick cash so I could afford to start playing on the professional winter circuit. There was a bursary tournament held every year and the top players won money. I came in third and won fifteen hundred dollars. That was more than enough to go out and play ten weeks in the United States on the PGA winter circuit. I was raring to go after that and headed right down to Florida when the time was right. And when I got there, wouldn't you know it, it was like they were waiting for me. It was as if they knew I was coming. Hoo! Just waiting they were. It's like they had sent a memo to the states that said, 'Keep your eyes peeled for Norman, he's on his way with a pocket full of cash and wants to compete!'"

"So, that was your first year to finally be on the PGA," I interject.

"Ohhh no! Not at all. Just the opposite. Just the opposite!" Moe shrieks. "More like they were waiting with their eyes squished closed and their fingers squeezing their noses shut. They said who are you? You're a nobody. You aren't a professional and you aren't an amateur. We don't know what to do with you. So, forget it, you can't play. Can't play!

"Oh yeah, that's right," I correct myself. "Your first year on the PGA wasn't until '59."

"That's right, but I stayed anyway and spent all the winter in '58 in Florida. Spent my time there wanting to play professional golf but wasn't allowed to. Wasted a year of what could have been the start to my pro career."

Moe takes a moment before he sums it up.

"It's stuff like that what makes you want to look over your shoulder to see if you have a target on your back sometimes. Seemed no matter where I went, some fancy pants, either amateur or professional, were in my way trying to stop me."

Moe takes the brass box and goes over to his golf bag, unzipping a side compartment, wraps it in a towel that was inside, and places it back in. After he zips it back up he pats the spot it's now safely secured in until he needs its powers the next time. "I'll keep it in here for now. Nice and close. It feels good knowing it's right there."

"So what did you do with the rest of the year then? Since you were technically neither an amateur nor a professional?" I ask.

"Oh! When I got back to Canada in the spring of '58 I was lucky enough to have another angel cross my path. Seems most people I met in the golf world were doing all they could to make me stop playing golf and wanted to make me go away. Luckily though, there always seemed to be at least one or two stray angels still out there to help keep me keep going. This angel was named Burt Turcotte. Burt was running the De Haviland Golf Club and he heard about my predicament and gave me a job. So now, by working there, I was officially a professional. I worked there for the spring, summer and fall and when the bursary tournament came up, I entered it again. I came in the top three again and had another fifteen hundred dollars in my pocket and was ready to go. This time I was going to play on the PGA circuit come hell or high water! I was going to get a taste of the big leagues once and for all and no one was going to stop me. The winter of 1959 was going to be the year I made my mark! Hoo! It sure was!

"You know that song by Bryan Adams called the 'Summer of '69'? The one that's a big hit on the radio right now? Well back then, I was so pumped up to play that I would have said they were gonna need another one. A new one called the Winter of '59. Oh sure! Just for me!"

42

SWEET DREAMS AREN'T MADE OF THIS

"I BET THAT MUST HAVE BEEN EXTRA SATISFYING WHEN YOU finally arrived, seeing you had to wait that extra year to get on the tour," I ask Moe.

"Hoo! You know it! Playing on the PGA tour was really something! Really something! It was exciting to be there! I mean, Hoo! Playing against the likes of Snead, Hogan, Demaret, Palmer, and Player!? Getting to see them every day, saying hi, knowing they know your name. Maybe, even saying hi to you first, now and then! Hoo!"

"It must have been intimidating too though, no?" I wonder out loud.

"Oh sure! But playing against them put energy up my spine! Made me play better golf too! I entered six tournaments that first year and made the cut each time. I even had the lead at one point in the final round of the Greater New Orleans Open and finished a respectable fourth. I made eleven hundred dollars. But the best part? Hoo! You wanna know the best part?"

"Sure, tell me,'" I reply eagerly.

"I was seven shots better than Arnold Palmer. Imagine that!? Seven strokes better than Arnold Palmer! That was even better than me being featured on the cover of Golf World Weekly the following week. They had an article on me with a picture of me holding four of my huge, long tees that the fans loved seeing me hit off."

While I am thoroughly enjoying these stories, it's getting harder to ignore that we're now in the full midday sun. I'm really starting to feel the heat of the day and I suspect Moe is as well, whether he is willing to admit it or not. As stubborn as he is it's not like the good ol' days when he could hit for hours and hours on end, feeling as fresh at the end as he had in the beginning. Even Moe can't fight the slippery slope of time and the wear and tear it has on our bodies.

Trying to find a way to minimize the heat I suggest, "Why don't we sit under a tree for a bit. I'd love to hear more about those first few years of getting onto the tour."

Still freshly invigorated with memories from his Masters box, Moe's mood is such that he's more than happy to comply and share.

Finding a grand oak tree with its thick limbs and lush canopy reaching out to the heavens, we settle under it, luxuriating in the expansive shade. While it is decidedly cooler than being in the blazing sun, once you added the humidity present, it is admittedly a less than ideal difference. Still, it was better than nothing. We both lean against the ancient, gnarled trunk, each opening a Coca-Cola, and slowly sip them, with Moe savouring every nip with the same delicious satisfaction as if it was his first taste.

"Dreams can be a tricky thing, can't they?" Moe offers out of seemingly nowhere. "Totally unpredictable. Sometimes they're so good they're better than you wished, and you have to keep pinching yourself. You have to keep saying 'thanks' to the universe. Then sometimes, they can start as you want and then go poof! Become nothing like you thought. Poof! Oh no! Nothing like you thought at all!"

"Why do you say that?" I ask.

"Because I barely arrived on the professional winter circuit and the big bosses sat me down right away and read me the riot act. Told me I already had a reputation for my playing, the way I dressed, the way I acted, and that I would have to change my ways if I was to play and stay on the pro tour. Oh sure! Told me that this was big business and big money. It was the tour of the world they said! The tour of the world! Said they didn't care how well I hit the ball. Oh no! Didn't care at all. Said that the PGA was trying to get big new sponsorships, and big-time money, and they had an image to project to get it. Everybody in the world was starting to watch, and it was either going to be follow their rules and do what you're told or don't even bother showing up! They weren't looking for any square pegs for their round holes. It was enough to drive a man to drink! Which I haven't, by the way. Never touched a drop in my life. Finally, I asked 'What do you want me to change? My life or the way I play?'"

"What did they say?"

"They answered back: 'BOTH! Both or don't bother.' Oooh boy! I wish back then I had chosen the don't bother. Sure did. Wish I had chosen the don't bother..."

As I look at Moe, I can see that his fists are tightly clenched, as this usually well-buried part of his past starts to unravel in his mind. It may all be in the past for him but I'm sure that it didn't make it feel any less real or like it didn't happen just yesterday. It's a few years of his life that he usually won't talk much about and so I know I'll have to tread carefully to keep him talking. I'm eager to see if I can learn anything new about this time in his life, with this door to this part of his past, temporarily open.

"Why do you say you wished you hadn't bothered? Wasn't being on the PGA your ultimate dream and goal?" pushing on carefully with my questions.

"Oh, it was! It was! But you see, suddenly, I wasn't able to make anyone laugh anymore. Wasn't allowed to have fun on the course. Oh no! No fun at all! They take it so seriously out there. They stopped me is what they did. They stopped me. Stopped me from being me. Or at least they sure darn tried. They didn't want any colour out there. They just wanted everything black or white. And preferably white. Sometimes, when a crowd is tense or bored quiet, I can't help myself. I just like to put a spark into them. I need to. And so...I do! Always have. Why not make the crowds smile and help them enjoy the time we have together? Why not be their get-out-of-jail card? But not out there. Oh no. Not on the pro circuit. Oooh no! The players think it's life and death out on the circuit. Life and death out there. If they hit a bad shot, they want to commit suicide! If I hit a bad shot, I just laugh. It's just a walk in the park! A walk in the park. Enjoy it all, I say. The good and bad. Put in the work and you'll always see way better than bad. Sure!"

A moment of silence comes over us both and as it does, Moe's eye accidentally catches the suit that is still hanging lonely in the distance. It starts to beckon to him like the scent of the Magnolias did at Augusta. But here on this golf course, at this moment, it is more of a stench than a perfume that is drawing his attention. It hangs patiently, waiting for him to come forward and try it on. Suddenly, the arm of the suit rises and waves for him to come over. Did it just do that for real, he wonders to himself? Surely it must have just been the heat playing tricks he surmises, giving his head a shake and rubbing his eyes. But then it does it again! It can't be! Then, on the third wave, he relaxes and chortles to himself as he realizes it's nothing more than the afternoon breeze catching it. A breeze that is picking up substantial speed late in this day. He wonders to himself if he should just give in already and go put it on. But he decides no. Not now. He's too comfortable sitting in the shadows and elects to sit, sip, and reflect just a bit longer.

"You okay?" I ask in response to his seemingly disconnected head shake and chuckle. "Is the heat starting to be too much for you? Should we go inside and enjoy some air conditioning for a bit?"

"Oh no, I'm fine. Just fine. It's nice just sitting here chatting with you, Nick."

"You be sure to let me know if you change your mind," I state firmly, with a hint of concern.

"I promise I will," Moe confirms back.

"So then," as I get back to our discussion, "It was the lack of fun or the less enjoyment of the game that eventually got to you?"

"Oh, there was that for sure. But the other problem was I could barely afford to be there. Oh sure! I mean it's one thing to be told to dress better...but how? How, when you have no extra money? I had just enough to eat, sleep and get to the next tournament. It was demoralizing to see all the big-name players buying hundred-and fifty-dollar golf shoes while I'm sticking mine together with tape, to keep the soles from flapping. Oooh sure! There I was often having a hot dog for dinner while they were having a steak and they're leaving half of it behind with a two-dollar tip!

"And! And...? Could they play any slower?" smacking himself in the side of the head with exasperation. "Jeeez!!! It was like playing with turtles. I mean hit the ball already! How many times do you have to swing the club before you hit the ball? If you know your swing -- *own* your swing, like I do -- you don't need a practice swing... or FIVE! Just trust it. Get up and hit it already! Shoot it already – or shoot me instead and put me out of my misery!"

Moe playfully makes a gun with his hand, points the imaginary finger barrel to his head, and pulls the thumb trigger, falling back fake dead on the grass, looking up at the sky through the thick branches of the tree.

"I remember in one PGA tournament, we were playing so slow, I was beginning to lose it. I had tried to make the odd polite comment to the other guys, hinting that maybe we could play a little faster, but it kept falling on deaf ears. So, I decided to go to my ball each time after I hit it and lay down in the middle of the fairway beside it. Just like I'm doing now. Just lay there, looking up at the sky. Having a quick lie down before my next shot, trying to send a message. Oh sure! I mean what choice did I have? Nothing else I was doing or saying was getting through. Hoo! My clothes were even starting to get green grass stains on them as if I was playing wide receiver in a football game. And it wasn't just the guys I was playing with either. Oh no! It was the guys in front of me too! Every few holes we would pick up a little speed and then the next thing you know, you're standing there looking up the fairway forever waiting for the guys in front to hit. To get on with it. 'Hit the ball already', I wanted to scream! Eventually, I just plain gave up. Oh sure! I gave up waiting and started driving my ball into the next group ahead. Once I felt I had waited long enough, I'd shoot. I wasn't trying to be inconsiderate. Heck, they were the ones being inconsiderate! I was giving them what was a fair amount of time. Thought maybe with my shot coming up behind them all the time they'd get the message. Heck, it wasn't like I was going to hit them. Oh no! I knew exactly how far my ball was going and to where. Besides, half the time they were in the rough anyway. My target was the fairway that they weren't even standing on! But did they listen? Did they take the hint? Oh no. Ohh, no! Instead, they decided I was the problem. I kid you not. They thought I was the problem. Told me to behave and golf at a normal pace. Since when was professional golfing supposed to be like you were walking in quicksand? *That* was supposed to be the *normal* pace!? Sheesh! It got so bad at one point in one tournament, the officials went and started parking a promotional car directly in front of the tee-off box for each hole coming up for me. I kid you not! To stop *me* from hitting too soon! Sure! As if *I* was the problem and not the other players! Oooh! And then! Oooh! Then? When they got to the putting greens it got worse! Got so bad you may as well have brought your lunch, sat down, and ate it. Heck, sometimes you could practically fit in a power nap too. I mean how many times do you have to read the greens before you putt? Walking up and down the path it's supposed to take, up and down, over and over, again and again and again? To take a look at each side of the hole or check the slope to the pin before you putt? Pick away every piece of fluff or dirt or pat down any bump that may be there? Half the time you'd think they were patting down invisible bumps too! Bumps made of air and imagination! I swear, if I had found a way to go first in all those tournaments I entered, I would never have lost! Just hit the bloody thing! Just hit it!"

Just then, a big warm gust of wind blasts through the golf course, rattling the arms of the trees and filling the air with the gentle sound of the leaves catching the breeze. Knowing the wind would affect his practice shots if it kept increasing, Moe's desire to share stories diminishes, and his need to get up and hit balls increases in direct correlation. Shade or no shade, heat or no heat, it was time to stop being so lazy and hit some balls.

Moe gets up and starts getting ready, still reminiscing as he does. Knowing it was pointless to try and stop him, and thankful I was able to get him to sit this long as it is, I stay sitting and continue to enjoy his storytelling of his past.

"But I did okay. I did okay. I never missed a cut that first year on the PGA. Not one. Even had some top 25's and a 4th partway into my second year. Did okay. Nothing to be ashamed of. I knew it was going to take time to adjust and get used to the routines and the different golf courses. Oh sure! You just don't show up and be the best, no matter how good you hit the ball. Oh no. No way! Just like the work you put in on the driving range, you had to put in the work on the courses you've never played before. Sure! Once you played a course then you knew more about it. Sure! And once I've played a course I remember every inch of it, including the exact length of each hole and where best to hit it. Yes, sir. If you asked me the length, or the par, of any hole on any golf course I've ever played on, I can tell you in a heartbeat. No need for me to look it up. I never forget. I was so eager to have a second chance at them all the next year I could hardly wait. Next year I would know even better where to hit it and score even better. Turn those top 25's into top 10's. Turn those 4th places into victories! Oh sure!"

Moe suddenly stops getting ready and looks vacantly up into the sky, before continuing.

"But in the end... in the end, I knew my heart wasn't in it. Things weren't the same. *Golf* wasn't the same. They were taking the fun out of the game. They were all way too serious acting as if it was life and death. It's like they thought they were all doctors, where every shot and every moment was like being in an open-heart surgery operation and without perfect success every step of the way, the patient was gonna end up dead! One wrong move and it was all over."

Just as I was about to interject, Moe stops me.

"Now, don't get me wrong, golf is everything to me too! But that's because it's my joy and my happiness. It's my *love*. It's the one place where I'm at peace regardless of my score. There's nothing bad on a golf course. Not ever. Of course, I always want to do good, play good...but just being out there? Hoo! That's plenty enough for me. Plenty enough! And they wanted to take all that away from me! Take it all away!!

"The one thing that became very clear, very quickly, was that while everyone on the PGA did have one thing in common --the love for the game of golf – it wasn't going to be enough. The love affair would never be enough because it was a different kind of love.

"I loved the game while they loved the money the game could give them."

43

SILENCE IS NOT ALWAYS GOLDEN

As Moe starts to fully get back at it, robustly striking golf balls into the increasing late afternoon breeze, he decides to work on his mid-irons as we continue chatting. He's thrilled I'm an eager audience watching him again and I'm still thoroughly enjoying his opening up to me. At the same time, I also can't help but notice that off to our left is still the undiscovered country of fine fabrics. Where the suit, tie and shoes sit uncomplainingly off to the side, ignored and untouched, eagerly anticipating their time will come soon.

Instead of commenting on them and interrupting the moment, I choose to bite my tongue for the time being.

"I did my best for as long as I could on the pro circuit, Nick. Oh sure! I tried. Tried hard. Tried to tell myself it wasn't about them. That it was about me and the game. That they couldn't do anything to destroy that unless I was willing to let them. To be strong. I'd tell that to myself a lot. Be strong. That you're the one lucky enough to know how lucky you are to be here. That it should be enough."

"But it wasn't enough, I'm guessing, was it?"

"Oh, it worked for a while. Worked for a while. Then one day... well...one day I guess I just had had enough. Just had enough. One of the boys I was playing with, during the final round of a tournament, was having himself a bad day and was letting everyone else know it. His face always had a scowl on it and there was lots of cursing going on under his breath. Meanwhile, I was playing really well and was looking to make some good money. Was maybe going to finish top three or better. Maybe even win! Some real good money. I knew I would play for sure next week in Pensacola. I was feeling good, and I wanted to share that feeling. Sure! So, I thought I'd try and cheer him up, as well as the crowd that he had got so uneasy watching him. I figured that since I didn't have a caddie that day -- in other words, didn't have anyone to stop me -- I'd hit a drive with one of my six-inch tees. Oh, the crowd loved it! Oooh sure! Was a big hit with them. Lots of cheers and applause. Made everyone happy again. Just like that! Poof! Picked everyone's spirits right up. Folks always loved it when I did stuff like that. It was instant feel-good medicine. It never failed. Never ever. Oh sure! They especially liked it off the Coca-Cola bottles though! *That* was their favourite. But I only did that on the practice range and never during a game."

"I remember you one time during a clinic," I interject. "You hit a ball off a pack of matches for the folks watching. You hit it so clean that the ball went right down the middle and the matches never moved. You hit them just enough to light them. Then you told the crowd *that* was the way to set a course on fire!"

Moe smiled. "Yeah, that was a good one."

"Anyway, sorry to interrupt," I apologize. "Go on."

Moe's smile quickly changes to a much sterner expression.

"Then...then...suddenly my cranky playing partner was coming at me full on. Rushed towards me like a banshee. Screaming at me! Oooh...screaming at the top of his lungs! Told me to stop clowning around and act like a professional. Completely ignored how happy I was making the crowd. Then, he comes up to me and says loud enough for everyone to hear, 'Wait until I tell the guys in the clubhouse about this, just you wait you fucking clown! We'll see how funny you think it is then,' and stormed up the fairway, getting as far away from me as he could."

"That must have been awful," I offer in consolation.

"My oh my, yes. Awful. What a moment that was. What a moment that was. And all those people? The ones who were just laughing and having a good time with me? They were stunned. Just stunned. They were just looking and watching. Looking and watching. Not saying a peep. Not a peep."

"So, what happened?"

Moe finally stops hitting balls, leans on his club and bites his bottom lip, almost enough to draw blood.

"Oooh. It was awful. Oh sure. Awful! One second all was good and then the next thing the rug was pulled out and everything went downhill fast. I was standing there not knowing what to do and so was the crowd. Nobody said a thing to help me either. After what he did and what he said and them all seeing it for themselves. Not one word in my defence. Not one word to support me. Just a few giggles and laughs. Laughs and giggles directed at me. Even though they all knew I did that shot for them. To cheer *them* up. I hadn't done that for myself. It was all for them! All for them! They knew it too. No way they didn't know it."

"That must have been extremely awkward for the rest of the game?" I ask.

"Oh sure! For me and the crowd. And not another word was spoken that day between my playing partner and me either. There wasn't a word of apology from him. He just kept being his miserable self, hole after hole after hole. Had I been able to speed up time by changing the hands on my watches I would have. He may not have said anything more to me for the rest of that final round, but that didn't mean that there wasn't a conversation going on. Ohhh, no. A lot was spoken in my head. Oh sure! Believe you me. I never stopped thinking and talking in *my* head! Never stopped for a second having a conversation with me! Never stopped thinking, what was I doing out there? It wasn't fun anymore! It was more like torture. Like that

Chinese water torture thing. Every round was becoming another drip, drip, drip of sadness. I was becoming so sad. How much more did I have in me, I wondered? Could I keep taking in all this unhappiness? Was this really what I wanted? Should I carry on and hope everything gets better somehow? Just keep my head down and keep going? That this was just one guy and his one opinion and to not let it bother me? Oh boy...life out there was eating me up. Eating me up. I couldn't do what I wanted to do anymore. It just ate me up and it really hurt."

A lot of what Moe is sharing with me right now are things I already know, but he is adding some important tidbits that I hadn't heard before. I have a feeling we may be about to break some important ground about his past that I have always wondered about. That maybe, I am going to finally find out what made him ultimately give up on the PGA, from his lips. I've heard a story or two over the years about the fateful day he made his decision, but it's said he has only told the true story once, to his close friends Audrey and Gus. As he keeps talking, I'm hoping that today, I may become lucky enough to be the third.

Just as I am about to press on with some pertinent questions, I hear a voice shouting in the distance. It's Allison from the ballroom.

"There you are, Nick! I've been looking all over for you!" she states with undisguised annoyance in her tone.

She sees Moe is with me and quickly shifts to a smile. "Hi, Moe! I didn't see you there. Hard at work are you?"

"You know it, Allison. I never take a day off from hard work."

"Good to hear. I'm having a busy one myself. And, I need Nick here to come back to the clubhouse and give me a hand with some things."

Allison turns back to me, "I thought you said you were just running out to your car for a second?" shifting back to her annoyed tone.

"I was...but then I found something, and I needed to get it to

Moe. Then we got to chatting...and well...sorry," I apologize, guilty as charged.

"Well, come on then," Allison insists, "We have plenty to do, and time is a ticking."

Sensing I am at the precipice of learning some valuable private history from Moe, I am not in any mood to leave just yet. "Sure, just give me a few—"

Allison cuts me off and is unwavering, as she tries to force a smile. "We don't have a few to spare. Nick, if you want everything just how you want it for tonight, you need to come back with me now. As in, right now."

"But...but..." I stammer, torn between my need to stay and talk with Moe and finalizing the details for tonight.

Allison states firmly. "Have you looked at the time?!"

"Oh shit," I mutter, as I look at my watch.

I take one more glance at Moe, who has a wry smile on his face as he says, "I think it's best for you to listen to the lady."

"Yes, listen to the lady," Allison repeats with added emphasis.

Caught between a rock and a hard place, I know the night ahead has to win out, and so I begrudgingly give in.

"Fine, let's go then," I sulk.

"See you later, Moe," says Allison cheerfully as she immediately heads off back to the clubhouse.

I hesitate for a second and look at Moe.

"Better go and do what you're told. I'm pretty sure you don't want her anymore mad at you than she already is," he laughs.

Knowing he's right, I follow off in step, feeling extremely annoyed I may have just missed a chance of a lifetime to learn something new about Moe.

As I walk away, Moe quietly chuckles and says to himself, "Hoo! And people wonder why I stay clear of the ladies."

44

WHAT'S SAID IN THE LOCKER ROOM, STAYS IN THE LOCKER ROOM

As Moe watches us both walk off, he plops down on one of the benches directly behind where he's been hitting balls. He sits not because of the heat, but from the sadness the memories he was just sharing with me envelopes him in.

There are a number of these benches placed on the driving range, equidistantly spread out behind the row of practice tee-off boxes. Each of them has a little plaque on them with a different golf tip on it and this one reads: "Keep your head down."

As Moe sits on the bench, he leans forward, placing his arms on his knees, lowering his head down just as the bench sign suggests. It's reminiscent of the same posture he had in the locker room following that round with the belligerent playing partner many years ago that he just shared with me.

Assuming this position instantly triggers memories of the transformational event that transpired on that same day following that round of golf. The memory cascades back to him in an instant. A memory that has been buried for a long, long time.

In the locker room after that final round in 1960, Moe was still feeling the demoralizing effects of the dressing down he had received on the course in front of all the fans. But, at the same time, he was also feeling pretty good, having just shot an excellent final round of golf. It would likely hold up as one of the best rounds of the day. There were still some players out on the course, but it looked like he would have a top-five finish at the very least. The player's locker room by this time was full of guys who had finished their rounds and there was a lot of good-natured banter and chirping going on. Moe of course was not part of it and only an audience to it.

What I want to share next is the account of what happened on that fateful day, as Gus and Audrey once told it to me years ago. The same story running through his mind at this moment and the one I was hoping he was about to share with me in his own words today if we hadn't been interrupted moments earlier by Allison.

———

AS MOE SAT THERE with his head down in the locker room following the tournament, he suddenly saw a pair of bare feet in thongs come into his view, standing directly in front of him.

Before he could even look up he heard a loud, terse voice.

"Norman, I got a beef to pick with you, and I'm sure I'm not the only one," the other player stated without trying to hide his disdain.

Moe froze, not sure what to do, still staring at the other golfer's thonged feet.

"Look at me when I'm talking to you!" the voice demanded.

Moe looked up and saw it was one of his fellow players, a towel wrapped around his waist, looking as if he was about to hit the show-ers. Not the belligerent golfer he had just played with but someone else. Someone more important. The rest of the locker room suddenly went silent, and all eyes were on the two of them.

"Just who-the-fuck do you think you are, Norman?! Do you have any idea where you are? Just take a look around this locker room. Take yourself a good, long, hard, look. This is the PGA! Not some rinky-dink, amateur, no-name, gong show up in nowheresville

Canada. What the hell do you think you were doing out there today? What was with all that tall-tee bullshit? Don't you EVER pull out one of your long tees like that again unless you want it shoved up your ass when you're done with it. Do you hear me?"

Moe was silent, despite his urge to defend himself.

"I said, do you hear me?!"

Moe defeatedly nodded his head yes, taking the time for a speedy glance around the room, confirming all eyes were on him. He went back to looking down at his feet, praying this would all be over quickly.

"I think it's time you got to know your real place around here. YOU, Norman, are a nobody! Do you hear me? A NOBODY! It's time for you to grow up. How they even let you in the parking lot -- never mind on the course -- is beyond me. You, are an embarrassment to both the game and the professional tour! I mean, look at you! What the hell are you wearing out there? Huh? Huh?! What's with the too-short-for-you plaid pants and the bloody turtleneck on such a hot day?! And the stink when you walk by? Man o' man! Do you even know what a goddam laundromat is? Jeezus! It's high time you learned to dress properly, like us! To act properly, like us! To be, like us! And for the love of God, SLOW-THE-FUCK-DOWN. Stop being such an idiot! No one cares how well you hit the ball Norman. Nobody! You hear me? NOBODY! All we care about is that you don't go and mess up the good thing we're starting to have out here on the tour. This is a well-respected, classy, and difficult sport and that's how the fans are going to see it. Lots of big money with deep pockets are about to turn this tour into the goose that laid the golden egg for a lot of us, and we aren't about to let the likes of you mess it up. Not a chance in hell are we going to let some loose cannon like you jeopardize what's starting to happen. So, either fall in line or fall out completely! Do what you're told or go back to where you came from. Got it?!"

Moe was shattered, his head spinning. Good thing it was between his legs, or he may have passed out. He remained paralyzed, unable to look up.

"I said, got it?"

Moe managed to weakly nod back again.

"Good! Don't you ever make me have to say it to you again," turning his back, appearing as if he was finally finished with his tirade.

Then he stopped and turned around.

"And if you're going to have that stupid smile on your face all the time, go and get those awful teeth fixed, will ya? Either that or be prepared to have one of us wipe it off your face for you, sooner than later!"

From out of the crowd of players watching and listening, hanging onto every second of the humiliating dress-down, a voice rang out, "And what about him not using a caddie?"

A few others made the sounds of agreement.

"That's right. Thanks, I forgot. From now on Norman, always use a goddamn caddie like the rest of us! Nobody carries their goddam golf clubs! That's not our job!"

Moe may as well have been a statue at that point, not moving an inch. Had Auguste Rodin wanted to make a complementary piece to his "The Thinker," he could have made one here and now of Moe, called "The Humiliated."

Moe's inaction not only empowered the player, but it also fueled him. There's nothing easier for a bully than when his victim doesn't fight back. The venom building up in the player angrily staring down at Moe has become so intense that he completely lost it.

"Look. The simple truth is, you don't fit in, and you never will Norman. My advice? Go back to the amateur circuit where no one cares, and no one is watching. Someone said you were some kind of idiot savant, and we should cut you some slack. Well, screw that! In my opinion, you're nothing more than some retard whose fifteen lucky minutes of fame are over. So, go home!"

Having crossed the morality line, the player started to leave but apparently, his false exits had not yet come to a close.

"Let me repeat myself one more time for you...," and then, in a very condescending tone, he taunted, "And, since I know how much you like things said over and over and over again...," as a few of the players in the room snickered at the personal dig, "Let me repeat: You don't fit in, and you never will fit in. So, just GO HOME and save everyone and yourself the trouble, you goddam clown!"

With that the player stormed out for the last time, leaving Moe in his wake. There were the odd muffled comments of agreement from assorted fellow players that followed his grand exit. Not many, but enough sadly, to let you know this opinionated player wasn't alone in his feelings.

Moe sat riveted to the spot. All alone. Stunned. Shell shocked. There was a long uncomfortable silence in the room as the moment settled and sank in for everyone. The response by the other players in the locker room was a carbon copy of what happened earlier with the fans on the golf course earlier. Nothing.

Slowly but surely the hush in the room dissipated and the conversations returned to normal as if nothing had happened. All the while Moe continued to sit there, head hanging, deflated in his silence. His entire being was shrouded in embarrassment, anguish, and hopelessness.

Eventually, Moe got the courage to look up and take a peek around the locker room again. He looked to all the other guys who saw and heard what had just happened hoping someone would say something. But there was not a word from anyone. Not a single word in his defence. No one to just say something as simple as 'sorry about that' or 'don't worry about that.' Nothing. Nothing but a few chuckles and snickers. They wouldn't look at him either. Not a single one of them. It was as if nothing had happened. Like he was a nothing. Like he didn't exist.

It couldn't be clearer right then, that if he vanished, no one would even notice. No one would even care. Truth is they'd probably be happy.

And that was it. At that moment on that day in 1960, his decision was made and his life changed forever.

———

"THEY WIN," Moe mutters quietly to himself on the driving range bench. "Or rather, they won. I was done."

45

TIE ONE ON

Feeling overwhelmed, as if that day had just happened all over again, Moe rises from the driving range bench and drains the last of his Coca-Colas. He slowly takes it over to the trash can and tosses it in. It catches the edge of the receptacle and hovers like a basketball on a hoop rim, giving it a fifty-fifty chance of dropping outside or inside before it teeters and successfully falls into the can. He stares at the trash can for a moment and suddenly with a loud wail resonating from within the depths of his soul, he takes a run at it and kicks it viciously, sending it flying topsy turvy into the air like a football on a field goal attempt, scattering its contents everywhere. When it finally comes to a rest he picks it up, and with one shrill and unforgettable howl, he tosses it as far as he can. The remaining contents spilling out as it makes an impact with the ground and rolls about. As it finally comes to a stop, he stands there, breathing heavily, his thick chest heaving up and down.

Attempting to gather himself together, Moe gradually starts to clean up the mess he's managed to scatter with the perfectly placed punt and toss. Any passing psychologist would tell you it's like symbolically seeing all of his emotional trash from the past that was once compacted down and hidden inside himself for all these years, tossed and laid out bare for all to see. And what a mess it was! He could just leave it there and do nothing since he was fortunate to be the only one at the range at this particular moment and no one would be the wiser. He could just walk away and decide it isn't his problem anymore. But he knows the odds are that someone will come along at any moment, see it, that they will know it was his mess, and then he would have to explain it all. So, it would probably be best to put it all back in, forget about it, and put a lid back on it.

It's not like he hasn't become exceptionally good at doing that all these years.

Having finally released some of the pent-up frustration that had been building up for so long, he decides it's finally time to give in to something else too.

The ever-beckoning suit.

While putting on the suit is hardly the same size of sacrifice as the one he made giving up professional golf in the USA, it is still going to be one, nonetheless. He feels comfortable wearing what he always wears, and this suit will put him off his game. Most importantly, it will put him out of his comfort zone.

Solemnly, Moe walks over to the clothes rack, takes off the tie, and inspects it. A brief panic wells up as he realizes he has no idea how to tie a tie. I, of course, was already thinking ahead, knowing Moe would have no idea how to tie a tie, and he smiles seeing it is already pre-tied for him.

"Angels always know how to look out for you," he says out loud to himself as he slips the tie over his head.

Just as it looks as if he's about to be a good sport and put it on properly, Moe jumps up onto the bench, turns the tie upside down and holds the wide end up with his arm, high above his head. It looks as if he is now in a noose about to hang himself on the gallows. He pauses there for a second, jumps off the bench, tilts his head, and sticks out his tongue as if he was hanging dead. After a second or two he can't stay serious any longer in this position and chuckles sadly to himself thinking, "They only wish...they only wish..."

With the distraction complete, he turns the tie around in the proper direction and puts it on properly. Once it is securely tight and centred under his chin he sticks the thin end inside the little loop behind the thick part of the tie and presses it down flat.

Clothing concession two is complete. The tie is on.

46

A PORT IN THE STORM

MOE DECIDED TO LEAVE THE PGA FOREVER, ON THE SPOT, ON that day in the locker room in 1960. He didn't play competitive golf for two years after that. He said those two years were the darkest days of his life.

Moe's comment to me, describing those two years, still sticks with me to this day. He said,

"For almost two years, I didn't know what to do. But I had lots of bad thoughts. A lot of dark thoughts. They say that everyone thinks of killing themselves once or twice in their lifetime. That thinking of killing yourself sometimes is perfectly normal. Well, for the first time in my life, I was feeling pretty normal."

Luckily, instead of getting into too dark a place, he immediately went to see two of his other so-called angels: Audrey and Gus. He showed up at their door unannounced that same night as the locker room carnage, and said, "I'm done. I quit. I won't ever play on PGA tour again. I won't ever play in the United States ever again. They broke me. I'm done. They win."

Audrey and Gus sure were good folks. They opened their door to him that fateful night and let him in, no questions asked. They let him stay with them for as long as he wanted and said that there was always room for him in their home. Moe was very fortunate they were there and were willing to give him the time and space to put himself together again. He desperately needed it.

He stayed for two years.

47

RUB FOR GOOD LUCK

FRESHLY HALFWAY DRESSED AND ON HIS WAY TO BECOMING THE "after Moe", in his new shirt and tie, and having achieved his six hundred ball quota, Moe grabs a red bucket lying beside a free-standing tap with a bright green rubber hose attached to it. He fills it up with water and splashes a bit on his face to refresh himself in the still sweltering heat. He gets a few drops of water on the new shirt and tie and quickly realizes this may not be the best of ideas and refrains from splashing any further.

He picks up the bucket and trudges back to the bench to set it down. Without stopping, he walks over to his golf bags and retrieves a club head cleaner, a small bottle of laundry detergent, and a white towel from the inside of one of them, before finally returning to his spot.

Placing a few clubs into the bucket to soak, he pulls one out. He grabs an item that looks like a golf ball but it's a club cleaning brush. He twists it until it separates, exposing the scrub brush hidden inside, sprinkles detergent on it, and starts scrubbing. As he does so, he talks out loud to himself.

"You never want to have dirty clubs when you start hitting your golf balls. And you never want to start the day cleaning them, instead of hitting them, either. You always want to be able to get at it right away and not waste valuable practice time. Your clubs must be as clean as your mind to start the day right."

"What was that? Are you talking to us?" asks a golfer in a red shirt who recently came to the range with his two other buddies to hit some balls.

Moe is embarrassed. "Oh, no! Sorry about that. Just talking to myself is all. Talking to myself. Sorry if I was bothering you."

"No worries. I just wanted to make sure you didn't think we were being rude and ignoring you if you were talking to us," explains the guy in the red shirt.

One of his golfing buddies, in a blue shirt, sees how vigorously Moe is scrubbing and offers in his French-Canadian accent, "You do know that a guy, over at the club storage, will clean those for you? You don't have to waste time doing it yourself, you know?"

"Oh no!" Moe scolds. "You need to clean your clubs yourself, just like you do your balls. You don't need others touching your stuff. Oh no! Your stuff is your responsibility. And, if you want to clean them properly, always visualize the good shots you're going to hit with them. Put those good feelings and thoughts into those clubs today and let them sink in overnight. Rub them in good and deep. Make sure your clubs are always ready for tomorrow, full of good shots."

"I cannot lie. That sounds like a good idea. Motivationally, I mean," blue shirt responds back to Moe.

"Ha, you're so lazy Marcel, there isn't a chance in hell you'd clean your own clubs! Who're you trying to kid!" red shirt taunts.

"Yeah, that's true, Harvey," Marcel good-naturedly chortles back. "You got me! How do you say...guilty as charged!"

"Although I have to say, with that slice of yours, you should try it anyway. It can't hurt!" Harvey grins.

Marcel punches him playfully in the arm. "Like you should talk, my friend."

Once Moe scrubs the first club clean he inspects it like a jeweller would with a freshly polished gemstone. His shots are so accurate that the centre of the grooves on the face of each club has a worn spot about the size of a quarter, and the rest of the surface is unblemished. The result of hitting the sweet spot of the club virtually every single time.

Seeing it meets his approval, Moe gives it a final rinse and dries it up with the towel. Before he's completely done with it, he kisses it.

While Harvey, Marcel, and the other guy have gone back to hitting balls, Harvey still notices the kiss and stops.

"Hey, you're holding out on us. It's not just about cleaning them yourself but giving them a little loving too, I see," he says playfully to Moe.

"Hoo! That's how you keep a good marriage going, always remember to kiss your loved ones once a day. It can work as good luck too. Not that I need it. Hoo! Not me. There's no luck going on in my shots!"

Moe places the cleaned club back on the ground and begins to repeat the process with the next one as the golfers go back to their practicing.

Despite the distraction the other golfers give him, Moe is still burdened by revisiting those dark days of his PGA past only moments ago. A dark cloud remains over his head as he thinks out loud to himself...

"Boy oh boy. Those PGA tour days sure ate me up. Ate me up. Wouldn't let me be me. Made me have to leave. Gave me no other choice. They put a hole in my heart."

He stops washing the club for a second and stares at it without really seeing it.

"I always thought a hole-in-one was an amazing thing. Oh sure. Unless the hole is in your heart...unless the hole is in your heart..."

He drifts off for a second, biting his bottom lip again, before resuming washing.

As Moe powers through, continuing cleaning his clubs one at a time, the three golfers pack up their gear and start to head off.

As they leave, Harvey stops in front of Moe and asks, "So, tell me...that tie you're wearing...is that some sort of good luck thing too?"

"Oh no, just wearing it for a friend. Wearing it for a friend," explains Moe.

"Ah, okay. Because my buddy Marcel here needs all the help he can get!" Harvey bellows as he slaps Marcel on the back. "I was going to tell him I had a suit tie, back in my car, and that he should wear it for our round later! Maybe shave a few strokes off his score!" following it up with a hearty laugh.

Marcel is none too amused. "Very funny smart guy."

The third golfer, who has been silent and has stayed in the distance all this time, pipes up, "C'mon guys, let's go already. I want to grab a quick something to eat before we tee off."

"Salut! Have a good day, my friend," offers Marcel to Moe.

"Yes, have a good one!" Harvey adds.

Moe nods his head cordially in return to them both.

As the three are leaving and are still in range of being overheard, Moe picks up on the other guy's last comments.

"I don't know why you two always do that. Start talking to strangers out of the blue like that. Especially you, Harvey. It's obvious that guy is a bit off...sitting there mumbling and talking to himself. And I mean, who cleans their own clubs? Never mind in a dress shirt and a tie! I wouldn't have given that guy the time of day."

While the comment is one of many Moe has heard a million times over, it still lands as hurtfully as always, and his scrubbing intensifies.

Unfortunately for Moe, as Harvey responds, they are now out of Moe's earshot.

"Well that's you," points out Harvey, with a strong judging quality attached to it. "You live life scared, and I don't. People interest me. All kinds of people. You just conveniently stick to your bubble. If we had more time, I'd have tried to get to know that guy better. He seemed kinda interesting to me."

"Yes, I agree," echoes Marcel.

"Whatever," he dismissively grumbles as the three head off and out of sight. "The weird ones are all yours. You two can have them."

48

SNOW ANGELS

IT'S NO SECRET THAT A LOT OF PEOPLE THINK MOE IS A BIT "off". Most people do, actually. I know it and he knows it. He's not dumb. He sees it and feels it. There's a long lineup of people thinking he doesn't fit in -- or can't fit in -- because he's different. And let's face it, the bottom line is, it scares them. Or rather, *he* scares them. And because of that fear, they feel *he* needs to change. That *he* needs to start trying to be more to be like everyone else and to fit in. But until there is evidence of that ever happening, they are steering clear of him.

As Moe eyes the next freshly washed club closely, confirming that it too passes inspection, he picks up the towel and starts drying it off. After it receives its kiss, he lays the freshly dried club beside him and moves on to the next, scrubbing this one with even more determination and vigour even though it is no dirtier than the others.

"A bit off, huh? I bit off, am I?" Moe grumbles to himself, the comment from that guy still hanging around his neck like an anvil.

"Who knows? Maybe that guy is right or maybe he's wrong," Moe continues to discuss with himself. "Who knows? Maybe it's just how I was born? How God made me? And if so, how can anyone argue with that? Or, who knows…maybe it *is* all my fault," becoming increasingly agitated. "All my own damn fault! No one to blame but me!"

Before finishing cleaning the golf club presently in his hands, Moe rises, grabs his half-finished Coca-Cola, and starts to pace. He's suddenly feeling overwhelmed and agitated and isn't sure what to do with it. Keep cleaning his clubs? Hit more balls? Put the suit jacket on? Get in his car and go home?

He chooses another easier option instead.

To take a walk.

As he begins, he has no destination in mind. All he knows is that he needs to burn off the bad energy that's building up inside of him like a locomotive and he knows that hitting golf balls is not the answer. You don't hit balls with bad energy. You only hit with good energy. And you don't clean them with bad energy either. You only clean them with good thoughts and good energy.

After aimless speed walking for a few minutes, Moe eventually finds he's come across the sand trap and chipping area again. He eyes the practice sand trap, jumps down into it, and lies down again. He doesn't make a pillow this time nor considers taking a nap but instead, rather, he starts moving his arms and legs up and down, side to side, making a huge indentation in the beautifully smooth bunker.

"Hoo! I loved the snow when I was a little boy," he thinks to himself, reflecting on the memories he had as a child. "I just loved the fresh white snow! Whenever it would start to snow me, and my brothers and sisters, would run out and try and catch the flakes on our tongues. And when it came down heavier, I loved lying down in it too, making snow angels with my twin sister Marie. We would make as many as we could until we ran in and got our mom so she could come outside and see what she always called our 'choir of angels!' There was nothing like it. I loved it! I loved how it could change how everything looked too. It was usually always so dirty where we lived in Kitchener, with all the factories and stuff spewing out pollution. It wasn't often we had the chance to play in white snow. Usually, it was grey or brownish. The Uniroyal Tire factory was just a block and a half away from our house too, and that sure didn't help. Oh no! Sure! But just like that, fresh white snow could make all the ugly and dirty look clean and new again. Clean and new. It was like magic. Especially when it was that thick wet stuff that clung to the trees. So pretty! My mom would always call it "the winter wonderland" and she would go walking through the streets with us looking at it all. The snow never stayed white long though. Oh no! Never stayed white long. But boy, you liked to be in it when it was fresh. Fresh and white! So when it did freshly snow out, you needed to get outside and enjoy it right away! There was no time to be wasting. Just like milk, there was a before-and-after date to it. And the tobogganing! Ohhh, that was the best! How I loved to go tobogganing with my pal Jimmy. Oooh! How we would ride down the big hill together after a fresh snowfall! Fastest of them all we were. Fastest of them all! We could run up and down that hill all day long. There was no stopping us."

Suddenly Moe bolts upright to a sitting position and the weight of the world looks to tumble down on him once again.

"Boy oh boy, I wish there was someone who could have stopped us though," he thought to himself. "Or, at least, stop me, on that one day. Oh how I wish. Ohhh how I wish. Maybe, just maybe, I wouldn't be who I am today if someone had stopped me and Jimmy."

49

IT'S ALL DOWNHILL FROM HERE

IT'S EXTREMELY HARD FOR MOE TO GO ANY FURTHER DOWN memory lane when it comes to this particular wintery day in his past. He's only told me the full story once. It was an event that may or may not have changed everything for him, and regardless of whether it did or not, there was no undoing it. So, he felt there was no point to keep bringing it up.

I think the hardest part of all is that no one will ever truly know how significant that day was. And like Moe says: Knowledge is everything. So, he did his best to block it out and not talk about it.

I, however, know it's something very important and that it needs to be shared with you.

Back on that fateful winter day in Kitchener, a five-year-old Moe decided to go tobogganing with his pal Jimmy and his sister, Marie. Jimmy and Moe had altered their normal sledding game plan and, instead of going down the hill in their own sleds – racing against each other -- they had decided to get into Moe's toboggan and go down together. They figured the weight of the two of them would give them a much bigger speed.

They were right.

The problem was that it made them go too fast, and they went all the way down the hill and up and over the safety hump nearby. The safety hump was a far way off from the hill, and it was put there to stop any of the sledders from going too far and into the street that went around the hill. But with their speed, they were going so fast, that they went right over the hump and flew right across it into the street.

Unfortunately, there was a price to pay for doing so as they went sliding directly under the car of a man named Mr. Berner, as he was pulling out of his driveway The sled and the two of them went slip-sliding right under his car in the blink of an eye.

It was scary for everyone having to helplessly witness what was happening as Mr. Berner continued moving his car backwards, without any hint of stopping. He kept going because he never knew Moe and Jimmy had gone under, despite numerous people yelling for him to stop – including Moe's sister Marie, screaming way off in the distance from on top of the hill.

Moe's said he was almost instantly stuck under the car and he couldn't move. He could see the tire treads and how they were coming for him very slowly but there was nothing he could do. At the same time, he couldn't see Jimmy, but he could hear him yelling. He could hear him screaming for Mr. Berner to stop the car. But Moe told me that for some reason he couldn't yell. That he couldn't shout out at all. He just kept looking at the tire coming at him until all of a sudden he could feel the rear car tire start running over his face. It was still so clear in his mind's eye that he could actually see the grooves in the tire running over his face to this day. He could practically taste the rubber too as he heard that crunching sound reverberate in his memory banks.

Moe told me, "I wasn't altogether sure if it was the sound of the snow crunching or if it was my face. All I knew was there was this crunching, crackling, and popping kind of sound as the tire slowly rolled over me. But what could I do? I was stuck there and I couldn't move, couldn't get out of the way! Weirdly enough, I wasn't feeling anything either, so I figured it was nothing to worry about. Once the light did come back and I could see again, and once the tire moved past and over me, I noticed I still couldn't see Jimmy anywhere. That did make me worry. Made me worry a lot."

His sister Marie -- who was still watching from the top of the hill -- said afterwards she thought they were goners for sure. She couldn't believe it when she saw both of them suddenly pop up as if nothing had happened and then ran home, crying scared to their moms.

Funnily enough, Moe said this wasn't the scariest part of the day. No, he said he was even more scared when Mr. Berner came by their house a little later.

You see, Mr. Berner did not come alone.

He came with a cop.

50

COME OUT, COME OUT, FROM WHEREVER YOU ARE

MOE THOUGHT HE WAS IN BIG TROUBLE NOW. ALTHOUGH HE knew he didn't mean to go over the safety hump and cause any trouble, it sure looked like he was in big trouble anyway. Every time the cops came to his house -- like when he broke the neighbour's windows once in a while with golf shots -- it never turned out good. Not ever. One year he broke thirteen windows trying to hit a ball between a small gap between the neighbour's houses. So, the family was suddenly starting to get to know the cops pretty well. And every visit always seemed to end up with Moe's dad being really mad and Moe's butt getting a real kicking.

So, when Moe saw the two of them at the door he just did the instinctive thing. He hid. He ran and hid under the sofa, keeping good and quiet.

Of course, Moe knew full well they would find him eventually. The problem was that the only real chance for escape was through the front door and that was where his dad was standing, blocking off any chance of getting away.

"You want to come out from under there please, Murray?" said the cop as he stood in the living room doorway having spotted Moe's tiny, socked foot sticking out from under a corner of the couch.

Five-year-old Moe didn't move, however, as he instead desperately tried willing himself to become invisible.

The officer moved further into the room, stood by the couch, and gently assured Moe, "You're not in any trouble this time, Murray."

Moe continued to will his invisibility but was getting the ominous feeling that these particular superpowers he desperately needed, would not be kicking in today.

"Murray, please come out from under the couch," repeated the cop. "I see your foot," as he gently nudged it.

Moe officially admitted defeat as confirmation that invisibility was not working was now verified.

"Murray, please do not make me ask you again," said the cop, still gently, but with a bit more authority this time.

"My name is Moe," he blurted out. This was the best he could come up with in response to officially being found and he remained stubbornly under the couch.

Patiently the police officer gave in. "Fine. Moe, then. Moe, will you please come out from under there? We just want to make sure you're alright."

"Where did Mr. Berner go?" Moe blurted, still firmly claiming his territory under the couch.

"He's in the kitchen talking to your parents. It's all okay, Moe. Honestly. Now come out from under there and let me see you."

Moe slowly but surely came out, staying closely beside the sofa.

"Good heavens, boy! The side of your face is all swollen!" reacted the cop with alarm.

He moved in and took a closer look at Moe, unable to completely mask his unease with the severity of the swelling he witnessed. He reached out to touch Moe's tiny, battered face, "Jiminy cricket son, that's a nasty one."

Moe flinched back, not wanting to be touched. Neither him nor the injury. "I'm okay. Really. I'm okay. Please don't tell my parents. PLEASE!"

"Look son, your parents already know what happened. Mr. Berner has told them everything. We all know it was an accident and now they need to take you to the hospital. Bloody hell kid, you need to get that checked out right away. That could be very serious!"

"No! I'm fine. I'll be okay. Just leave me alone. Please! PLEASE!"

Like he was shot out of a cannon, Moe bolted back under the sofa as close to the back wall as possible, making sure his foot came with him all the way this time.

"You stay there then, and I'll have a talk with your parents," he ordered as he left the room. "Don't you be going anywhere though, or you will find yourself in trouble."

As soon as the officer left the room, Moe scurried out from under the couch and eavesdropped on the conversation between the cop, Mr. Berner, and his parents in the kitchen.

"I found him. He's hiding under the couch," said the cop.

"That little bugger," grunted Moe's dad as his temper instantly flared and he lunged for the living room.

The cop instinctively recognized the risk in the temporarily unhidden fury in Moe's dad and stood directly in front of him, stopping him from proceeding any further.

"I know you're angry Irwin, but he's fine where he is. He's not going anywhere. Right now, you need to prepare to take your kid to the hospital. Murray's face is a mess."

Moe's father stopped proceeding any further but retained his full inner anger. Behind him, worry and concern quickly formed on both Moe's mother and Mr. Berner's faces.

"Don't be foolish. We're not taking him to the hospital," declared Moe's father firmly.

Sensing the urgency, Moe's mother tried to negotiate, "But if the officer says he needs to go to the hospital, maybe we need to take him..."

"We're not taking him to the hospital, Mary. We can't afford that, and you know it!"

"Perhaps I can offer some assistance with that then...," stated Mr. Berner.

"Thanks but no thanks. You've done enough already. Look fellas, this is my kid, and I'll look after him as I see fit. I'll decide what he does or doesn't need, and he doesn't need to go to the hospital. If he's good enough to play goddam hide and seek then he doesn't need a bloody hospital!"

Moe's father stubbornly crossed his arms and dug his heels in. Both Moe and his mom knew that look all too well.

"But Irwin, we haven't even seen his face to know yet!" she pleaded.

"Mary, enough. This discussion is over."

"But Irwin, please...," trying desperately one more time.

"I said discussion closed!"

Knowing it was futile to proceed any further as it would only make things worse, she gave in and frustratingly held her tongue.

Knowing he had won this battle, Moe's father turned to the cop and Mr. Berner and started to usher them out the door. He wanted them gone and silenced as well. Now.

"Thanks, fellas, I appreciate your concern and for letting us know what happened. I'll take it from here. I'm sure Moe will be just fine and there's nothing to worry about. I'm sorry to have taken up so much of your time."

"I do wish you would reconsider about the hospital, Irwin. It doesn't look like something you should ignore," reiterated the cop one more time as he tossed a disquieted look to Mary as well.

"Probably turns out to be nothing more than a black eye," responded Moe's dad flatly.

The cop pressed on, "I think it could be a lot more than that by the quick looks of it I had."

Moe's father kept strategically herding them out and managed to get them onto the outer front steps, "I appreciate your concern officer.

And don't worry Mr. Berner, I'm sure it was Moe's fault and not yours. That damn kid is always doing something he shouldn't be. You both have a good day."

As they hesitantly walked away and down the steps, Mr. Berner tried one last time. "You know where to find me if you need my assistance in any way…"

Moe's father nodded and with a patronizing smile closed the front door, solidly locking it shut, the enemies now safely out of his castle.

Without even as much as a glance towards the living room, he immediately yelled out, "If I were you boy, I'd stay under that couch for the rest of day!" and headed directly upstairs, taking his undisguised building rage up with him.

Once Irwin was safely out of sight, Moe's mother cautiously went into the living room. She saw Moe was standing sneakily by the door and quickly realized that he had overheard the entire conversation. She tried desperately to hide the fear in her heart as she saw Moe's swollen face. It was every bit as serious as the cop said and she knew she should take him to the hospital to get him checked out immediately. She also knew that it was true they couldn't afford to. But even more so, that her husband would not allow it and that the repercussions that would follow if she disobeyed him would be severe.

So, she buried what she knew was the right thing to do, damming up the wall of tears that were desperately wanting to flow forth, and managed a gentle smile on her face as she told the biggest lie of her life.

"Oh, Moe. That's not so bad. Let's go put some ice on that and help the swelling go down. That's not so bad at all."

51

LABELS ARE FOR SOUP CANS

A FEW DAYS PASSED BY AFTER THE TOBOGGANING ACCIDENT, AND Moe's parents never did take him to the hospital to get his face properly looked at. His folks didn't have the extra money to go to the hospital and he understood that. It wasn't free to go to the emergency room back then like it is today, and it was often a difficult choice many a family had to make when it was already hard enough to make ends meet.

Sadly, his mom always said afterwards that she regretted not taking him to the hospital that day or the next. She always wondered if maybe he would have turned out differently if she had taken him. She always swore one side of his face was always a little bit more pushed up than it was before it got crushed. His brother said Moe's voice started to change after the incident too, and that he started to talk faster. He also said Moe started repeating things like he hadn't before.

But Moe had a counterargument for all that. He would say, "Who knows right? Who knows? I was just a little kid after all. I wasn't even in school yet. Nothing was set in stone yet about me.

Nothing was set in stone. I was just becoming me! I was still developing. Who knows how I was or wasn't gonna turn out. That's just nonsense playing a game of what if. What is, is what is."

You have to admit, he did have a solid point.

Some people will say that Moe is "different" – for lack of a better word -- because he suffered some form of a brain injury from the tobogganing crash. Others will say he might have been born with autism and is on some level of the spectrum. There are even others who want to add to that list and say he has Asperger's Syndrome. In any event, Moe never went to a doctor in his life, so without doing a barrage of tests there's no way for anyone to truly ever know.

I've always found it intriguing how putting a finger on what Moe may or may not be, seems so important to so many. How preoccupied many of us often are, trying to make a diagnosis on someone, so then we can decide how we want to treat and interact with them. All because they seem to be a little different than most of us.

If you were to ask Moe about this, here is what he would tell you:

"Who cares?! Why is everyone all worried about wanting to know what makes me different? To put some kind of label on it. A label on *me*! Wanting to either make me be like everyone else or put me in a certain group of different people? To make me fit in. Fit in somewhere. Never noticing that, just maybe, it's a good thing being different. Hoo! Oh sure! That maybe that's what makes me special in the first place. That maybe I like being me! That I like being different! Or to stand out at least. In a good way, of course. In a good way! The best ball-striker in the game! That's me! The best ball-striker in the game. And that's not just me saying that. Oh, no! I'm just repeating what everyone else says. The way I see it, it's not a terrible thing being different. Not bad at all. I mean, why all the fuss trying to fix what really ain't broke in the first place?! Who says being different means you're broken? Why the need to fix or put a label on everything that isn't the same as everything else? Hoo! It's crazy town. Oh sure. Crazy town. Completely bonkers when you think about it! Just treat me and look at me like you would everyone else and be done with it already."

Pretty hard to argue with that, isn't it?

52

TALK THE WALK

Having sufficiently calmed down from being called a bit "off" by the golfer earlier, Moe extricates himself from the sand trap. Before he heads back to the driving range, he grabs the rake, ready to remove his angel indentation and pauses, wondering if he should leave it there or not. In the end, his compulsion to follow the rules, to make sure the trap is better than he found it, wins. He restores it to its former condition and begins his walk back.

As he does so, he hears a voice from behind him hollering, "Did you get all those clubs cleaned and happy-ready for a good game of golf tomorrow?"

Moe turns and sees it's Harvey – the guy in the red shirt from before.

"Almost. Almost!" Moe replies. "Still a few more to go. Just needed a little break."

"Are you heading back to the range now?" inquires Harvey.

"That's the plan. Why?"

"Do you mind if I walk back with you then? That's where I'm headed too."

"I thought you have a game this afternoon?" questions Moe, with a strong hint of him not really wanting Harvey's company. At least not after what was said earlier.

"I do. I just forgot my water bottle back there and I need it for my game. I know...most guys like to be drinking beer out there instead... but I take the game too seriously, I guess," he laughs. "I can always have a few beers after the game if I want. I'd just rather be at my best when I'm playing, so water it is."

Despite Moe's initial impulse to reject the invitation for the walk, he's pleased to see how serious Harvey is about his game. And, being a non-drinker himself, constantly annoyed by the drunks he sees on any course by the twelfth hole, he begins to reconsider.

"You sure you want to walk with someone who is a bit 'off' though?" Moe asks, with a mischievous glint in his eye.

Harvey stops in his tracks.

"Aw, man. You heard what my friend said didn't you?" Harvey shakes his head with anger and embarrassment. "He can be such an ass sometimes. I mean he's normally a really good guy, but he does have his dickhead moments – pardon my language. If we had more time earlier, I definitely would have liked to have stayed and talked to you more. Now to be clear, I'm not an ooga-booga kind of guy, in that I don't believe you can just will things to happen, but I do believe in the power of thought. I think there's some merit in putting good thoughts into your clubs as you clean them. I'd like to hear what else you do to mentally help your game. Although I do have to confess, I'm pretty lazy and still like my clubs cleaned for me," he snickers.

Ignoring the joke, Moe gives it one more quick thought before he starts walking away, at his usual fast pace.

"Well then, come along then. Pick up the pace. Pick up the pace. I don't have all day to waste, and you still have a game to get to."

Talking that as a yes, Harvey quickly catches up and they begin their walk back together.

After a minute of silence, it dawns on Harvey that he was going to have to be the initiator of any conversation.

"I'm Harvey by the way," he offers, extending out his hand.

"You can call me Moe," as he reaches and shakes Harvey's hand back, ignoring the slight wince on Harvey's face that was so common from this otherwise simple ritual greeting gesture.

"Yeah, I know. I know your name. I didn't put two and two together when I first saw you earlier...but then I saw that photo of you back in the clubhouse. Congratulations!"

"Oooh, you did now, did you?" Moe smiles. "And thank you!"

"You've sure won a lot of tournaments in Canada, haven't you?" Harvey praises.

"Ohhh sure! Won my share. Won my share," being careful to not sound too full of himself.

"Won your share? That's an understatement. You were amazing by the looks of things! That must have been something, winning like that all the time," Harvey gushes.

"Oh sure. Winning is great, sure. But don't be fooled. There's a price you have to pay for that to happen. Oh yes, a big price. It's a lifetime of endless hard work, complete dedication and an unwavering desire to succeed. And then when you do, you still have to be aware that the golf gods will take one more chunk out of you, for good measure."

"What do you mean?" asks Harvey, giving Moe his absolute attention.

"You see, winning means having to give some of yourself up. And not just some, but lots. You have to pay a price. There's no free ride to winning."

As they continue to walk, Moe's hand plunges into his pocket and he grabs one of the two golf balls that always reside there, unconsciously playing with it in his hand, passing it over and over again through his fingers like a skilled magician would or professional card dealer would with a deck of cards.

"All I really ever wanted to do in life was do my best. To just show up and play. Play the game. You see, that was something I could control. Something that was all about me. Nothing else. Just me and the ball. Just the way I liked it. Just proving to be the best ball-striker in the game was plenty. But being good also meant you won. And if you won, then you had to talk. Oh, sure! Whenever you win they make you get up in front of everyone and give a speech when you get your cheque and your trophy. There's no such thing as win and go home."

"Well, that can't be so bad! It's gotta be kinda cool being the king of the hill and everyone knowing it. Having all your subjects gathering around you, hanging on your every word," Harvey replies.

"Hoo! Boy oh boy, have you got that wrong! So wrong! There's nothing worse than having to give a speech! NOTHING! I hated having to get up in front of everyone like that. I hated it! I would rather stick pins in my eyes than get up in front of a crowd and talk."

"Oh, now I see what you're saying. Yeah, I hear a lot of people aren't too keen about talking in front of a crowd," he sympathizes.

"That was me! I was so shy. So shy. Now, on a golf course, I was never shy. Oooh no! If I was in motion or swinging the club I was a-okay. Then I felt I could do things that no one else could. I was invincible. Nothing can go wrong on Moe's golf course. But when I would win a tournament and the golf club was now out of my hand? Hoo! When I suddenly saw them all? Everybody? Seeing them for who they were? Crowding around me to hear me speak or want a picture or an autograph? It was terrifying."

"Yeah, I can see how that can happen to someone."

"Nothing but a bunch of judges they all were. Judging *me* instead of my *game*. As soon as I signed my scorecard, I couldn't wait to get away from everyone. Get away before some committee guy got his grip on me and made me give even more of me away. Sometimes the thought of winning and having to be put on display was enough to make me want to lose. And boy oh boy, I love to win, so that sure tells you everything about that feeling. About that fear. Oh sure."

"Did that ever happen? Did that pressure ever make you lose or did the joy of always winning triumph?" Harvey asks.

"Oh sure, it cost me. Cost me more than once. In fact, it cost me the one professional tournament that was ever on the top of my list to win – alongside The Masters, that is -- which is The Canadian Open."

"No kidding!" Harvey exclaims with wonder. "It affected you winning the Canadian Open?!"

"Oh, sure! It was also the only USA-PGA sanctioned tournament that I ever played in after I left the States. I mean heck, everyone wants to win their country's national title, but best of all it was held here in Canada. I can still remember that Canadian Open in '63 like it was yesterday."

"Can you share that story with me? That would be amazing to hear about it," Harvey begs.

Not one to shy away from telling a golf story – good or bad – Moe is happy to oblige.

53

THE CANADIAN OPEN

"WELL..." MOE CONTINUED, "IT WAS THE LAST DAY OF THE tournament, and I was playing some really great golf. I went into the last round three shots back of the leader. Things were starting to get really interesting when we rounded for the back nine and my caddy was pumping me up big time.

"Way to go, Moe!' my caddy said. 'Let's keep this going! It's a race between you and Ford now. Just nine holes to go. You got this.'

"My caddy could sense all the momentum was now with me and that victory was there to be tasted.

"Starting to be a walk in the park. A walk in the park," I grinned back.

"You've got him good and worried too. He's trying to hide it, but I can smell it,' my caddy kept encouraging as he went to my bag and pulled out a club. 'You should go with the driver,' he told me.

"So, I took the club, quickly teed up the ball and hit it. I didn't even bother to take the time to watch it. Why bother? I knew it was gonna be a walk in the park from here on.

"Nice shot, Moe! Another one right down the middle!' my caddie said after my shot. He even raised his hand for a high-five, which I gave him back.

"Then, as we headed off to where the ball landed my caddy teased me by saying, 'I hope you're getting that speech ready!'

"Well, that just stopped me dead in my tracks. 'Speech ready?'

"Sure, Moe!' my caddy explained. 'Just picture it! There's going to be fifteen thousand fans screaming and chanting your name around that last green. All of them waiting to hear their new champion speak! It's all in your control now Moe. This is your chance. Your destiny. Embrace it! You can do it! It's everything you've worked so hard for, right at your fingertips.'

"Then, my caddy went on even more, 'And that's nothing! Imagine what it's going to be like when they ask you to drop the puck at the next Leaf's game at The Gardens! Or do the coin toss at the Grey Cup. This is a life changer, Moe. A life changer! Let's bring this baby home! You've got this!'

"Then he offered a club for my next shot, telling me, 'Aim for about ten feet to the left of the pin and let the slope of the green do the rest of the work.'

"My next hit was well struck to the middle of the green, exactly where the caddie suggested and rolled close enough that it should have been an easy two-putt for par. With a superb putt, it was a birdie.

"My caddy never stopped encouraging me. 'Let's drop this baby in, Moe,' he said. 'Let's start to seal the deal! Time to open up some breathing room!'

"Sadly for me, neither the par nor the birdie happened and I three-putted for a bogey, falling one back of Ford. Next thing you know, my putter may as well have been a wet noodle. A wet noodle! I three-putted six times on the back nine and lost the match. Six times! SIX! I couldn't swing the putter. I was paralyzed. I was terrified. It all started to hit me. All I could think about was that number: Fifteen thousand. *Fifteen thousand* people! I was going to have to accept the trophy and give a speech in front of fifteen thousand people! End up at center ice at a Leaf's game! Every one of them was going to want a piece of me. Looking at me. Watching me. Judging me. One more big chance to make fun of me."

Harvey is spellbound, not wanting to interrupt and get in the way of the story and there is a moment of silence between them as they continue their walk as he waits for Moe to continue.

As they arrive back at the driving area, Harvey figures Moe is done, and he attempts to break the ice. "Wow, that's something. Knowing you were that close, and then let your mind take it away. Golf sure can be cruel."

"It sure can sometimes. It sure can," Moe agrees.

"Ah, there it is!" as Harvey points to his water bottle and walks over to pick it up.

"But eventually, I learnt to get better at it. At winning and what came with it. Oh sure. I had to. I had to! I read some books and listened to some audio tapes on public speaking and self-confidence by Tony Robbins. Besides, aw heck, I was so far ahead, so often, it was getting impossible to even try to fake losing! I finally learned that if I was going to win, I would have to learn how to talk in front of a crowd. How to say thanks and accept the cheque and trophy. So, I did. So, I did. My only regret is that I didn't learn how to do it earlier."

"By the look of your winning track record, you figured it out soon enough!" Harvey praises.

"Better late than never right? Better late than never," Moe smiles.

"Well...I better head back Moe," Harvey says with some regret in his voice, as he was enjoying chatting. "I should be teeing off soon. Thanks for the walk and the story. It really was a pleasure hearing it and for you to be willing to share it with me." Then a smile comes over his face. "And I promise, if I ever stop being lazy, that I'll try and use your theory about rubbing good thoughts into my clubs when I'm cleaning them."

"As you said to your buddy, you never know what it might do, unless you try it!" Moe winks back. "You go enjoy your game now."

"And you the rest of your day, Moe. Especially this evening. Good on ya! Congratulations again."

As Harvey wanders off to enjoy the rest of his day, Moe looks at the few clubs remaining to be cleaned. Without delay, he sits down and immediately gets at it. As he scrubs away, the frown he had on his face earlier is now gone and it's replaced with a smile.

Time to put those happy thoughts back into his clubs like he's supposed to.

54

OUT OF THE MOUTH OF BABES

Having cleaned all of his clubs and put them all away, and with the driving range once again empty of any other golfers, it's finally time. Time to address the ultimate challenge of the day: The suit-in-waiting.

Starting with a deep breath, Moe strolls up to the suit, leans his putter up against the rolling rack it hangs on, kicks off his shoes and takes off his plaid pants. He lets them drop to the ground, exchanging them for the dress pants, and pulls them on. He pauses one last time as he spies the jacket with trepidation.

With a deep swallow, he gingerly takes the jacket off of its hanger and puts it on. Assuming its rightful place on him, he stands rigid, unable to move, feeling it smothering onto himself like hot wax from a candle dripping onto his bare skin. His first instinct urges him to tear it off immediately, throw it into the trash can and be done with it. But he refuses the impulse. Instead, he holds his breath, willingly accepting its grip, although still fearful it will be like a boa constrictor, slowly sucking the life out of him until he drops dead.

Standing still, terrified to move, thinking he might rip or tear the fabric if he does, he doesn't risk moving a muscle. Surprisingly though, once he relaxes, realizing the world wasn't coming to an end after all, he admits it feels much closer to a nice embrace rather than the cloistering straitjacket grip he was anticipating. It actually feels kind of good! Every bit as good as that awkward, yet rewarding hug from his sister, many years ago when that infamous letter arrived.

As he stands experiencing all the unexpected positive feels of the new suit, two young boys suddenly go running by.

As they pass, one of them tosses him a welcoming, "Hey mister!" and waves, as he tears past.

The other immediately follows up with a hearty, "Nice suit!" as he dashes by in a blur.

Moe happily tosses back, "Hey boys! Thanks!" waving back in return.

As they remain on their chase one of them yells back, "No problem!", while the other screams, "Looking goooood!"

Moe smiles to himself. He continues watching them as they continue their sprint, both laughing unabashedly with childhood glee, not a care in the world between the two of them.

"Boy oh boy, I love kids," he thinks to himself. "Love them! They're the only people I ever feel comfortable with. The only kind of human beings I can talk with and can always trust right from the start. Just the kids. Oooh yes! Just the kids. They just see you for who you are, accept you for who you are, and find a way to fit you into their world."

Moe's grin stays firmly on his face as he watches them run off, that is until a frown starts to set in. "Finding reasons for keeping people out is something you're taught," he says to himself. "No way we're born like that. Oh no! That's something we learn from adults. Kids are always jolly. None of the fear has set in. All they see is the good. All they see is the good..."

Then breaking back out into a smile again, he points towards the two boys and says to himself, "Now those two kids...they know how to live on the Moe Norman golf course. They just live happily and everyone is welcome to join."

Moe runs his hands over the fabric of the suit again, still taken aback at how good it feels. He could almost get used to this. Almost. But he had better not get too used to it because a suit like this isn't something he would ever be able to afford.

Financially, Moe is in quite a tight spot. Players never made much money back in his days, not nearly like they do on the professional circuit today. A player nowadays can make more money winning one tournament than most of the guys his age made in an entire career. And now Moe is even too old for the senior's tour, which is often the only way for some of them to start making a living again. For some, it's even better than their glory days. All Moe really has as a source of income is doing the odd golf clinic now and then in Canada, and when he went to visit Audrey and Gus in Florida. They were even kind enough to do a fundraiser for him so that he could pay off some debts. But he's already back in the hole. It's tough. Really tough. Each day is a challenge just to get by. He knew full well he certainly wouldn't be wearing a nice new suit like this if it wasn't for someone buying it for him.

55

TIME'S UP

HAVING FINALLY COMPLETED ALL OF MY REQUIRED TASKS FOR the big night that was finally about to start and having cleaned up and changed into my own suit, I head over to get Moe, eager to get the ball rolling. As I stroll along the path, I'm quietly praying to myself that he has done everything I have asked of him. If there is one thing I can predict about Moe it's that he's unpredictable.

As I dodge two young boys racing past me on the walkway, I see Moe off in the distance running his hands over the quality cloth of the suit I bought for him.

As I approach I can't help myself, "Wow! Look at you! Looking good, Moe!"

"You think?" he replies, caught between being embarrassed at being seen wearing it, and his pleasure at knowing how happy I am to see him in it.

"Are you kidding me? Like the superstar you are! Damn, I have to say it, you clean up good!"

"You think so? You don't think I look like a dummy?" he responds with a blush.

"Are you kidding me? I might have to give a call to GQ and get you a photoshoot."

As much as I want to enjoy his transformation, I quickly have to shift my intention since I know there is little leeway in the time we have to spare. I appropriately take a more serious tone.

"It's time. Are you ready?"

"Oooh boy...oooh boy," Moe responds in a fluster.

"It's all going to be fine, Moe. Just enjoy it," as I place my hand reassuringly on his shoulder. "It's been a long time coming."

Moe takes a deep breath and releases it. "Okay, I'll try. I'll try."

Seeing he has a golf club still in his grip, I try to remove the one-of-these-things-just-doesn't-belong-here item.

"Here, give me the putter. You won't need it. I'll look after it for you."

"Oh, nice try, Nick! Nice try! I already gave you a putter by the Bow River in Calgary a long time ago. One is plenty, don't you think? One is plenty, don't you think? Getting a little greedy aren't you?" he teases, hiding the putter behind his back.

I'm about to reply but Moe cuts me off.

"I'd like to take the putter with me if I can. If I can. I'd like to hold it."

"Of course, sure thing, not a problem," I give in, knowing it's like a third arm for him.

"Oh I forgot; I need one more thing. One more thing. Give me a second!" shouts Moe as he runs back to his golf bag and quickly grabs a few items from inside and shoves them into his pocket.

I can't see what he was grabbing but it takes all of about five seconds so I doubt it can be anything all that important. Besides, I don't have the time to get into any debates over it. We're seriously on the clock now, so no harm, no foul. Hopefully, this is the last of any more delays.

"Okay, I'm ready!"

"I'm not quite so sure about that...," as I look down at Moe's stocking feet. I should have known there had to be something.

"Something wrong with the shoes?" I ask.

"Hoo! Right! Don't want to forget those do we? If we're going to do all this dress-up, we gotta do it right, don't we?!" as Moe races over to the rack and pulls the new shoes and socks out of the box, and slips them on.

"Hoo! Fits like a glove. Fits like a glove!" he expresses with glee as he ties them up.

With everything now finally on his body, Moe stands straight and tall as if ready for full military inspection. I oblige and do a full three-sixty around him.

"Better be careful there buddy. You're looking so fine that the ladies are going to be all over you!"

Moe turns beet red and is visibly mortified by the thought.

I can't help but laugh at his immediate anguish, "I'm just pulling your leg, relax! Okay, let's head over to the clubhouse."

I grab his plaid pants and old shoes and socks from the ground and put them on the rolling rack while he grabs his clubs and does the same. Once all is carefully secure, I start to push them back to the clubhouse. As we begin walking I can't help but notice that for the first time in my memory, I'm the one walking the fastest and he's having to keep up with me. I also can't help but acknowledge that Moe's face gets a little more serious with each step.

He knows there's no chance of turning back now or backing out, nor that I would let him even if there was. Tonight is here and as of right now it's every bit as "game on" as it has ever been in his life or in any tournament he has ever played in.

As we walk I remind him, "This is your last chance to run anything by me should you want to. Do you know exactly what you have to do? Any questions? Any thoughts? I'm all ears if you want me to be."

He remains stoically silent as we continue our way back.

56

A GRAND ENTRANCE

Upon arriving at the clubhouse, we quickly drop off the rolling rack and the various items on it and head directly towards the main banquet hall. There's a string quartet playing by the bar area in the lobby and a buzz is in the air. Everyone walking about is dressed up in suits and elegant summer evening dresses. Placed directly outside the door to the hall is a big photo of Moe with his full name under it: Murray (Moe) Irwin Norman.

"Hoo! Will you look at that! Will you look at that! Fancy!" whistles Moe as he sees the picture.

As we stand looking at the portrait, a loud kerfuffle breaks out behind us, and we both turn around to see what the fuss is all about.

It's the three young rich guys from earlier in the day, being their usual careless, obnoxious, and boisterous selves. I see they are in suits as well. Of course, they spot us and immediately start heading over our way with mischief in their eyes.

Oh great, I think to myself, are these three stooges going to be a problem tonight as well?

As they stride over I'm undecided about what to do. Go on the offence and cut any confrontation to the quick or go on defence and usher both of us into the ballroom to disappear into the growing crowd gathering there?

It turns out I needn't do anything.

The three get close to us and abruptly stop, frozen still as if there was a powerful forcefield holding them back.

Maybe Moe has superpowers after all, I joke to myself. Perhaps he's turned them on, and now they can't move, or they can't see him.

But they do see him. They see him very clearly.

They look at Moe, and then me, and stay unreservedly silent. Something that up to now I would have thought they were incapable of. Then, somehow I manage to adorn the invisibility superpowers Moe lacked as a child and I disappear before them, becoming no interest to them whatsoever.

The three look at Moe, they look at the large photo, and they look at Moe again, until

Captain Obvious breaks the awkward silence.

"What? You gotta be fucking kidding me. *You're* Moe Norman? *The* Moe Norman?!"

We say nothing in return. We don't have to.

"Holy shit!" blurts out one of the others.

"For real?" completes the third.

My cocky grin grows by the nanosecond, and I do nothing to hide it. I'm fully energized to see these three weasels cower in recognition. I could have marinated forever in their realization that they had been abusing the most important person at the golf club today. I also probably could have spent a good five minutes ripping each one of them a new one with a good long dressing-down speech to humiliate them even further. But I didn't need to. "Less is more" they always say, and I couldn't think of a better game plan.

So, I keep it simple.

"We'd love to stop and chat boys, but we have much more important things to attend to. And as you can guess, much more important people to engage with. Enjoy your evening."

That was all they will get from either of us and with that point scored – which was more like a game, set, match moment -- I put my arm around Moe and usher him into the ballroom. The three shell-shocked dudes watch as we go in, mouths wide open and dumb-founded.

"You know," says Moe quietly to me, "If golf balls weren't so expensive I'd have shoved one into each of those dummies' open mouths."

We both have a good laugh and while we do, unbeknownst to us, three sets of parents come rushing up behind the little prep boy gang of three. They too are all dressed to the nines for tonight's event.

"What was that all about son?" says the father of the ringleader, with enthusiasm.

Then his wife chimes in, "Wasn't that Moe Norman? You boys were talking to Moe Norman? How exciting! What did he say to you? What were you boys talking to him about?! Don't leave a thing out!"

I'll never know what their answer was, but you can bet all the money in the world that the truth never crossed the lips of any one of those guys for the rest of the night.

57

SEND IN THE CLOWN

As the army of catering staff complete their call of duty, removing all of the plates following a wonderful and elegant dinner and their numbers start to diminish on the banquet hall floor, it signals their job is near done. My remaining task is making sure that everyone is readied and armed with a fresh glass of wine or after-dinner cocktail and I'm sufficiently satisfied it too, has been fulfilled. It's officially showtime. I gesture to Allison with a thumbs up, who is poised at the ready. She nods her head to Gary who operates the control panel, and he lowers the lights in the hall to alert the crowd that we are ready to proceed.

A spotlight comes up on a stage, focused on a lecture podium emblazoned with a Canadian Golf Hall of Fame crest on it.

As a hush comes over the room, I walk up to the podium. To be sure the microphone is working, I give it the prerequisite few taps.

It's working.

"Ladies and Gentlemen, honoured guests, and fellow members thank you so much for coming out on this wonderful occasion. It's a special evening and we are all assembled here to pay tribute to a very special man and his many accomplishments. With no further adieu, it's my great honour to introduce to you the latest member of Canada's Golf Hall of fame. Winner of fifty-five professional golf tournaments, including eleven Provincial Opens and two Canadian PGA Championships. Who, as an amateur, was the winner of two Canadian Amateur Championships and many others -- too many to count. Who, as a senior player, was the winner of a record eight Canadian PGA Senior Championships. An incredible and unmatched career that includes thirty-three-course records, and numerous rounds of fifty-nine – including one at the age of sixty-two! -- and not to be glossed over, an incredible seventeen hole-in-ones. With all this being said, it is now my great privilege and honour to introduce you to the man considered to be the best striker of a golf ball, in the history of the game, Mr. Murray (Moe) Irwin Norman!"

Everyone in the hall instantaneously rises to their feet and Moe is given a thunderous standing ovation. As they stand and clap Moe walks hesitantly from his table towards the stage, adorned in his brand-new suit, the putter still clenched firmly in his hand. He humbly acknowledges the crowd with a shy nodding of the head here and there, as he makes his way. Without saying a word he arrives at the stage and woodenly stands beside me.

We both look out at the crowd, two men in fine suits, standing side by side as the crowd continues to clap. While our fashion look is complementary, what is going on inside of us could not have been more contradictory. I'm beaming, never more thrilled to be alive. It means everything to me to be able to be with Moe on this special and historic day and see this finally happen for him. Nor could I be prouder to be one of his few close friends. Moe on the other hand looks as if this may be the last place in the world he would rather be and that he may be rueing the day we ever met.

I lean into him and speak into his ear so he can hear me above the noise, "Congratulations, Moe. This is long overdue. Look how much they love you. I'm so proud and happy for you."

Moe looks back at me, directly into my eyes as if it was the easiest thing in the world for him to do and the fear wanes into an appreciative smile, "Thank you, Nick. Thank you. This is all because of you."

"No, it's not. It's all because of you. Your time has come my friend."

We shake hands, which evolves into a brief hug whether he likes it or not, and I step back, letting Moe have all the well-deserved spotlight to himself, heartily joining in on the relentless applause. Once the applause runs its due course and the people begin to take to their seats again, a representative from the Hall of Fame steps up and presents Moe with a framed certificate of his entrance into The Hall. It's accompanied by a picture of him swinging a club in his glory days as a young professional on the Canadian tour.

"Oooh! Thank you! Thank you. Hoo! I was sure much better looking back then. Oh sure! No sign of this belly I got going now or the grey hairs! Hoo! No sir! I like it."

The audience laughs at his self-deprecating comment, and I can see it helps put Moe a little bit more at ease as well.

Another item is wheeled out covered in a velvet sheet. When the cover is pulled off it reveals the plaque that is to be permanently installed in The Hall of Fame. It too is accompanied by a photo, in this case, it depicts him in a bright red turtleneck in his record-winning senior playing days.

"Hoo! I guess I spoke too soon. Spoke too soon!" Moe blurts out. "There's the grey hair and the belly. Hoo! There they both are. Not gonna let me run from them are ya? Hoo!"

Again the crowd bursts into laughter, eating up his good honest nature like candy. It strikes me how different his life may have been had he only realized all along how much he was – or could have been – loved. Or better yet, had we allowed it to happen. I may be speaking for myself, but it's always far more refreshing and rewarding when you meet someone who is unedited, honest, and forthright in how they present themselves instead of the usual calculating, veiled image we get from most of our public figures or sports heroes.

Knowing it's important to keep things moving along, and that there was still a lot to cover over the evening, I return to the podium.

"We all know Moe isn't that fond of making speeches, so maybe I can help postpone that pain a wee bit longer for you Moe. But just a wee bit longer though -- we *are* going to want to hear from you! But first, we have a special surprise. Ladies and gentlemen, I am pleased to introduce to you Wally Uilhein."

Moe shoots a puzzled look my way as Wally walks up to the podium to a round of applause and adjusts the microphone. I smile and give Moe an all-knowing wink back.

I'm loving every moment of this.

"Good evening everyone. I'm Wally Uilhein, and for those of you who don't know me, I'm the President and CEO of Titleist Footjoy. What an honour it is to be here tonight and what a pleasure as well. It's a thrill to be in the presence of some of Canada's greatest golfers and such a great ball-striker as you, Moe.

"Now, I know you and I have never met before in person Moe, but I feel like we have. I know a lot about you as you have earned yourself quite a reputation."

"Hoo boy! Now I'm in trouble. Hoo boy! " blurts out Moe without thinking, to which the crowd roars its approval.

"I can say without reservation that the best players in our game, both in the past and in the present, do not hesitate to say that you are the best ball-striker this sport has ever seen. And I do mean ever. That you deserve to be mentioned among names like Hogan, Nelson, Jones, Snead, Palmer, Nicklaus, Player, and Trevino."

The crowd interrupts with more well-deserved appreciative applause.

Moe looks down at his feet and closes his eyes. It may come across as humility -- and on some level it is -- but it's also because he thinks if he opens them and looks up he will see this is all a dream. Did they just say that? Did they just mention his name in the same breath as the greats?!

"I also know that in your day the financial rewards for a

successful golf career were nothing like they are today. That making ends meet in the latter part of a sporting life can sometimes be difficult. Traditionally, society offers scholarships to talented people, particularly at the beginning of their careers. The goal, of course, is to give them a better chance at success. But it seems we never consider talented people often enough at the back end of their careers. We forget, that being very good at something or doing good things, doesn't always translate into financial security. As a society, we tend to forget about people when they are no longer front and center or before us anymore 'doing their thing' for us all to see.

"Well today, we would like to change that. On behalf of Titleist and the worldwide golf community, we wish to present you with this back-end-of-life scholarship. Can you step forward please, Moe?"

Moe is still looking down, eyes closed.

"We aren't putting you to sleep now are we?" Wally jests. "Moe?"

Moe opens his eyes and looks at me and I gesture to him to go over to Wally. He continues to look at me and I gesture again and mouth strongly, 'Go! Go!'

He hesitantly obeys and goes up to Wally.

"Moe, please accept this cheque, payable to you, in the amount of five thousand dollars. An amount to be repeated every month for the rest of your life. We offer this to you with deep gratitude, respect, and thanks. Congratulations again on your long overdue induction to the Canadian Golf Hall of Fame, from fellow golfers all around the globe."

Wally holds out the cheque for Moe to take. Moe doesn't move. He's frozen dumbstruck.

"Oooh! I ... Oooh!" not knowing what to do as he stares at the cheque.

"If I were you, I'd take it," Wally smiles.

Moe takes the cheque and stares at it. The crowd applauds.

As the crowd continues to cheer the moment, Moe looks at me utterly flabbergasted and I shout out to him over the din, "I guess this will help make sure you get a good upgrade or two at your motels from now on. Maybe even your first off-the-assembly-line Cadillac!"

Moe beams at the thought.

As the applause dies down and the room goes silent, Moe remains numb, looking at the cheque.

"Oooh! Hoo! For real? This is for real? You wouldn't be jerking around an old-timer like me for fun, now would you? Would you?"

"Yes Moe, it's for real," says Wally emphatically. "Once a month for the rest of your life."

"Hoo! I better stay around a little longer than I intended then huh? Shouldn't I?"

It won't come as any surprise that the audience gushes again in delight. Unbeknownst to him, he's on a roll without even trying.

"What do I have to do for it? What do I have to do? What's the catch? If it's having to hit your golf balls I've sure got no problem with that! Hoo! No problem at all. Titleist is the only ball I'll ever hit. The only ones."

Wally gives out a pleased chuckle, "Well Moe, I can't lie. I do like to hear that!"

Turning more serious, "But no, there is no catch. Nothing at all. Just continue to be you. We at Titleist – heck, I bet it's safe to say everyone in golf -- just wants you to keep being yourself."

"Nothing? I don't have to do anything?!"

As if he is waiting for Allen Funt from the Candid Camera TV show to appear at any moment, still looking unconvinced, he turns to me, "You're sure there's no catch, Nick? This isn't some kind of prank? Because it wouldn't be funny."

"No catch, Moe. And no, it's not a prank. They just want you to continue being yourself. To continue sharing you and your love for the game like you always have and in your unique way. And believe me, that is not nothing. *That* is something quite special."

The crowd once again lets out enthusiastic appreciative applause.

Moe studies the cheque, as I thank Wally and he returns to his seat. I return to the podium and finally say the words that Moe has been dreading.

"So, Moe...I'm sure this crowd would love to hear a few words from you now. You are the reason why they're here. What do you think folks? A few words from Moe?"

I start clapping and the crowd wholeheartedly joins in, standing up again in unison encouraging him back to the podium to speak.

As the applause rings out, I can't help but feel relieved. Here we finally are. After a long day and an even longer life journey to get here, it's officially Moe's time. Of course, that also means it's do-or-die time too. Put up or shut up as they say -- with shut up not being an option from my side of the equation. I'm both terrified and excited as to what comes next. Will he pull it off?

After the applause ends, Moe stands at the podium, staring out blankly, saying nothing.

I can sense immediately that "Houston, we have a problem..."

As a diversion, I slink up to the podium, reach into the shelf on the inside, and pull out a Coca-Cola that I had strategically stashed there earlier in case it was needed. I give it to Moe, and he straight-away takes a big sip. He swallows but still says nothing.

Trying to stall and give him a little more time, I point to the putter, certificate, and cheque that are still clutched in his hands, "Let me hold those for you."

Moe gives me the certificate and reluctantly, releases the putter. He takes the Coca-Cola and puts it back on the podium. Referring to the cheque he says, "This I can look after. Oooh yes! This I can look after myself."

He folds the cheque, kisses it, and puts it in his pocket as a few appreciative chuckles resonate from the audience. Gary dims the house lights even more as I back away leaving Moe centred in a tight spotlight. The stage is all his. The moment he had always dreamed of has arrived and as excited as I am for him I also pray that we are not about to see another meltdown as with his first go-around at The Masters.

He taps the microphone hard, making a huge thud sound. It blasts a high-pitched squeal, and he reacts backwards with a jerk. "Hoo! That was loud! Sorry about that. I think that's what you're supposed to do before you talk right? Hit the mic? Don't know why, but everyone does it. So, there ya go!"

The crowd is silent, and I suspect more than one person in the audience is wondering how this is going to play out. My nails are already beginning to dig into my palms as my fists are clenched tight with worry.

"Oooh! Hoo! I'm shaking like a leaf right now! Shaking like a leaf. Just like that first time I teed off at The Masters. Oooh, they always say the longest walk in golf is the walk from the driving range to the first tee. Yes sir, the longest walk of all. But today...Hoo!...today... today I would have to say it was beaten by that walk from the driving range to this podium."

He clears his throat as his mouth goes completely dry on him and he takes another good gulp of Coca-Cola. I start to worry I may have made a critical mistake in only hiding one of them inside the podium with the way he is quenching his nervous thirst. He takes another sip and pulls out a hankie to dab his forehead. As much as he tries to pretend there's no one out there and to incorporate all the public speaking tips he gleaned from his self-help tapes, books, and videos -- he always found the idea to think the audience were all in their underwear was preposterous -- he knows full well they are out there in the sea of blackness before him. Staring at him. Suddenly, it feels like his inability to speak in public is as bad as it ever was.

He takes a deep breath and tries again. "I...umm...I..."

The torturous sight continues unabated as Moe continues to stand bare before the crowd, appearing completely lost. It dawns on me that he hasn't prepared a thing. He hasn't considered what he was to say tonight, and he hasn't written anything down either. This wonderful night is about to do a one-eighty and turn into a complete disaster! I knew I should have made him think about what he wanted to say and write something down!

"I...uh...," continuing to pathetically stumble.

Moe takes yet another deep breath, never relinquishing his vacant stare. All the while, I want to shoot myself in the head and be done with this unravelling nightmare I've irresponsibly let happen. Why wasn't I more demanding about him writing something down? Maybe I should have written something for him, just in case? Why didn't I force him to tell me what he was going to say?

"I...uh...uh..." stammering on a road to nowhere.

The tension is building in the room and the uneasiness everyone is experiencing is becoming palpable. It's evident he needs help. Everyone is on pins and needles at this point and a few coughs are starting in the audience which is always the truest sign that people are becoming uncomfortable.

Thankfully, I give my head a shake and stop stupidly and self-ishly thinking this is all about me and how it will all be *my* failure. This moment isn't about me, it's about Moe. How can I help him? What can I do?

Then it hits me.

I quickly grab Moe's putter, go up to the podium and hand it to him. Moe takes it, looks at it, and briefly gazes at it. Suddenly, as if a curtain had just been pulled from over his eyes, or as if some magical elixir went from the club into his veins, his demeanour instantly changes. The blank stare vanishes, the uncertainty dissolves and the impish grin emerges as he relaxes and becomes his old self.

The flood gates open.

"Hoo! Oooh. How I dreamed of this day. Holy doodle! How I dreamed of this day. To know that I was accepted by all of you. That my swing was appreciated. That I was respected. Oooh, how I have dreamed! As far back as those days when I was just a kid. When my brothers and dad would ask why I wanted to play such a sissy sport like golf? Why not play a man's game, like hockey? But golf was always my thing. Always my thing. From the first day I swung a club and hit a ball I instantly knew it was something that made me feel free. Oh sure! It was golf that taught me how to believe in myself. Taught me who I was."

Moe recites his favourite poem that he said always described who he was now because of his commitment to practicing and trusting in his swing:

"I have a little robot that goes around with me.

I tell him what I'm thinking I tell him what I see.

I tell my little robot all my hopes and fears.

He listens and remembers everything it hears.

At first, my little robot followed my commands but after years of training,

It's gotten out of hand.

He doesn't care what's right or wrong or what is false or true,

No matter what I try now he tells me what to do.

"Hoo. I've tried at times to be like everyone else. Oh sure! Sometimes tried real hard. Real, real, hard. But I've learned it just doesn't work. It's just the way it is. It's just the way I am. I know I'm not like everyone else. I don't look like everyone else, sound like everyone else, talk like everyone else, swing like everyone else...heck I can't even dress like everyone else. Except for tonight of course!"

He runs his hands down the chest of his suit.

"Just look at me in this will ya! Hoo! Me looking like a million bucks. But don't get carried away that this is a sign of things to come! Oh no! This is all Nick's doing. He picked this suit out and strong-armed me into it. Oh sure! Strong-armed me right into it. Probably gonna be a one-night-only kinda deal. I hope you've kept the receipt for the suit Nick, so you can return it afterward!"

Someone shouts out from the audience, "I don't know about that Moe, now that you're getting five grand a month forever!"

The crowd laughs in agreement.

"Hoo! Right? Isn't that something? Isn't that something! Hoo! That's gonna be a game-changer for sure. A game-changer for sure!" Moe turns to the side of the stage where I'm standing watching.

"Thanks, Nick! Thanks for everything. I don't know what I would do without you in my life. You're my truest guardian angel."

I smile and nod back and inside my brain, all I could do was keep screaming, "Look at you! Keep going buddy, you got this. You got this! You've really got this!"

"Golf is happiness. That's the biggest thing I've ever learned. Oh sure! Golf is happiness. It's intoxication without the hangover. It's stimulation without the pills. Some say it's a boy's pastime, yet it sure builds men doesn't it? It cleanses the mind and rejuvenates the body. It's all these things, and many more, for those of us who love the game. Oh sure! Golf is true happiness. True happiness. Sure, it may be defeating at times, but it generates courage. You can cheat and steal for many things, but you can't with a golf swing. No sir! To achieve a great golf swing, you have to work at it. And work hard. You have to make life sacrifices. Like most things you love, when you work extra hard, eventually it takes you to even greater heights and greater joys. Golf's price may be high, but its rewards are richer. Just like tonight..."

Moe takes another sip of his Coke and continues.

"Boy oh boy, I'm a lucky man. So many gifts golf has given me. So many gifts. And now you all. Hoo! Giving me this honour tonight. Hoo!"

Barely able to get the next words out.

"Maybe...maybe even love me a little bit. Maybe..."

He takes a second to collect himself, wipes his forehead again with this hankie, reaches into his pocket, and brings out three golf balls. One orange and two white.

He takes time to look at them.

"Earlier today when I was hitting balls on the range, when I was reflecting and thinking on my life like Nick asked me to do, and I was thinking about what I was going to say to you all tonight, I threw this orange ball away."

He holds up the orange ball.

"Oh, sure! Just carelessly threw it away. Thought about how

much I hated these things. How they didn't make any sense. How they were different and were a mistake. But you know what? Now I see that it really isn't so bad, is it? Not so bad at all. It gives colour to the game. Gives colour to the world! How can that be a bad thing?"

He takes a moment and studies the orange ball with more intensity.

"You know, I think I'm going to keep this one after all. Sure! Keep it after all," as he puts the orange ball back in his jacket pocket.

"Now, as for these two?" as he stares at the two remaining white ones in his hand, "These two are a dime a dozen! A dime a dozen. Not nearly as interesting. Just more of the same. Aren't they? Just more of the same. Who wants them? I don't."

Moe moves away from the podium and methodically heads down the stage stairs until he comes to the table where the three young rich guys from before are sitting, with their parents. He hands one ball to the ringleader and the other to his father.

"You have them. Seems more like something you're looking for."

Moe returns to the stage, retaking his place behind the podium. His anxiety seems to have completely disappeared into the ether. If you hadn't known the truth of his fear, you would never have guessed it now.

"It took me quite a while to figure all this out. Took me all the way to tonight. Oh sure! Knowledge always does that. Always takes time. But it's always worth it. Isn't it? Always worth it in the end."

Moe steps away from the podium and moves to the front edge of the stage as the spotlight follows him. He pulls the orange ball out of his pocket again, holds it outstretched, high in the air for all to see, and studies it further one last time. He takes an extra-long pause in doing so. Finally, he looks down at someone in the audience, close to the stage, extends his arm down, and holds out the orange ball to them.

"You want this one?" he asks gently.

The audience member is unsure what to do or say.

"Don't worry. It doesn't matter. You can't have it. This one is mine. I've earned it. Hoo! Oh, yessiree. I've earned it."

Moe takes the orange ball and sticks it on his nose.

It's an orange clown nose that he had hidden in his pocket all along. It looks exactly like the orange golf ball we just saw minutes ago. It was what he had grabbed at the last second from his golf bag just moments before heading to the banquet hall with me.

He doesn't move a muscle after that, standing confidently, proudly, and tall at the edge of the stage, letting himself be seen by all.

As is and always will be.

He basks in the spotlight, surrounded by the darkness, looking like a royal and regal statue. His clown nose on and holding his putter as if it was his sceptre. Slowly his one-of-a-kind smile grows larger and larger until that toothy grin arrives at its fullest effect.

"In closing, I want to thank you all, for today and all the days before it. From the bottom of my very full heart.

"Murray Moe Irwin Norman."

"Moe the Shmoe."

"*Your* Clown Prince of Golf."

"What more could anyone ever ask for."

He takes a bow.

EPILOGUE

AFTER SPENDING A LIFETIME OF BEING TOLD NO, THAT HE didn't fit in, that he didn't meet the standards, that there was something wrong with him and that he needed to change -- despite all of his outstanding and unrivalled life accomplishments – Moe Norman's long overdue entrance into the Canadian Golf Hall of Fame finally transpired when he was sixty-six years old.

Moe was also inducted into the Ontario Sports Hall of Fame in 1999 at the age of seventy.

Moe was then finally inducted into the Canadian Sports Hall of Fame in 2006.

He would never know it.

It came two years after his death.

As his fellow professional golfer Ken Venturi with fifteen professional wins and one major said: *"Because Moe is eccentric, he never got the credit he deserved or played the kind of golf he was capable on tour."*

Or as Lee Trevino opined: *"I don't know of any player ever, who could strike a golf ball like Moe Norman. If he had just had some kind of . . . handler, someone to handle his affairs, everyone would know his name today."*

I find it sad that many of you who have read to the end of this story have never heard of Moe Norman. Or that if you had, they were just odds and bits of his wacky life stories, tossed casually around at a golf course. Because there is no doubt in my mind he is one of Canada's greatest athletes and treasures and he deserves a much better fate.

I believe that the fact he is nothing more than a footnote in our sport's history is a disappointing reflection on how we as a society, more often than not, see and treat people different from us. This is not just a sports issue of course, and it happens in all walks of life.

Luckily there has been some progress since Moe's days. People are more aware of those on the spectrum or those who are different for some medical reason and why, and they make an effort to accommodate their special needs. We even have had sports fans embrace the less-than-perfect players, such as John Daly on the PGA. But there is no question we still have a long way to go. Embracing those who think like us, who look like us, or who seem "perfect" still seems to be our first choice of fan worship and are the ones professional sport and media wants to promote.

Wouldn't it be nice if the next time a Moe comes along, we don't hear about him or her, long after the fact? That instead, we revel in their gifts, and we do it in the present. That we celebrate their eccentricities, their differences, and their unique views. That we embrace them and let them know how thankful we are for sharing their talents, knowing that we all become better when we are being open to what is less familiar. To help us all expand and grow.

It's disheartening when you stop and think about how many other great and ground-breaking gifts, minds, ideas, and personalities the world has missed out on because we squirrelled certain people away or kept them out of sight. Too busy focusing on the messenger rather than the message they have to offer. Too determined to keep things as they already are.

Sure, I suppose there's always something comforting in unanimity and commonality. It makes us feel safe knowing exactly how things are to be and where boundaries lie. But that doesn't necessarily make it right, does it?

And sure, there's strength in naming something different so you can address it. Even perhaps to help, repair, treat or fix it if needed. *If needed*, being the critical point

But never should it give you or anyone the power to change, deny, or destroy -- something or someone -- only because you are scared of it. Because it's foreign or wasn't what you thought something "should be."

It's a careful and delicate and often destructive dance, isn't it?

Wouldn't it be nice if so many of us weren't so focused on fixing what's different from each other or stubbornly digging our heels in on what we think we know, and instead we enthusiastically allowed differences or new ideas to make us stop and reflect and go "Hmmm ... interesting...now, what if..."

Wouldn't it be wonderful if instead of only just a few angels being scattered here and there to help the outliers or fringe players in society, that there were choirs and choirs of them? Choruses of angels poised to make the world a better place by willingly including, accepting, and helping everyone? Regardless if they look and act just like us or not. To unabashedly give everyone a real chance to do it their way and see what becomes of it?

Imagine for a moment what Moe may have accomplished and what we could have learned had we started appreciating him when he was six years of age, instead of sixty-six.

As one of Canada's greatest golfers, Mike Weir said: *"The world missed out on a little bit of genius."*

ACKNOWLEDGMENTS

First and foremost I have to thank my mom and dad for introducing me to golf and stirring my passion for the game. And beyond the golf course, to have always unwaveringly encouraged me to trust my own heart and instincts. To always follow the beat of my own drum and whatever path I choose, to just go for it.

To Pat and Doug, who played endless rounds of golf with me as kids at Victoria Beach, while most other kids were enjoying the beach. And to Lloyd Smith who managed the course at the time, encouraging and taking great delight in seeing youth like me take up the game.

To June and Pat for allowing me to be their "coach" and for the many years of fun it brought.

To Allison, Graham, Allan, Lorraine, and Gary who have golfed every morning in the summer with my mom for decades, and always allowed me as an adult to tag along when I visit home. And to the many other "regulars" we meet every morning who are part of the experience as well.

To my dear friend Richard McMillan, who – when he learned of my passion for Moe's story – told me to stop talking about it and write it. Rick is no longer with us, but I know that without his friendly push this novel would never have happened. He never did get to see this version as the first incarnation was as a live theatre play, and as covid dashed the chance of live theatre coming back any time soon, it has evolved into this novel instead. The play still does exist, and hopefully one day it will find its place on the stage once the pandemic is over, and we are all able to safely gather indoors together again.

To Sonia for her eagle eyes. Practice, practise, practice. And Patti for her final step wisdom.

And finally to all the sportswriters who have shared and documented Moe's often forgotten stories so wonderfully in the past. I am too young to have experienced him myself, in the flesh, and it is their columns, articles, interviews, books, videos, and personal tales that captured my imagination and spurred my love for Moe and his incredible life journey. It is their passion for him, and the game, that has compelled me to want to do my part to spread the word as well, with this fictional telling of his story. There are many publicly shared stories out there about Moe, but I must single out Lorne Rubenstein, Tim O'Connor, Todd Graves, and Jack Kuykendall at the top of my list for giving me the most fuel for my fire.

ABOUT THE AUTHOR

Andrew is an artist in the truest sense of the word, having had a wonderful career as an actor and singer, and now as a visual artist and writer. While the bulk of his professional acting career was on the stage, playing lead roles in plays such as THE LION KING, BEAUTY AND THE BEAST, LES MISERABLES, SEUSSICAL, SWEENEY TOOD, FIDDLER ON THE ROOF, THE WIZARD OF OZ, PETER PAN and THE HOBBIT -- to name but a few -- he also appeared in both TV and Film in productions including MURDOCH MYSTERIES, HEROES REBORN, CINDERELLA MAN, THE FIRM, QUEER AS FOLK, SUGAR-TIME and RELIC HUNTER.

In the early 2000s, Andrew decided it was time for a change and began to move away from the complicated life and travel of being an actor and embarked on a visual arts career. It has exceeded his wildest expectations. He regularly participates in art shows and exhibitions, is represented by numerous galleries, and his work is found not only in corporate and private collections around the world but also has been given as gifts to Ministers in Canada's Parliament. You can learn more about his work on his website :

www.astelmack.com

While this is Andrew's first novel, he is no stranger to writing. In fact, after a long hiatus, he is thrilled to finally be putting his English degree in Theatre and Drama back to work! He has two more novels and plays in development, including one for younger audiences.

Andrew now splits his time between his live/work studio in Toronto, Canada and his hometown Winnipeg. His May to October is spent at his beloved Victoria Beach where he blissfully paints and writes the warm summer months away. And lots of golf, of course.